122686

Utopian Literature

Advisory Editor:
ARTHUR ORCUTT LEWIS, JR.
  Professor of English
The Pennsylvania State University

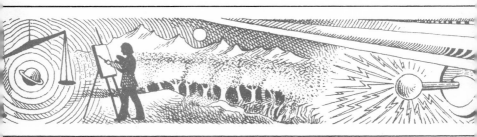

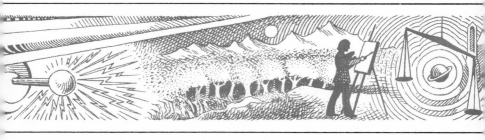

The Scarlet Empire

David M. Parry

ARNO PRESS & THE NEW YORK TIMES
NEW YORK · 1971

Reprint Edition 1971 by Arno Press Inc.

Reprinted from a copy in The Pennsylvania State University Library

LC# 77-154456
ISBN 0-405-03538-1

Utopian Literature
ISBN for complete set: 0-405-03510-1

Manufactured in the United States of America

Publisher's Note: This edition was reprinted from the best available copy

THE SCARLET EMPIRE

"I only spoke for the youth," she began. *Page 34*

THE SCARLET EMPIRE

By

DAVID M. PARRY

WITH ILLUSTRATIONS BY
HERMANN C. WALL

INDIANAPOLIS
THE BOBBS-MERRILL COMPANY
PUBLISHERS

PRESS OF
BRAUNWORTH & CO.
BOOKBINDERS AND PRINTERS
BROOKLYN, N. Y.

CONTENTS

CONTENTS—*Continued*

THE SCARLET EMPIRE

The Scarlet Empire

CHAPTER I

WHEREIN I TAKE THE FATAL PLUNGE

As I sit on my broad veranda gazing out to sea I live again through those strange events which make the past appear as some fantastic dream. For many years I have shrunk from taking the world into my confidence, for I have feared abnormally the ridicule of men. But now why need I care? My part on this stage of life is nearly played, and to me applause has lost its charm and scorn its sting. So, while waiting for the final curtain, I shall employ myself as suits my fancy. I shall write the tale of my life, or rather of that remarkable period which began with my twenty-fifth year and which was heralded in by the following announcement in one of the popular dailies:

"Yesterday afternoon, about two o'clock, a young man at Coney Island was seen to jump off the long pier which richly deserves to be called the Suicides' Promenade. His body was not recovered, although

Officer Michael Rafferty of the Broadway squad, who was having his day off and who happened to be on the pier at the time, made a gallant and desperate effort to rescue the youth. It is regarded as remarkable that after he sank into the water his head did not reappear at the surface, and it is the theory of Officer Rafferty that the body must have been caught by a strong undercurrent. Inquiry at Precinct Station No. 7 later disclosed that John Walker of 407 East 38th Street is missing and there is evidence to show it was he who so successfully sought a watery grave. Walker was said by his landlady to be a rather quiet individual but with strong views as to the evils of the trusts and the hardships thrust upon the poor of this day by the money kings. It is supposed that he tired of life's struggle and sought release in death from the sufferings entailed by poverty. He had no known relatives."

I have this item framed and hanging in my library. It is now forty years since it was printed. Little do those who happen to read it imagine that it refers to me — to me, the hale and portly man of business, the owner of this magnificent home, with all its cooks and butlers, the well-known financier and respected citizen, the Honorable Cyrus J. Brown. But truth is often stranger than fiction, and this item of news certainly

does refer to me. Were Officer Rafferty alive to-day
I think I could prove to him that I have knowledge of
what happened on the pier that day which only the
man who jumped to his supposed death could possess. But, unfortunately, the worthy Rafferty has
been gathered to his fathers, and thus I am de-
prived of producing the only human witness, aside
from myself, who could in any degree testify to the
truth of what I now relate. I confess that I feel some
misgiving lest I ask too much of the credulity of men,
but the word of a gentleman is not to be lightly
questioned. I shall, in this story, be as veracious as
my memory of those distant events will permit.

I remember distinctly that prior to my memorable
visit to the pier I was in somewhat indigent circumstances. These circumstances compelled me to fast for
protracted periods, and my clothes became faded and
threadbare. For weeks I spent my waking hours in
walking the streets and communing with myself as to
the selfish aspect of worldly affairs, the lack of wisdom
displayed in the management of things in general, and
the manner in which a man like myself would set things
right if mankind would only permit it. I had become
an inner member of an organization which had for its
purpose the reformation of society in such a way that
no one would have more of this world's goods than

another, and all would know the luxury of leisure and high living. Sometimes in the evenings we would make speeches on the street corners, and though, like the abolitionists of old, we were greeted occasionally with derision from those who were hostile to our propaganda, yet there generally gathered about us a knot of eager-eyed men who drank in our fervid eloquence with insatiable thirst. By degrees I became deeply and more deeply immersed in my chosen pursuit of righting the evils of the day, and as my means diminished, the less diligent I became in my search for remunerative employment. Thus in time I learned that the reformer's path is strewn with thorns, and as I took my last saunter on the pier my soul was possessed with bitterness. It was no wonder that, reaching the place from which to jump, I addressed the universe in the following strain:

" Hell no longer has terrors for me. I have lived on the earth — there can be no greater hell than that. What fools these mortals be who prate about their liberties! Liberty to starve, liberty to slave, liberty to kill one's self — curses on such liberty! They say that the majority rules. What a delusion! Why, if the majority rules, should a few be allowed to reap advantages not enjoyed by the majority? Why should penury and plutocracy grow side by side? Why should parasites pass their days in sumptuous idleness, while the majority become bent with ceaseless toil? Yet these deluded pack-horses for the few fail to see that the majority rules only in the abstract, and they refuse to allow those who would aid them to come to their relief. The world is sadly in need of reform, but it refuses to be reformed, therefore will I bid it farewell. I go where I no longer shall be a slave to beings no better than myself, where all are on a par, where in truth the majority rules — I go to enter into the democracy of the dead."

I turned to wave a last farewell to earth when I saw Officer Rafferty closely observing me, and then, without more ado, I made the fatal plunge.

CHAPTER II

The skeptical will doubtless contend that a man who dives into the ocean and fails to reappear in a few minutes must necessarily be counted among the dead. I, too, long entertained the same belief, and naturally I expected that once in the chilly water I should quickly be rid of life's cold felicity. As the poet has it:

> "Life is a dream of cold felicity,
> And death the thaw of all its vanity."

A thought that touched my saddened soul was that I should soon be gone and that my requiem would be sung only by the waters dashing against the pier.

But what was my astonishment, when, after sinking like a plummet for what seemed many leagues and yielding to the dreamy sensations that come to the drowning, I awoke again to life, finding myself stretched on a slab of rock and gazing at a fish-like creature that stood leaning over me and holding in its finny arm a knife! Was I dreaming or was I really about to be served for a meal by this denizen of the

6

deep? I was so dazed that I shall be pardoned for having an indistinct memory of all that occurred; but nevertheless I can recall the fascination with which I gazed on the creature. For a moment it held the knife poised over my heart and I thought my end had come. Instead of a murderous blow, however, I was conscious only of the ripping of the clothes across my chest and then of being rolled and thumped until the blood coursed through my veins and my restoration to consciousness was complete. Now I saw I was no longer in the sea, but in a chamber of solid rock, and that the light did not come from the sun, but from streaks of incandescence in the ceiling. I breathed again — inhaling long and deep. I was not dead — I was alive — how strange, how wonderful! I turned my eyes on my finny rescuer, and while it was still pounding my body I made a curious discovery. It was a human being! The fins were not fins at all, but hands and arms and legs. The head, true enough, resembled the head of a fish, but beneath it, through a transparent part of the scaly hide, I could see the features of a man.

"A man within a fish!" I exclaimed in the first moment of my surprise.

"Yes," replied the creature with monosyllabic brevity.

" Rather warm in that hide of yours, is it not? " I remarked inanely, my mind not yet fully awake.

" It is," he rejoined.

He continued industriously to belabor my body, and though I wished to ask him many questions the physical punishment I was undergoing made conversation difficult. At last he desisted, and standing erect, threw back his fish-head, or rather hood, exposing to my view a kindly countenance and a well-shaped head covered with a shock of long black hair. He was blowing like a porpoise, which showed he had not stinted his energy on me. I liked this man on the instant, and my heart went out in gratitude to him for what he had done. My desire for death was completely gone, and, feeling again the value that a normal man places on his life, I already looked back with shame and repugnance on my attempt to die.

" I can not express my debt to you," I said. " I am only one of the common herd who, penniless and hungry, drop themselves into the sea, but now I know that no man should throw away his life. I am indebted to you for saving me, not only from death, but from the crime of self-destruction."

" You are a citizen of the upper world," he responded, " and of course do not know that all men are penniless in the country to which I belong. Money

I thought my end had come. *Page 7*

is of no value whatever among us, and as for self-destruction, rest your conscience, for that is not counted by us a crime."

"For the love of Heaven," I cried, bewildered by his words, "is this not some cavern along the coast, and are you not a citizen of the United States?"

He looked, I thought, in pity at me and replied:

"I know nothing of your United States. I am a fisherman, sometimes a surgeon, and I am connected with the Fishery Department of Atlantis, or, as it is often called, the Scarlet Empire. This chamber is not on the coast but at the bottom of the sea."

I was too stunned to reply.

"I foresee," he continued, "that you will ask me many questions. So let me tell you that the Scarlet Empire is a social democracy, the most advanced form of government in history, and since you, being a barbarian, only newly come from the bleak wilderness beyond the waters, may not understand what is meant by social democracy, I must say further that ours is a land of many laws and that among these laws is one limiting the number of words which a man may speak in a day. Do you observe this little instrument?" At this he pointed to a small object that hung close to his throat. "That is a verbometer — it is a curious contrivance too intricate to explain and the inspectors of speech alone have the knowledge to read from it the number of words it registers. I am limited to one thousand words a day, and you should be aware that I have already consumed much of this quota on you."

" What! " I exclaimed, incredulous.

" I see you are slow to believe me or else you criticize by innuendo one of the laws of the Democracy. It is dangerous even to hint a doubt as to the righteousness of any law. The majority rules in Atlantis, and the individual must obey implicitly. The law placing a limitation on speech was based on the discovery made generations ago that an unrestrained tongue leads frequently to crime and conspiracy; besides, there is the further consideration that it is not just. save where the occupation makes exception necessary, for one individual to talk more than another — it is not in consonance with the fundamental idea of universal equality which the Democracy seeks to enforce."

" Pardon me," I said meekly, " I did not intend to criticize — I was only voicing my surprise."

" Let me warn you, then, against being too curious or too much surprised — it may get you into trouble," he returned, standing with his arms akimbo and looking me over critically.

" I am obliged to you for your warning," I said

faintly, feeling a sudden drowsiness. "I do not wish to impose on your fund of words, but I should like to know the name of my rescuer."

"I have no *name*," was the reply. "My *number* is 713. Tradition has it that in ancient times my family name was Brine, or at least my wife so asserts in private. You are the first man I ever saved — I have come across others like yourself, but never succeeded in resuscitating them. I should judge you are a rather hardy individual, although your muscles are somewhat soft, as though not inured to hard labor. I see you are sleepy, and I am also near the end of my string of words. There is one thing more I will tell you, though, and that is that you are the only foreigner now in Atlantis — some years ago there were a few of your United States people here, but they have long been buried."

As I dozed off I thought how strange it was that I should meet a surgeon in the likeness of a fish at the bottom of the sea, and that he should speak the English language. It was beyond comprehension. Then, too, what a wonderful country this Atlantis must be! A social democracy — exactly what I had been dreaming of for years! I should surely see many marvelous things and have experiences that would fill books. But what if I should never be able to return to the surface? I could make no use of my knowledge. This was a disconcerting thought, and the law as to the limitation of daily speech also jarred unpleasantly. What a ridiculous law! To think that I, who had spent my life in shouting my opinions from empty barrels on street corners and in pouring my wisdom into the ears of any chance acquaintance that would listen — I whose chief occupation had been that of talking from morning till night, must now perforce be silent. What absurdity was this! With the most fantastic notions surging through my mind, I fell into a deep sleep.

NOTE: It is perhaps judicious that I enforce my own testimony in this chapter respecting the existence of human beings living in the sea as fish by quoting from Berosus, who, writing of the ancient days of Chaldea, says:

"In the first year there appeared, from that part of the Erythrean Sea which borders upon Babylonia, an animal endowed with reason, by name Orannes, whose whole body (according to the account of Apollodorus) was that of a fish; that under the fish's head he had another head, with feet also below similar to those of a man subjoined to the fish's tail. His voice, too, and language was articulate and human, and a representation of him is preserved even unto this day. This being was accustomed to pass the day among men, but took no food at that season, and he gave them an insight into letters and arts of all kinds. He taught them to construct cities, to found temples, to compile laws, and explained to them the principles of geometrical knowledge. He made them distinguish the seeds of the earth, and showed them how to collect the fruits; in short, he instructed them in everything which would tend to soften manners and humanize their laws. From that time nothing material has been added by way of improvement to his instructions. And when the sun set, this being, Orannes, retired again into the sea, and passed the night in the deep, for he was amphibious. After this there appeared other animals like Orannes."

CHAPTER III

I TAKE MY MEDICINE

I must have slept very soundly, for when consciousness again returned I found that I had been transferred without my knowledge to a comfortable cot in a dry room. The place had no windows and its solid walls appeared to be made of scarlet-colored marble. But what particularly aroused my wonder was the manner in which it was lighted. Running like a border around the ceiling was a narrow band of great luminosity. So intense was this line of light that I could not look at it steadily enough to determine its nature. I noticed, also, that the air was pure and that the temperature was mild and pleasant. There were some fifty cots in the room, and from this I inferred I was in some hospital ward or army barracks.

While speculating vainly as to my immediate future, a door at the opposite end of the ward opened noiselessly and there appeared a figure arrayed in a scarlet robe belted at the waist. I looked and saw it was a man. His countenance, though not unpleasant, had an impassive and somber cast. What interested me most about him, however, was the breadth of his forehead, which I took to be an indication of unusual intelligence. With a bare nod by way of greeting, he approached my cot and began to make an examination of my physical condition. He felt my pulse, took my temperature, examined my tongue, sounded my ribs and exercised all my limbs. Not a word did he say, but after each medical test he made notes on a tablet he carried. I resolved to remain patient until he grew ready to speak. At last, when he seemed about to depart, he said:

"Stranger, you will have to take prescription No. 49."

"But, Doctor," said I, "I never felt better in all my life."

Without deigning to reply he rang a gong and there appeared a young man, who was also arrayed in a scarlet garb. Receiving a written direction from the doctor, he took himself away and in a few seconds reappeared with a bottle of black fluid, on which I could make out the number, forty-nine. Filling a small glass, he held it to my lips, and, not wishing to appear discourteous, I swallowed the dreadful dose. It was as vile a compound as I had ever tasted, but I refrained from comment. I was then left alone for perhaps half an hour, when again came the young man with the black bottle in his hand.

"It is time for another dose," he said indifferently.

I replied that I felt very well and did not care to take more.

"But you must!" he said.

I thought of positive refusal, but again I was influenced by a desire not to offend, and I swallowed the mixture with as good grace as possible.

Once more I was left alone. But behold, at the end of another half-hour, in walked the young man for the third time with the black bottle! I began to hate this taciturn individual.

"I will not take any more of that abominable stuff," I cried; "and that settles it!"

The young man elevated his eyebrows with just a suggestion of interest and then departed.

I had scarcely time to meditate over my show of independence when there appeared six men, headed by the doctor.

"I learn, sir," he began, "that you decline to take your medicine. This is an unheard-of act of rebellion! Are you aware that not for five hundred years has any one refused to obey the State physicians?"

I was not aware of it, and said so.

"Well, sir," he continued, "you know it now!

Your late arrival in Atlantis alone excuses you for this heinous offense."

" But I am an American citizen," I hotly exclaimed, " and if I do not care to take medicine no man or government, sir, can compel me to take it ! "

I immediately regretted this outburst. In a twinkling the six men had seized me and pried open my mouth as a veterinarian would open the mouth of a horse, and down went an excessively large dose of the nauseous stuff into my stomach. I struggled the best I could, but it was of no use against such odds. Puffing and blowing, and feeling as though I had taken an emetic, I was finally released. This time it seemed that I had aroused a latent spark of interest in the doctor, for he tarried after the others had gone and delivered himself of what must have been a lengthy speech for him. He said:

" My dear young man, you are certainly out of the ordinary ! Your case has a number of strange points about it, and I foresee that I shall be called on to prepare an extended thesis. In this Democracy, which has stood the test of centuries, the individual yields implicit obedience in all things to the majority. You must acknowledge, even though you are an American, that the will of the majority must be considered supreme. The individual is merely one atom of the whole. The majority knows what is good for all, and when it speaks the individual must yield his opinion. If the various individuals were allowed to follow their own notions as to what they should or should not do, it is plain to be seen that anarchy would result. Now this prescription to which you have objected was discovered thousands of years ago, and it has come down to us with all the rest of the blessed heritage of those days. Its efficacy has been proved in millions of cases, and is not open to argument. The majority has decreed that it should be prescribed whenever the heart beats abnormally. To prove this, I have only to refer you to medical edict No. 489667542. You thus see that in this land the most solicitous care is taken of the individual, and you need never worry your mind as to what you shall eat, drink, or do."

As the doctor proceeded I began to see my error, and before he had ended I was very contrite.

"Doctor, I wish to apologize for my rudeness," I said. "It was inexplicable. For years I have dreamed of a social democracy, and now, when I find I actually live in one, it ill becomes me to be dissatisfied with my lot. I agree with you. The individual has no rights which are not subordinate to the will of the majority. I am mighty glad I am here."

"I see that you are perfectly sane, after all," he

replied. "At first I began to fear that your mental processes were not as they should be. Your eyes appeared to be normal, although a little brighter than they ought to be, but this I attributed to fever or excitement. I shall be very happy to report that you are convalescent and that it will not be necessary to send you to the insane asylum."

While we were talking there had entered another man, who stood listening to our conversation.

"This is the chief inspector of the young men's dormitory, in which you are now a resident," said the doctor to me. Turning to the inspector, he told him there was nothing alarming in the case and that he would later make a full report. The two then departed, and every half-hour afterward I took my medicine without a murmur.

CHAPTER IV

IN WHICH I EAT

It may have been the effect of the medicine or it may have been merely the reaction due to the strenuosity of my experience — at any rate, it seemed that I should never get enough sleep. Now and then I would awake to consciousness, only to fall back, after a few moments, into deep and dreamless slumber. It was as if I lay in some leafy shade on a balmy day, endeavoring now and then to open my eyes, but always succumbing to the general somnolence.

Hours must have elapsed when at last I sat up in my cot wide awake. A full realization of what had happened came to me, and my strange surroundings aroused in me nameless fears. I looked about the room. The light was shining dimly and I concluded that it was night. I began to discern figures lying upon the cots and I thought I could detect the sound of breathing. So I had company and a goodly amount of it. But how did all these men retire without my being awakened? Should I disturb them? No, it would be better to wait. However, I felt very hungry.

Why had no food been offered me? Could it be possible, I asked myself, that these people meant to starve me?

I continued for an hour or more to torment myself with these and similar questions, and it seemed as if I must cry out, if only to vary my train of thought, when suddenly a bell in a corner of the ceiling began to ring out clamorously. I never felt so much like applauding in all my life. The bell worked wonders. The sleepers arose almost with one accord and began to move about. At the same time the light grew bright, and as I glanced upward I saw a curtain, which had caused the dimness of the sleep-time, roll up at one side of the room. I waved my hand in greeting to my room-mates, but they gave me in return only a solemn nod. What queer beings these men were! Though, as I could see, they were young in years, they appeared to have lost all zest for life. But the doctor, who soon approached me, seemed quite cheerful, as though he entertained some pleasant anticipations not shared by the others.

"So you are awake this time without doubt," said he. "You have had a rest of sixty hours, and I believe you are in pretty fair condition now —thanks to the medicine!" There was the suspicion of a smile about the corners of his mouth, and I liked him the better for it. I believed the doctor and I were going to be friends.

"Doctor, I'm starving!" I said.

"Ah!" he replied. "Appetite is a good thing within bounds. Enough of it assists in the digestion of the amount of food necessary to support life, but too much of it is a sin of the flesh which you must restrain and overcome. But of that I shall speak more fully later on. I am to tell you now that I have been deputed as your special overseer to teach you the ways of the life and the laws of Atlantis. For this purpose a special dispensation has been granted me by the popular assembly to talk as much as needs be to enlighten you as quickly as possible."

"I am glad to hear that, Doctor," I replied.

While we were talking I saw that those about me had each robed himself in the common scarlet raiment. The doctor handed me a like garment, and when I asked for my own apparel he informed me that no distinction in dress was permissible in Atlantis. I took the clothes and put them on without further demur. I found that they were as soft as silk in texture and almost without weight. When I had nearly finished my attire the bell once more began to ring.

In answer to my inquiry, the doctor told me that the first bell was rung at seven o'clock and was the signal

for all to rise. The second bell, he said, was rung at
seven thirty, and indicated the time of prayer.

"You must begin now to fall into our ways," said
he. "Every person, at the ringing of the second
morning bell, must face the east and, stooping well
forward, remain in silent prayer for sixty seconds."

A quick glance about me showed that all were
doing this, and I did likewise. At the end of perhaps
a minute I straightened myself, but saw that I was a
little too soon. A man immediately approached and
called for my number.

"Number?" I said in bewilderment.

The doctor interposed.

"He has not yet received a number, and is but newly
arrived among us," he said, at the same time displaying
a document to the man, who, after seeing it, noted
something on a tablet and bade us adieu.

"That was an inspector of prayers," the doctor informed me. "He will report you for not praying the
required limit of time, but I think under the circumstances you will get only the minimum punishment."

The doctor then took occasion to whisper in my ear
that during prayers I should count two hundred leisurely and thus I should come to gage the time for de-
votions with great accuracy.

I began to feel that I should have to tread a dangerous path in my new life, and I made up my mind to place full trust and reliance in my preceptor.

We all now filed out through the door and entered another apartment somewhat like the first, only much larger in size. This room was crossed lengthwise by four tables, along the sides of which were benches. The tables and benches were made of the same scarlet substance of which the walls and ceilings were formed. Every one sat down and the waiters brought in some copper plates and eating utensils. Small cups were also passed and in each of these was poured a steaming fluid which filled the air with an aroma that magnified my appetite.

" This is fish gruel," said the doctor, " and one cup is allowed for breakfast. We shall also have an egg apiece."

I think there must have been about five good swallows in the cup, and it was gone in less than a minute. I noticed that the others took longer time with their portion. In fact, they nursed it and were loath to see it disappear. Some of them even dipped their fingers into it and then licked them with much relish.

The waiters next brought around the eggs, which much resembled hen eggs, but the doctor told me they were laid by an animal that burrowed into the bed of the sea. I found the egg quite palatable, and when

I had consumed it I wished dearly for another or for a replenishment at least of my cup of gruel. I did not have the courage, however, to ask for more, and was quite pleased with my timidity when I witnessed the ignominious failure of a young man to obtain a second portion. Instead of boldly asking, like Oliver Twist, he played some conjurer's trick with his cup and declared to the waiter that he had not, as yet, had his gruel.

"You must have received it," said the waiter.

"You are mistaken," was the reply. "You certainly see I have no cup."

It was evident that all this was highly unusual, for the attention of the entire company was drawn to the circumstance. Now I saw an inspector hurry to the young man's side. There was some sharp questioning by this dignitary, and then an order to his attendants to search the blouse of the youth. The cup was found. The evidence of duplicity on the part of the unfortunate young man was too conclusive to admit of denial.

"Why did you do this?" asked the inspector severely.

"I was hungry, sir, and wanted more," meekly came the answer.

"You will follow me," commanded the inspector.

The young man arose and, surrounded by several sub-inspectors, left the room.

I asked for an explanation.

"He is under arrest," vouchsafed my guardian. "He has committed one of the most serious crimes known in Atlantis — that of seeking to obtain more than one's just portion of food."

"What will be done with him?" I asked.

"I shall take you to his trial, if you choose. It will further enlighten you as to the excellence of our Social Democracy."

CHAPTER V

We lost no time in following the prisoner and his guard. In fact, the doctor said we must hurry, as justice was swift and certain in Atlantis.

For the first time I passed the portals of the dormitory to the outer world. As I did so I stopped, overcome with awe. It was as though we had stepped into some vast cathedral. The dormitory stood on a small eminence and from this vantage-point I looked down a vista of titanic columns, which rose to a dome of immeasurable height. About each pillar ran a line of light — a shining vine — winding upward until its brilliancy contracted to a thread and lost itself in the upper air. The dome was faintly disclosed by lights which shed their rays like distant stars. I judged that the pillars were from an eighth to a quarter of a mile apart, and I could see that there were rows beyond rows to the right and left of those immediately in my line of vision. But though each column bore its garland of light, so wide was the surrounding space that the general effect was scarcely equal to that of the

27

full moon, and in this half-light the columns shimmered like colored marble and were dimly mirrored in the smooth and glossy flooring of the mighty naves. At intervals, running transversely across the vista down which I looked, were channels from which shone forth floods of light, and these channels I came afterward to know to be the streets of Atlantis. In the day-dreams of my boyhood I had often pictured sea caverns with crystal walls and sweeping distances, but no stretch of my imagination was ever comparable to the reality that now confronted me.

I know not how long I might have stood spellbound by the grandeur of the scene, had not my conductor laid his hand on my shoulder and enforced on my mind the necessity for haste. He grasped my arm, and, permitting myself to be piloted, I soon became aware that we were threading our way along an Atlantian thoroughfare. This highway was like a trough cut through walls of granite or coral, I could not tell which. The walls did not rise more than fifty feet at any place, and I noticed that at more or less regular intervals doors had been hewn into them, leading, as I correctly surmised, to store-rooms and places of abode. The street was some fifty feet in width. The center was used by vehicles, while on each side pedestrians were coming and going as in every city I have ever visited. The lighting system was well-nigh perfect, luminous arches stretching from wall to wall at frequent intervals.

The vehicles in the street drew my attention. They were constructed in strange designs, and what particularly excited my curiosity was the lack of all visible motive power. From looking at these I turned to regard the people about me. I became impressed more and more with the remarkable similarity in their appearance. What a dull, listless, lethargic race, I thought. In vain I looked for some one with a sprightly step, or with a glint of interest, hope or purpose in his countenance. Not one among them gave me even a passing glance, and I felt in truth an alien among a people I could not understand. Then a new thought flashed on me and I exclaimed:

" Doctor, I have not seen a single woman! "

At this my friend seemed about to laugh outright, and I believe he would have done so had he not been in Atlantis.

" Use your eyes," he replied. " There is one! " and he pointed to a figure walking directly in front of us.

" I thought *that* was a man! " I exclaimed.

" We are all on a level here, you know," said the doctor.

" Truly, the leveling process has been carried far!"
I replied.

" In ancient times," he remarked, " woman was an
object of beauty. I have read that she once decked
herself in gaudy colors and had a care for her com-
plexion and the dressing of her hair, that she might
catch the favor of a lover, but now there is no necessity for such enticements, as the State manages the
marriages, thereby rendering obsolete the barbarous
custom of being wooed and won."

" But how mannish, how slatternly they look! To
think they should wear the same garb and cut their
hair like the men! How outrageous ——"

" Silence! Your tongue will get you into trouble.
We are now at our journey's end."

With this interruption of what I immediately saw
would have been a treasonable utterance, the doctor
led the way through a doorway in the coral wall and
we found ourselves in a well-lighted hall. Here were
a number of benches facing a rostrum and occupied
by some fifty individuals, but whether the occupants
were male or female I could not tell until I had looked
closely into their faces, when I found that most of
them were men. Deep quiet pervaded the place.

In a few minutes a man ascended the rostrum and
took his seat on a small dais in the center.

"We are just in time," whispered the doctor. "That is the judge."

"Bring in the culprit!" commanded the Court in a loud voice. I noted that his Honor had a muscular frame, a bullet head and a stolid countenance. If physiognomy counts, thought I, this man must be a model jurist! But I had little time for reflection, for the young man in whom we were interested was being dragged forth like a felon about to be executed, until he stood with trembling knees and hanging head before the court.

The judge glowered at his victim.

"What's the matter with you?" he bawled. "Why don't you stand up? I've a mind to imprison you to teach you respect for the court. Clerk, enter a decree of three days."

A man sitting at a table began to write. Another of somewhat heavy build now advanced to the platform, and said:

"Your Honor, it is my official duty to inform you that the criminal now confronting you is No. 489744 X Y Z, and that he is domiciled in the dormitory for young men, No. 457. He is guilty, sir, of attempting to cheat the State and his fellow men by falsely pretending that he has not been served with gruel this day."

The Court frowned heavily and said: "That is a most damnable offense! Proceed!"

The prosecutor then detailed with minute particularity all that had occurred in the breakfast-room and wound up his remarks by demanding a full vindication of the majesty of the State.

"What have you to say for yourself?" commanded the Court harshly, addressing the prisoner.

No. 489744 X Y Z held up his head and showed a face pale with fear. He caught his breath once or twice and meekly replied:

"I was starving, your Honor!"

"You were starving, were you?" roared the judge contemptuously. "I sentence you to go without gruel for thirty days. Perhaps that will teach you that our Social Democracy is ——"

Suddenly the clear note of a woman's voice rang out:

"Have mercy, sir, have mercy!"

The judge, amazed, stopped speaking and the audience rose to its feet. The figure of a young woman was advancing down the aisle to the platform. I could see nothing exceptional about her at first, but when she came nearer I noted with admiration the grace and dignity with which she walked, and, looking into her face, I thought that I had never seen a countenance so noble and beautiful. As she came forward a number of men seemed to block her path and without a moment's hesitation I stepped to the front and said:

"Gentlemen, please make way!"

They parted to the right and left, and as she passed she gave me a little smile of gratitude that filled me with strange emotion.

"What a vision!" I muttered, and then I felt the doctor give me a warning clutch on the arm. Startled as from a deep abstraction I looked swiftly around, and saw that the people were gaping at me as well as at the girl. A murmur of whispering was in the room, and suddenly the judge burst out in thunderous voice:

"Arrest both the woman and the man who have just spoken. My court is being made a Bedlam. Is this a conspiracy against the State? Officer, if any one dares even so much as whisper, take him to jail immediately. Authority must be respected."

The judge's face was red with anger, and I dreaded the outcome. Intense silence had followed his outburst. Then he snorted again and the whole audience seemed to quail before him.

"Since some semblance of respect for justice is again established," he began ironically, "I shall deal first with you, woman. Meanwhile let the youth stand where he is. What said you just now about mercy?"

He turned his purple visage on her. Again she had become the center of all eyes. I looked enraptured at her — surely she was a goddess descended from the skies!

"I only spoke for the youth," she began in a sweet voice which showed no sign of wavering. "May I not speak for him?"

Could any one resist such an appeal? I held my breath, waiting for the reply.

"Let's hear what you have to say!" exclaimed the judge, and though he spoke roughly I was certain he was not so unbending in his sternness as he had been a moment before.

"You are a good man and a just judge, I am sure," she went on, her face becoming radiant. "You will be merciful to this boy, will you not? I beg of you to reconsider the decision you were about to pronounce. I do not ask you not to administer justice. The defendant has been guilty of a serious offense and should be punished, but then it is his first offense and he should be dealt with kindly. Mercy, you know, makes justice gracious, and I plead that as you would be judged with compassion in the hereafter you now be lenient with the frightened youth before you."

I drank in every word. It was not perhaps so much the substance of what she said as the manner in which

she said it that went straight to my heart. I looked
at the judge, and saw with thankfulness that the stern
lines of his face had relaxed. I knew then that woman's charm had tamed the outraged dignity of the
brute. I watched him anxiously as he hesitated, one
moment seemingly about to yield and the next putting
on again a frowning front.

"You speak in riddles," he said at last, as he nervously drummed upon the arm of his seat. "What can
I do?" he mused, not taking his eyes from the beautiful face before him.

Then she smiled. It was the final undoing of the
Court.

"What is all this, anyway?" he exclaimed, as if
bewildered. "What was it I said — thirty days?"

"Yes," said the clerk.

"Your Honor ——" called out the prosecutor, now
aroused from his trance.

"Silence! Make that thirty a three. The prisoner
shall go without gruel for three days — and — remit
the prison sentence. Away with him!"

The young man quickly recovered his courage sufficiently to say:

"I thank your Honor."

"*Thanking* me?" roared the Court. "Enough of
this! Out of my sight!"

Then turning to the prosecutor he exclaimed savagely:

" Clear the court-room! This unseemly business must come to an end. Release the woman and also the man. The court's adjourned."

There was a scramble for the door.

I looked after the girl as she passed from the hall. Those nearest the door fell back, giving her a wide berth as though they feared her. What incomprehensible conduct! Then as I passed out I heard the strident voice of the prosecutor exclaim: " Your Honor, the woman is an atavar."

" Atavar!" The word rang in my ears.

" Atavar!" The word filled my heart.

CHAPTER VI

The doctor hurried me along the street for a considerable way before he uttered a word.

"Doctor, why such haste?" I said. "I should like to have another look at that young woman. I do not think I ever saw any one so fair; and how brave and good she was in coming to the assistance of that friendless boy!"

"Yes, you would like to see her," he replied, "and speak to her, too, no doubt. But have you not seen enough of Atlantis to know that inspectors are everywhere? We have not heard the last of that trial, if I know anything at all about this country. Social Democracy received a serious shock in that court-room to-day! You do not realize it, but I do. Such a court scene has not occurred here in a decade, and serious trouble is sure to result."

"But was she not beautiful?"

The doctor gave me a searching look.

"As you value your freedom, man, be careful!" he answered. "I warn you! Danger dogs every step of

37

the man that admires a woman in Atlantis. If I mistake not, you are already in peril, and I know full well
that she whom you call beautiful will lose her freedom
in an hour. How any woman of her power should be
out of custody I can hardly understand. There must
be something wrong in the nicely adjusted machinery
of the State. It was long ago seen that in woman lay
the principal danger to social democracy. Swayed
by impulse, unreasoning, and delighting in inducing
men to act contrary to their judgment, it would only
require a few such creatures as you saw to-day to
wreck our entire political and social system. The
judge, who proved himself so defenseless against that
woman's smile, is a marked man. He himself is now,
probably, wondering at his own conduct, and will,
most likely, have further opportunity to reflect behind
prison walls."

"I in danger, and she to be imprisoned!" I said
aloud. I could hardly comprehend all that the doctor
said.

"Silence!" he whispered fiercely in my ear. He
looked uneasily about. Close behind us walked several
men. Inspectors, I said to myself with considerable
uneasiness.

"Doctor," I said, raising my voice, "I do not think
that the young man got all he deserved. Thirty days

on short rations was only fair punishment for such an offense."

"You are right!" replied the doctor with bolder utterance, "and I am glad that you so quickly appreciate the value of our institutions. I am indeed sorry that you witnessed such a miscarriage of justice on the first occasion of your visiting a court."

I felt some shame in the course of dissimulation I had suddenly embarked upon — shame because it seemed as if I were playing traitor to a girl who would scorn deception. But the knowledge of danger will sharpen a man's wits, and I realized, too, that once in prison I should be unable to help myself or to help others. To help others! Yes, for from that moment a firm resolution possessed me: I would do all in my power to assist the girl, and if she were imprisoned I would never give myself a moment's rest until she was released. Could it be possible the doctor was right? Was she really about to be sent to jail? It seemed too preposterous to be true. What kind of country was this that tried to crush out womanly sympathy, and looked on noble and generous deeds as unpardonable offenses? Was all this essential to social democracy?

These thoughts deeply troubled me, and I remained silent for the rest of the journey back to the dormitory. We had no sooner reached it, however, than I was accosted by the inspector who had noticed my lapse at prayer in the morning.

"It has been ordered," he said without preliminary remark, "that you shall go without dinner because of your violation of Rule 32 in the code concerning prayers."

I remembered what the doctor told me as to the result of my being reported.

"You see," he said, "you have been kindly dealt with, as I predicted. For such a minor offense, particularly when the extenuating circumstances are quite obvious, the formality of a trial is waived and the minimum punishment is fixed when the report is made. This saves people a great deal of time and inconvenience."

"I am happy," said I with some bravado, "that such consideration has been shown me. It speaks well for the lenient character of your laws."

The doctor regarded me for some time out of the corner of his eye.

"By the way, Doctor," I remarked, "what is the religion of Atlantis? What do the people say when they pray?"

The question seemed to puzzle my friend. He cleared his throat deliberately and then said:

" To tell the truth, I do not know what they do say when they pray. Perhaps they say nothing. As for myself — well, you see, it is this way. Our ancestors centuries ago lived beneath the sun and worshiped it. They turned to the east each morning when the globe of fire appeared and made their supplications. This practice became a habit, which has come on down to the present day. There is a general feeling — call it superstition, religion, or whatever you please — that calamity would overtake the nation if the habit were broken, and the majority long ago decreed that every individual should conform to the custom, this being on the theory that if it was good for one it was good for all, and that if it was beneficial for the common welfare none should escape in contributing his share in making the benefit as large as possible."

The explanation struck me as having some curious aspects, and I remarked:

" It looks as if religion may correctly be said to have gone to seed, in this country."

" I suppose that would be a valid conclusion," said the doctor indifferently, " but hereafter you must not neglect to pray in accordance with the laws."

Although the subject would have been interesting under other circumstances, I found my thoughts reverting constantly to the scene in the court-room, and

I noticed also that the doctor's mind seemed to be else-where. After a pause I suddenly asked:

" Who is she? "

" I do not know," returned my friend, " but you will find out in due time. Indeed, we shall not have long to wait."

He spoke truly, for scarcely had he uttered the words when an inspector entered the room and commanded us to follow him.

CHAPTER VII

A JOURNEY IN THE GARDEN OF EDEN

The inspector did not conduct us to the exit of the dormitory which we had previously used, but led the way through several rooms and halls and finally up a small flight of steps, when, on opening a door, we were ushered again into the silence of the pillared dome. Once more I stood transfixed by the scene, but this time, owing, no doubt, to the changed mental attitude with which I regarded it, I felt that I was gazing on the cold magnificence of some mighty mausoleum. A chill went to my very soul. For one moment I entertained the thought that perhaps, after all, I did die when I jumped into the sea and that this was merely some purgatory reserved for those who commit self-murder.

" Step this way," said the guide.

After a short walk we came to a car that much resembled those used on our own street railroads. There were the tracks also. We got aboard, the signal was given, and soon we were speeding past the shimmering columns with their spirals of light. Faster and faster we went. For some time we crossed over lighted streets in rapid succession, then a space with no streets, and then again more streets. Another interval without them, and then we were flying over a maze of them once more. We were passing through villas and towns. But one very odd feature was the almost total absence of noise. The doctor and I talked without the least difficulty of making ourselves heard.

"How fast are we traveling?" I asked.

"About one *farsakh* or league a minute," he replied.

I made a mental calculation.

"Two hundred miles an hour!" I exclaimed. "I suppose this is propelled by electric power?" I continued.

"No, electric force is little used in Atlantis. We derive all our energy and heat and light from radium."

"And, pray, what is radium?" I asked.

I had never ridden on electric cars, and all my knowledge of the possibilities of electricity as a motive power had been obtained from the casual reading of experiments in the laboratories. As for radium, I had never even heard of such a substance.

"You do not have radium on the surface of the earth?" queried the doctor, noting my perplexity.

"No," I replied, "we use steam power on the earth."

The doctor smiled with complacent superiority. "This shows," he remarked, "that your civilization is much behind that of Atlantis. I dare say that your people will in time come to use electricity and finally radium, perhaps. You are, indeed, much more fortunate than your countrymen, for you will now enjoy a state of development far in advance of anything dreamed about on the earth.

"Perhaps you do not know it," continued my friend, after a few moments of silence, "but Atlantis is the birthplace of invention and scientific discovery. Before the deluge, when she sank into the sea and became a kingdom of the under waters ——"

"Oh, I remember! I remember!" I exclaimed excitedly. "The name of your country seemed familiar to me, but I could not place it. I am in the long-lost Atlantis, that island of antiquity which became submerged in the sea before the dawn of history. What relief this information gives me! I began to fear that I was in some limbo of ——" I was about to say purgatory, but I checked myself in time and said "Heaven" instead.

"As I was saying," continued the doctor, disregarding my interruption, "the upper world owes much to Atlantis. It was here that man first began to develop an intelligence. There is a legend, the truth of which

I can not vouch for, that these gigantic columns which you so admire are the petrified forests of the Garden of Eden. You can not see their branches here below, but if you could ascend " — he pointed upward — " you would find that great limbs spread out in all directions, supporting a dome which seems a mass of foliage and mineral matter impervious to water."

"How strange and weird and miraculous!" I whispered, stricken with awe.

"Miracles were performed in ancient times," continued my guardian, "and why should one not have happened in the Garden of Eden? At all events, we must believe the evidence of our eyes."

Again I lapsed into silence, watching the speeding scenery with new emotions. I noticed that we were now in a region of hills and valleys, with few and scattered signs of human activity. Was I really in the primeval abode of man, where Adam and Eve once lived in blissful ignorance of right and wrong?

The doctor recalled me from the deep reverie in which I had become immersed.

"Yes," he said, "the world owes much to Atlantis. Her people were the first to construct ships, the first to engage in commerce, and the first to plant colonies on distant shores. At one time she ruled all Europe and America. But the deluge and the earthquake came and in a night she disappeared, and with her were buried the records of the early civilization of man. Her colonies survived, however, and though they knew little of the learning, the great inventions and the advanced character of her governmental institutions, yet this little they preserved and transmitted to posterity. The Phenicians, for example, were a colony of Atlantis, and from them the world obtained the alphabet, the first and perhaps the most marvelous invention of all ages. But the credit for this invention belongs to Atlantis."

"I remember now," I said, "that students of antiquity can not trace the development of the Phenician alphabet. It seems as though it sprang suddenly into existence."

"How could such a thing be?" replied the doctor. "The Phenician alphabet was the product of centuries of slow development here in Atlantis, and when you come to examine the ancient records you will be able to note backward the slow evolution of each letter from its original outline of a human face."

"Wonderful!" I exclaimed.

"Then, again, you perhaps know," continued my learned friend, "that there is a hiatus in your history between the Stone Age and the Age of Bronze. Before men could make bronze it would have been nat-

ural for them to work in copper, since bronze is made
of both copper and tin. Yet you find no relics of a
Copper Age in Europe. But these relics you will find
in Atlantis and also in the lands of the Aztecs and the
Incas of America, two of her ancient colonies. Speaking of the Incas, they alone seem to have preserved
some of those governmental and religious institutions
of the old Atlantis, for I have read with interest that
their government approximated a great deal nearer to
social democracy than that of any land of which we
have knowledge."

"How is it," I asked suddenly, "that you possess
any knowledge of the upper world at all?"

"Why, my dear sir, you are not the only visitor we
have had from the upper world. Our Fishery Department in the past has rescued a number of schol-
arly men from death in the sea. Again, we have
many chests of books in the Hall of Curiosities that
have come down to us with wrecks of ships. Was
there not a great man of your country whose name
was Captain Kidd?"

"You know about him!" I exclaimed.

"We have many books inscribed on the fly-leaf with
his name, and property of many kinds that evidently
belonged to him may be found in the Hall of Curiosities."

"Were any of his friends among those who were rescued?"

"Yes, at one time quite a number. I believe that Captain Kidd must have been a great socialist."

"Yes, I believe he was. He certainly entertained ideas of common ownership, that would have done him credit in a pure social democracy. I have no doubt he would have been a valuable acquisition to Atlantis, had he ever made you a visit."

"He must have been one of those great characters that live before their time," commented the doctor. "But I was speaking about the advanced civilization of Atlantis at the time of the deluge. The inventive faculty of her people was at that period in full activity and continued so for several generations. Although they were shut off from communication with the outer world, they quickly readjusted themselves to changed conditions. It may have been that a miracle was wrought in their behalf to save them from extinction, but at all events, discoveries in electricity and radium were made simultaneously with the submergence of the country. Radium is a mineral which is found in large quantities in mines in the interior. It has a variety of wonderful properties. It is self-luminous, and under its rays vegetation grows, as I suppose it does under the rays of the sun. With it the problem of existence was solved for the buried people of this country."

"And did the inventive epoch come to an end?" I asked.

"Yes. Not for some thousands of years has there been any new invention in Atlantis. It is thought that all possibilities in this line of development have been exhausted. The last great invention was that of Social Democracy. At the time of the deluge a fierce conflict raged between the adherents of individualism or barbarous civilization and a new party that stood for equality between man and man and the amelioration of the inequalities of Nature. This party grew stronger with the passing years, and after some centuries of conflict established itself in power and founded the Social Democracy which now exists. With this crowning achievement of the brain of man the state of perfection was attained, and although there is a department of invention in the State, those assigned to labor in that department have produced no improvements of any kind for centuries past, which certainly is ample proof that the limit of invention has been reached."

"I hope," said I, "that the solution of the problem of social government will not always remain a secret of the ocean depths. If I ever find my way back to the surface, I shall revive the fame of Atlantis and shall incidentally make myself famous. I shall take the lecture platform and —— "

" I see," dryly remarked the doctor, " that individual initiative and egotism form a substantial part of your character, despite your belief in social democracy."

" I ask your indulgence, Doctor. I spoke thoughtlessly and by force of habit acquired in a society where man must fight and scheme for his own selfish ends. I am sure I shall be well content to live in this land of perfection, where I need no longer strive for fame or for a livelihood."

The inspector accompanying us had taken no part in the conversation, but I noticed that he pricked up his ears when I made my little lapse into the language of the struggling world above. But my subsequent remark drew from him a word of approbation.

" I think, sir," he said, " that you will make a good citizen of our land."

He then fell into the customary silence of the Atlantide. Remembering that there was a limitation on the amount of daily speech, I did not regard his taciturnity as strange, and in my heart I thanked the higher powers, whoever they were, for having, for my sake, removed the restriction in the case of the doctor.

Off in the distance I could now see a wonderful column of light, which shone with almost the brilliancy of the sun.

" What is it? " I exclaimed.

" That," replied my guardian, " is a monument erected to the Federation of Labor of Atlantis. The Federation was one of the chief forces which brought about the Social Democracy, and it erected the monument in honor of itself at the time it was at the height of its power. We shall sometime inspect it if you wish."

I saw it for only a brief period, as intervening hills soon obstructed the view. But never, thought I, had I seen anything more beautiful or grand. So absorbed was I in contemplating it that I did not catch all of the doctor's next remark, but one sentence recurred to me long afterward. It was this : " Beyond the monument several miles is the wonderful Crystalline Wall, which keeps out the sea."

Suddenly the car came to a stop and we alighted.

" Our destination," announced the doctor.

We had traveled for several hours.

CHAPTER VIII

THE CAPITOL OF ATLANTIS

Within a short walk of where the car stopped a massive rock with perpendicular sides rose to a considerable height above the surrounding plain. Innumerable lights shone from windows that seemed mere apertures.

"An Atlantian skyscraper!" I exclaimed.

"It is the Capitol of Atlantis, the headquarters of the various departments of inspectorships," said the doctor. "It is a wonderful structure, hewn out of solid rock, seven hundred cubits in length, four hundred in depth, one hundred above the surface and one hundred below. It was constructed in the old days before the Social Democracy. How the ancients succeeded in carrying out such a colossal undertaking is to-day regarded as an inexplicable mystery."

"It must be in a class with the pyramids of Egypt," I interjected.

"The records show that it cost one hundred thousand talents of copper," continued my friend, ignoring my reference to the pyramids. "These records also

53

tell us that it was seventy-five years in course of construction. But how the rock was hewn out and many other interesting details were left untold. The story of the building, as preserved in the archives, is mostly one of scandal and gross plundering of the people's earnings. One set of officials after another grew rich off the job."

"It certainly is a splendid monument of ancient civilization," I said, admiring its vast dimensions. "But the Social Democracy, I suppose, erects buildings like it now without working any hardships or injustice on the people."

"You are wrong, my friend," replied the doctor. "There have been no such buildings erected by the Social Democracy, and, in fact, very few buildings of any kind. Still, I have no doubt that were the State to-day to attempt such an architectural task the people would enjoy considerable advantage over the ancients, as happily boodlers and grafters are now wholly unknown."

The entrance to the Capitol to which our guide led us was wide and spacious. A stream of men was going in and another coming out. A man standing in the middle of the entrance as we approached called out:

"Your cards! Show your cards!"

The doctor and the inspector produced two pieces of pasteboard.

"This man," said the doctor, pointing to me, "has no card for —— "

"Both of these men are in my custody," interposed the inspector, "and this is my authority." With this he presented a paper, which the guard scanned. Then we were allowed to proceed.

"Must you have a card in Atlantis?" I asked the doctor as we passed down a long hall or rotunda.

"Yes," he replied, "we all have cards. This is mine."

He handed me the one he had shown the guard. I read on it the following:

SOCIAL CITIZEN No. 311897 M N P Q.

HABITAT, DORMITORY FOR YOUNG MEN No. 457.

OCCUPATION, PHYSICIAN AT DORMITORY.

The card was also stamped with a circular seal with the words: "Issued 4-11, 2456, Department of Registration."

"You will note," said the doctor, "that this is a white card. That color indicates that as a citizen my record is good.   Should I be convicted of a serious offense this card would be taken up and a green one substituted.   If I should again be convicted of a flagrant infraction of law, I should receive a black card in place of the green one.   The holder of a black card is the object of special surveillance, and, like the ex-convict of the old days, he is regarded as guilty of any charge filed against him until he produces indisputable evidence of innocence.   But if his conduct for an entire year proves exemplary he may in most cases secure a pardon, when a white card is again exchanged for the black one."

"How admirable a system!" I exclaimed.   "It re-minds me strongly of the labor union cards in Amer-ica.   A man can not work in a good many places up there unless he holds a card which shows him to be in good standing in a union."

"The same custom exactly that prevailed in Atlantis before the Social Democracy," returned the doctor, much interested.   "The more I learn about your civ-ilization the greater the number of similarities I note between it and the civilization which prevailed for a few generations prior to the advent of social equality. It was from the union card that the idea of citizen-ship cards sprang.   In effect this card is an evidence that I am a member of the State in good standing, and am, therefore, entitled to food and lodging and the right to use the highways and enter public buildings when my purpose is legitimate and does not interfere with the performance of my duties or the duties of others."

"Do you have to show your card often?" I asked.

"Rarely, except when traveling. The inspectors one meets every day soon come to know one. But when a man leaves his usual environment he must be prepared to display his credentials on frequent occasion."

"Suppose a man loses his card?" I ventured to suggest.

"In that case he is immediately arrested and remains in prison for two weeks, pending an investigation of his record and a search for the card. If the card is not found he is released and a conditional card is issued to him. These and other precautions are necessary since the cards of malefactors are occasionally forfeited and the State must be reasonably sure that lost cards do not find their way into the possession of these outcasts."

"What happens to the man whose card is forfeited?"

"He either starves to death or is devoured by

wild beasts which haunt the dark and dismal caverns
beyond the confines of Atlantis."

A shudder went through me as I heard this remark,
and for a moment forebodings of coming danger oppressed me.

Then my mind reverted to the girl of the court-
room, as, indeed, it was constantly doing, and now
I began to wonder whether I should meet her in
the inquisition chamber which I surmised was our
destination. For some moments the possibility of
seeing her soon made me so preoccupied I was
only half conscious of the scene about me, and it
required much exercise of will-power before I could
bring my mind back to a consideration of my immediate surroundings.

We were threading our way through a crowd of
silently-moving men — what a hive was this Capitol of
Atlantis! I glanced up and down the great hall, and
everywhere the light shone on polished porphyry and
marble. At intervals were strangely-worked columns,
hewn apparently from the solid rock, while in niches
along the walls were many statues. These figures,
on close examination, displayed antique workmanship
and the disintegrating marks of time.

"Sculpture is one of the lost arts," remarked the
doctor, who observed my examination of the statuary.

"We do not waste our time on such things now; besides, the knack of making them seems to have departed from us. Men have been assigned to art work in the past, but their productions were so poor that the State was finally forced to close its studio departments. These marble figures are now looked upon as relics of the barbarous age."

From looking at the statues I turned to reading the signs over the many doors that opened into the hall. Among these signs were the following:

Department of Sleep Inspectors.
Department of Time Inspectors.
Department of Highway Inspectors.
Department of Bath Inspectors.
Department of Laundry Inspectors.
Department of Marriage Inspectors.
Department of Vocation Inspectors.
Department of Vital Statistics.
Department of Dormitory Inspectors.
Department of Cooking Inspectors.
Department of Agriculture Inspectors.
Department of Light Inspectors.
Department of Heat Inspectors.
Department of Sanitary Inspectors.
Department of Medical Inspectors.
Department of Speech Inspectors.

Department of Fisheries Inspectors.

Department of Etiquette Inspectors.

Department of Eating Inspectors.

Department of Inspectors of Inspectors.

Department of Inspectors of Inspectors of Inspectors.

I grew tired of noting these signs. Men were constantly going in and out of the various doors, and through these doors I caught occasional glimpses of walls of books and files and countless desks, with men writing and handling documents. Now and then we came to transverse halls, which were, to all appearances, like that in which we were walking. Finally we reached a broad stairway and began an ascent of five flights.

"Are all these floors occupied by departments?" I asked.

"Yes," the doctor answered. "There are ten floors and subterranean basements, and although the building is so vast, such is the size of the State's business that many departments are forced to occupy outside buildings."

"Marvelous!" I exclaimed. "I estimate that each floor must cover about one hundred and eighty-five acres and that this would make almost three square miles of floor space in the structure. The business of governing in Atlantis is most certainly stupendous."

"What else could you expect, where all the responsibility for the welfare of the individual is assumed by the State?" replied the doctor. "You must remember that the State controls and directs the entire energies of the people, cares for them from the cradle to the grave, enforces equality among them and neutralizes the inequalities of Nature. The individual no longer needs to cudgel his brain about anything, — the government does all the planning and thinking. Of course the work of the government must necessarily be great, but, immense as it is, many economies of time and labor have been secured over the old system. Many useless occupations have been abolished, as, for example, those of the speculator, the banker, the politician, the jobber and the middleman in all lines, as well as those that pampered to the expensive whims of the idle rich. The Social Democracy has carried to its logical conclusion the tendency toward concentration in industry which developed under an individualistic régime, only instead of a few individuals controlling capital and production the State controls them. It is now a case of monopoly run by the government for the people in the place of monopoly run by individuals for themselves."

"Such a government is one of which I have dreamed for years," I replied. "Therefore my great curiosity, I think, is pardonable."

"Curiosity in a stranger like yourself is to be condoned," put in the doctor, "but it is not permissible, except in the fifth degree, among the people of this country."

"So you recognize degrees in curiosity?" I muttered. "But since I do not know what those degrees are, I will ask you how many inspectors there are in Atlantis."

"In a population of four million in the five provinces there are one million inspectors," he said. "Of course I use only round numbers, but what I have said is approximately correct."

I was fairly stunned by this information, but veiling my surprise, I said:

"Your system of inspectorships must be one of the wonders of the world, but perhaps you will be interested to know that in America we have a few inspectors ourselves. For example, we have there what are called walking delegates. It is the business of these gentlemen to go about among the people to see whether they are working too industriously or for less pay than the unions stipulate they must earn. They also inspect the union cards held by the workers, to make sure that no one works who does not possess one or who is in arrears for dues for the support of the delegates. Those who do not come up to the requirements demanded by the delegates are branded as ' scabs ' and are either physically chastised or driven away from the job and warned never to return. The walking delegate also enters the offices of the employer and lays down the law to him as to whom he shall employ and how he shall run his business. In case the employer is recalcitrant the delegate calls all his men from their work and sets a guard about the plant to prevent its further operation until the employer returns to reason and accedes to the desires of the delegate. I imagine that your very complete and comprehensive inspectorship system is merely the walking-delegate system in full bloom."

"True," replied the doctor. " I wonder sometimes at your sagacity. The historic fact is that before we had the inspectors we had the walking delegates. At first the delegates, backed by their unions, assumed the duty of looking after the interests of the laboring classes. Some elements of the population demurred to their interference, but they gradually became more powerful, nevertheless, until at last all resistance was brushed aside, and, by natural stages, the present system was established. Thus it was that the chaotic conditions resulting from every man's doing as he pleased and thinking only for himself, without regard to his brother man, passed away to make room for the present ideal state, in which there is absolutely no strife of any kind and every man participates equally in toil and in the fruits of toil."

"I should like to put another question to you right there," I interrupted. "Where I came from, the job of walking delegate was much sought after. I should think that every man here would want to be an inspector. How do you manage such an important phase of human nature and still maintain equality?"

"That is a natural query, but it is a little difficult to explain in a few words. In the first place, all occupations are assigned by lot, and it is not within the power of any man to select his own vocation. In the second place, every individual gets exactly as much food and clothing as another, whether he be an inspector or a washer of dishes. In the third place, the hours on duty vary with the different occupations, being longest with inspectors and government officials, and shortest with those who dig in the mines or do other hard labor."

"How about the glory of being a dictator?" I queried.

"Glory, did you say? There is no such thing in Atlantis."

The doctor spoke with so much scorn that I thought it discreet to drop the subject.

CHAPTER IX

THE COURT OF INQUIRY

Reaching the top floor of the Capitol we passed through several apparently never-ending halls until we came to a door over which I marked the words: The Court of Inquiry. Entering we found ourselves in an anteroom, and there sitting in gloomy silence was the judge who had that morning fallen from grace. We had scarcely taken seats when the outer door re-opened and there entered as ugly a creature of the feminine sex as I had ever seen. She hobbled with a staff, and turned up to me an evil face, from which the flesh had shrunk away, leaving only folds of skin to hide the bones. Her eyes were like those of a basilisk. I could not look on her without a feeling of disgust and loathing.

We remained in utter silence while now and then I glanced at the door in the hope that the girl would come in whom my thoughts centered. But in this I was doomed to bitter disappointment, for she had not appeared when the door leading to the court-room proper was opened and we were beckoned to enter. We found ourselves in a room in which was a table piled with books, behind which barricade sat five men. In front of them were a few benches and to a space on one side of these we were assigned.

"The judge of the lower court will stand," said the chief of the five judges. The man complied as he was bidden, looking very grave.

"You are aware that the laws of Atlantis were made to be enforced, are you not?" continued the justice.

"Yes, your Honor."

"Do you know what the laws are?"

"Yes, your Honor."

"Do you understand the theory of the law?"

"Yes, your Honor."

"Let us see. Should any individual have more food than another?"

"No, your Honor."

"Why?"

"Because if one man ate more than another he would consume more of the products of labor than another and inequality would at once be established."

"Suppose one man weighs one hundred and twenty-five pounds and another two hundred and fifty pounds. Should the heavier man whose appetite, let us say, is the greater, have more food than the other?"

" No, your Honor, it would not be just."

" State some of the beneficent effects of the equal distribution of food."

" For one thing, it enables the State to calculate exactly how much food will be required and thereby to regulate the amount of labor engaged in the various food-producing industries. For another thing, it tends to correct the errors of Nature. Under a system that would allow men to eat their fill the natural result would be great inequality in men as regards the amount of food each would consume. This was the condition in ancient times. Some men were big, and some were little, some had keen appetites and some had small ones. Now all this is changed. By virtue of the policy of compelling men with little appetites to eat their proper amount of food and forcing those who crave for more to be satisfied with what is their just share and no more, the inequalities of Nature as to the physical size and appetite of different individuals is being largely modified."

" That is correct. Now, again, as to these natural inequalities of which you speak. State more specifically how the system of equal distribution of food corrects them."

" First, by tending to make lean those who are

predisposed to obesity, and to make fat those who would be lean were they not compelled to eat all the food assigned them. Second, by eliminating from the race all individuals for whom the amount of food allotted them is not sufficient to sustain life and also those on the other hand whose constitutions can not assimilate as much food as they are required to eat."

"Do you believe the State to be justified in thus enforcing a rectification of the mistakes of Nature?"

"I do. Equality is more precious than all else. The distress of overeating, the pangs of hunger, even a few lives must not be permitted to stand in the way of the establishment of equality. The majority have rights which must be made secure, though the minority suffer thereby."

"Now, what is the punishment fixed by the law for those who do not observe in letter and spirit the principle of equal food consumption?"

"For those who utter any complaint about the food supply the penalty is from one to ten days on half-rations, according to the nature of their remarks. For those who express doubts as to the virtue of equal consumption the penalty is imprisonment and bread and water for from one to six months. Open denunciation of the principle of equality as to food distribution is deemed treasonable and is punished by long imprisonment or withdrawal of citizenship card. In extreme cases the criminal shall be thrown to the kraken of the sea. Where the offense consists in merely asking for more, three days without the article asked for is the penalty. Giving another a portion of one's food is punished by compelling the offender to live for from three to fifteen days solely on the article of food which he gave away. Accepting a gift of food deprives the individual of the kind of food he accepts for from three to fifteen days. Where the individual committing these minor offenses adds deceit and lying to his act, he is guilty of a crime and in his case the penalty for the simple offense shall be multiplied from ten to twenty times at the discretion of the court."

"Stop there. You seem to know the law and according to your own statement just made, No. 489744 X Y Z should have been sentenced to go without gruel for at least thirty days. You seem to appreciate the fact that to grant the right of one individual to eat more than another would be to undermine the foundations of the State."

The five judges bent their heads together. A deep silence fell over the court-room. All eyes were fixed on the defendant, whose face was blanched and whose lips were bloodless. The chief justice again turned to the culprit.

"I have one more question to ask you," he said. "Do you know what the law says shall be the punishment of a judge who does not deal out justice in accordance with the laws?"

"Yes, your Honor," replied the wretched jurist, with a quiver in his voice. "In cases where there are extenuating circumstances, such as a good record in the past, or temporary aberration of mind, the punishment is withdrawal of citizenship card for ten days. To this shall be added incarceration in an insane hospital for six months, or for such additional length of time as may seem necessary for the rehabilitation of the mental powers of the delinquent. In flagrant cases the offender shall undergo the extreme penalty of having his membership card forfeited for ever."

It was painful to watch the efforts of the man to master himself. Only a few hours before he was playing the rôle of a tyrant, and now his knees shook and his twitching features betrayed the deadly fear which he vainly strove to hide.

"It is well that you have not attempted to evade responsibility by a plea of ignorance," replied the chief justice. "Such a plea, of course, would not have received consideration, as the law will not take ignorance as an excuse, but nevertheless it is to your credit that you did not seek to justify yourself by pleading it. It is also duly noted by the court that you did not attempt to put on the bold front of injured innocence, and likewise that you have made no utterance of protest against the laws and institutions of the Social Democracy, or given expression to any such heresy as, for example, that put forth by the atavar in this case, that justice should be tempered with mercy. But while this court is ready to see extenuating circumstances in your case, it, of course, has no alternative save to render judgment as fixed by statute. The decree is that your citizenship card shall be forfeited for ten days and that you shall be incarcerated in insane asylum No. 59 for six months."

Harsh though the sentence was, I believe it came as a relief to the prisoner, for his face brightened as though he had been reprieved from death. He followed an inspector of the court out of the room, and that was the last I ever saw of this swashbuckler of a judge. I felt a pity for him, for I now believed that the severity of his outward bearing was but a foil for a tender heart. I was recalled from my musings by the strident voice of the old woman, who had accompanied us into the presence of the court.

"I am — 46987 B C G, and am overseer of insane asylum No. 97," she was telling the chief justice.

"What do you know about this atavar who created such a scene this morning?" queried the justice.

The question at once riveted all my attention on the woman.

"This hussy you speak about," she continued, with an evil leer, "is No.—7891 O C D. She has always given considerable trouble, but your kind-hearted inspectors of asylums took it into their heads some time ago that she was under the law entitled to more freedom of action than I was giving her. It is true she has not committed any act that showed she was an atavar for three years past, and although the law does say that after three years of good conduct the inmate of an asylum may receive a day off from the institution once a month, yet I have known from the first that she was of the incorrigible kind. I have ways of telling that the law does not take note of. I can see it in their eyes. I knew this hussy was playing a part. She was that careful in what she did that I could not get any proof of her perfidy. But she showed quickly enough how two-faced she is when the chance came. You men are blind as bats! If it wasn't for a few women like myself the Social Democracy would soon go to pieces on the rocks. A pretty lot you are to make laws that allow such dangerous characters to roam at will as this creature with her frills and her notions! I called the attention of the inspectors to the careful way in which her hair was combed, and do you know she made them believe that she gave no heed to her hair and that it lay so naturally! The noodles — they were ready to believe anything she told them. But she's safe enough now, I can tell you! You'll not have any more trouble from her. I've got her confined in the solitary, and she'll stay there the full limit of the law if I have my way." And she chuckled fiendishly.

"Stop!" commanded the justice. "You are not the Court. It is evident from everything about this case that the woman in question is an atavar, and one of a dangerous kind." Then turning to his confrères, he said:

"Do you think we should summon her?"

"If I can put in a word there," interjected the old woman, "I would advise you not to do so. You men are all alike — if she comes here who knows but that there will be other judges to have their cards forfeited? I warn you she is dangerous. She

combines witchcraft with her atavism. She will throw
a spell around you and you will no more realize
what you are doing than did the judge you have
just sentenced."

At this the judges held a whispered consultation,
the conclusion of which was announced by the chief
justice:

" The Court has decided that it knows sufficient
of the evidence in this case to regard it as proved
that No.—7891 O C D is an atavar, who should
be closely confined, and, accordingly dispensing with
the presence of the accused, we decree that she shall
be placed in solitary confinement for six months, and
as for you, you termagant, beware! She must receive her due allowance of food and be treated in
accordance with the law — no worse, no better."

The old witch made a mock courtesy, and I saw
there was a covert sneer in the look she gave the
court before shuffling from the room. During her
examination it was with great difficulty I prevented
myself from committing some overt act of indiscretion. I could have throttled her with no more com-
punction that I would feel in killing a snake.

To think that the girl was in the power of this
diabolical creature! In solitary confinement, too, and
doomed to stay there for six months! My thoughts

were such that, had it not been for my good friend,
the doctor, who in warning pinched my arm, I should
have lost all prudence. As it was, when the chief
justice beckoned to me to stand I had quite recovered
command of my wits, and I listened to him with
all the demeanor of a respectful citizen.

"We have before us a full report of your life
since you came among us," said the judge, "and
we have permitted you to witness the administration
of justice in the cases of this weak judge and this perverse girl. We understand that you believed in
Social Democracy while a citizen among the individ-
ualists on earth, and that you are strongly in sympathy with our institutions. It is true that you have
committed one or two small lapses from the path
of loyal rectitude, but some latitude is by law allowed
strangers like yourself in their novitiate. In the main
this report is highly commendatory, however, and
although you displayed some solicitude for the girl
in the court-room this morning, we presume that
your conduct was partly the result of the habit
acquired on earth of being chivalrous to the other
sex. That you did not fall so much under the spell
of the girl as did the judge is proof of your loyalty
to the State, and this proof is reinforced by remarks
which you were overheard to make on your return

from the scene of trial. We have decided, therefore, that there has been nothing in your conduct, so far as this case goes, to make you amenable to any of our laws, and you are released from custody."

"I am duly sensible of the honor the court has paid me," I replied with fine dissimulation. "Truly your institutions far exceed anything that I have ever dreamed of, and I am very glad, indeed, of the privilege accorded me of being a citizen in a State where equality reigns supreme. I can well appreciate that this equality is so precious that it is necessary to maintain the strictest surveillance over those who show marked attributes of individuality unfortunately inherited from their distant ancestors."

"Well said, young man!" remarked the justice. "Those with marked individual traits of character are the most dangerous delinquents that the Social Democracy of Atlantis has to contend with. Yes, we keep a very close watch over those who show the symptoms of atavism, as well as those possessing a perverse disposition. You seem to indicate a very commendable interest in our admirable system of government. I hope that you will soon be assigned to some occupation and receive a wife. I believe in young men settling down early in life, and so does the Social Democracy."

With that we departed and returned the way we came to the dormitory. There I went without my evening meal in accordance with the punishment that had been meted out to me for having been too quick with my prayers.

CHAPTER X

I awoke with a start the next morning. I had been dreaming that I had risen from sleep and witnessed the rising of the sun. What tricks the mind will play us when the conscious self is still steeped in slumber! It seemed so real, that dream. The eastern sky was brilliant with the colors of the dawn, while in the west a star or two twinkled through the dwindling shadows of the night. I could hear the twittering of birds and could see long stretches of meadow partly hidden in the morning mist. I thought I drew deep breaths of invigorating air and that I exulted with nature in the birth of a new day. The sun, in all the panoply of his mighty greatness, emerged above the horizon, and then, alas, I awoke — awoke with a bell ringing in my ears, to the sickening reality of the radium-lighted dungeon of the sea!

I groaned involuntarily. That I should have to pass the rest of my days in Atlantis seemed now a fate most unbearable. Then came the thought of

Atavar — I knew her by no other name — imprisoned in some black hole with an evil hag as a jailer. My thoughts ran in bitter channels. I began to revile in strong terms the Social Democracy — I who once was proud to pose as a martyr to the cause of socialism. Thus does experience often cause us to reject and scorn views once deeply cherished. Believe in a system which found it necessary to entomb innocence and beauty in living graves as the most dangerous enemies of the State? No, never! I continued in this wise to reason with myself and from that day to this I have always been thankful in my heart that sane judgment thoroughly triumphed at this critical moment in my life.

I glanced about at my comrades of the dormitory. These creatures, what are they? I asked myself. Miserable wretches, with souls withered into nothingness, moving like automata through their aimless, barren lives, slaves to their laws. Laws! laws! laws! Was there ever before in all the universe a country where man-made laws had embalmed in mummydom an entire race?

The scales fell from my eyes and I beheld how, in their delirious pursuit of equality, the Atlantides had founded a despotism so complete that it was stifling all the faculties which distinguish man from the brute.

Surely, I said to myself, if Satan has a kingdom he has it here in Atlantis.

These reflections were interrupted by a diversion in the sleeping ward. My comrades here and there were rising from sleep, when six men entered the room, and, proceeding to one of the cots, lifted up the form of a man and carried it out. I noted that the arms and legs of the man hung lifeless, but I inferred that he was only sick and was being removed to the hospital ward. No one appeared to give the episode a passing thought. After the morning meal the doctor showed me to his laboratory — a small room with many shelves filled with books and filing-cases — and it occurred to me to ask about the young man who had been removed.

" Why, my dear friend," responded the doctor, " he was dead ! "

" Dead ! " I echoed, horror-stricken.

" Yes, dead. He had strangled himself with a cord in the night."

" My God ! Suicide ? "

" Do not take it so hard," went on the doctor in quiet tones. " It is nothing, this thing of suicide."

" Nothing to kill one's self ? " I asked in amazement.

The doctor looked on me with a strange light

in his eyes. He lowered his voice to a whisper. I feared he was not quite right in his mind.

" Think," said he, " of the restful oblivion of the grave, where consciousness is freed from the misery of this damning monotony. I have closed the eyes of many a youth who with his own hand sought the happiness he could not find while living. When I see them meditating from day to day on the doing of the deed, do you think I interfere? Not I! I would assist them if I dared. Before you came I, myself, was merely putting off from time to time the accomplishment of my own freedom. Do not look so pained. I tell you that suicide is a brave, noble act, and those that commit it are to be envied, not condemned or pitied."

The doctor paused and, picking up a bottle filled with small black pellets, continued:

" Here is a deadly poison sufficient to emancipate a thousand men from the misery of existence. Take one of these pellets and you can not live an hour."

He stroked the bottle almost lovingly, and then, opening it, took one of the pellets, and handed it to me.

" Take that," he said. " Some day you may appreciate the gift as a favor."

I accepted the pellet mechanically and hid it in a small pocket in my robe.

"Is there no law against suicide?" I asked, not knowing what else to say.

"Law! Of course there is a law. It is a model enactment — explicit, comprehensive and punitive to the last degree. There is no loophole to be found in it."

The doctor smiled grimly and continued:

"But when a man makes up his mind to die he defies all laws. For one supreme moment he asserts his independence as an individual, and while it is true he dies yet he performs at least one act in response to his own will. Those that fail in the act are of course imprisoned, but they usually succeed. The chief effect of the law is to make them succeed."

"Doctor," I responded, "you do not seem to be yourself this morning. Why should you, who are such a good citizen of the Social Democracy, utter sentiments that sound much to me like blasphemy? Do you know that you have practically advised me to commit self-murder?"

"There, now," he replied in whispered entreaty, "do not use harsh terms. I did not mean to shock you. But remember you are still a stranger to this country. You will understand when you have been here a while longer."

He gave me a searching look and I saw that his

hand trembled and that some strong emotion seemed to be mastering him.

"It is time for me to speak plainly to you," he whispered with intensity. "I believe I can trust you. I have studied you and I know there has been rising in your mind an abhorrence of this country and its laws. Is it not so?"

"Yes," I said.

"I knew it, I knew it!" he replied excitedly, fixing my eyes with a steady gaze that read my very soul. "Now will I make a confession to you. Know, my dear friend, that I who outwardly am the most loyal of the loyal, am at heart the State's most bitter foe. I am an atavar!"

"An atavar! you an atavar!" I was altogether incredulous.

"Yes, an atavar," he reiterated, throwing back his head defiantly. "An atavar of the most dangerous kind, for I have hidden my secret until this moment from every living soul, waiting patiently for the time when I might strike a blow which would tell."

He began to pace up and down the room, continuing his confession in intense but low-pitched tones born of years of caution.

"I had almost despaired when you appeared. Year after year have I hoped to find some one in whom I could confide. Some there were who would have gladly listened to me, but I feared their indiscretion. Others there may be who are living a lie as I am doing, but if so, they, too, must fear to confess their secret and so I do not know them. But with you the case is different. You have inherited qualities of self-reliance and resourcefulness. In your blood is that determination, that will that conquers obstacles, and you possess confidence in the dictates of your own judgment and the power of your own right arm. Generations of men, molded in the storm and stress of individual freedom, have bequeathed to you strength of character not to be found in any of those native to this land. I feel that I make no mistake in opening my heart to you. Long have I bided my time, and at last my patience is rewarded."

I listened to the doctor's speech in growing wonder, not unmixed with joy.

"And you are an atavar!" I repeated.

"Yes, an atavar, and I am proud to own to it. You have my secret now. One word from you and I should be thrown in prison to remain until my bones mingled with the earth. But I know you will not betray me." The doctor paused.

"Nothing could make me disclose such a secret.

You may depend on it," I reassured him. He continued:

"The knowledge came to me that I was different from the others when still a child in the public nursery. I chafed under the restrictions placed on our play, and the clock-like precision with which our lives were regulated was irksome to my spirit. But I uttered no complaint. I used my mind and saw that to complain was to be punished. So I left complaining to others, and while my heart rankled against the restraint on my freedom I posed as a youth most obedient to the State. When I grew older I met by accident a girl whose sadness of face and gentleness of manner touched me deeply. I imposed on my good record and so managed to see her secretly. But it was an idle dream. She was taken from me and mated to another. Because of my defiance of the marriage code I was imprisoned for many months and when at last I was discharged it was with a decree that never should woman be given me to wed. Little did my judges dream how well their judgment attuned with my desires, else they would have forced upon me some supercilious creature to mock the memory of her I had lost. Long years have I brooded on the wrong committed against us, and now so whetted is my wish for vengeance that I would deem it the highest privilege fate could grant if I could with my life accomplish one small thing toward the destruction of this cursed Democracy — this damnable Democracy, which, like an octopus with a million tentacles, is throttling the manhood of our entire race. Ah, my friend! Forgive me for the feeling I have shown — there is a cause, there is a cause!"

There were tears in his eyes. In my great pity for him, I grasped his hand and said: "My dear Doctor, I am deeply grateful for your confidence. I who was so lonely in this new world am made to feel again the touch of human sympathy. We understand each other."

The doctor with an effort recovered his usual serenity and busied himself with his bottles. Soon he was speaking again.

"I have something more to say," he went on, "and that is that you, because of your power to think and act for yourself, are capable of coping with any man or set of men to be found in Atlantis. Because of my knowledge of the place and its ways I could give you good counsel, and, between us, who knows what can be accomplished?"

He looked anxiously into my face. I pondered for several minutes and then replied:

" My friend, I do not censure you for wishing to revolutionize this kingdom of the sea. But my judgment says no. It can not be done. I have marked our young comrades dragging themselves away in the morning to their daily labor like felons marching to the prison factories. There is no material there with which to build our revolution. They would not understand — they can not understand. Your atavars, too few in number, are either dead or buried in dungeons we can not open. Besides, Doctor, I have had my fling at reforming people against their will, and it is a thankless task. Do not fondle an impossible hope within your breast. Rather let us think on what may be done."

" And what is that?"

" Why not escape? A few thousand fathoms above our heads there is the land of the sun, the land of life, of vigor, where each man fights his own battles and revels in the strife. There the individual is sovereign, and the State his servant, not his master. Here the State is supreme, and the individual, living no longer for himself, loses those faculties of mind and heart which have raised him out of savagery. Let us plan to leave these people to their fate if we may."

The doctor shook his head.

"What you propose," said he, "is more impossible than that which I propose. No living being has ever escaped from this country to the upper regions. Long before you could reach the surface, even supposing you escaped the krakens, the argonauts and other creatures of the sea, you would be dead from lack of air."

"Possibly you are right," I replied. "But then we shall study the matter, and not give up hope too soon. I came, why should I not return? But mark you," I added after a pause, "I must find that beautiful atavar — she must be rescued, do you understand? and if we find means of escape she must go with us."

"You are talking wildly. It is impossible," returned the doctor.

"Well, if impossible, then be it so, but it sometimes does one good to discuss the impossible. In the meantime while I am here I shall remember the adage, 'When in Rome do as the Romans do.'"

The doctor sighed, but before we left the laboratory we clasped each other by the hand in token of the new bond of friendship between us.

CHAPTER XI

THE WEALTH OF THE ANCIENTS

That day the doctor and I began a series of inspection tours, which, during the course of several weeks, took us over much of the country and greatly increased my knowledge of the people and their customs. I had one ulterior motive in these daily trips, and that, needless to say, was the finding of the institution in which the fair atavar was immured. The doctor sympathized with this aim, and, though we rarely spoke of it, he was as assiduous as myself in seeking out the prison-house. We were under the disadvantage of not daring to make inquiries as to the object of our search, for, had we done so, we must have aroused the suspicion of the inspectors. But as it was, my insatiate thirst for knowledge respecting the institutions we came across was looked on as a subtle tribute to the civilization of the times and resulted in the widest latitude being accorded me in carrying on any investigation I might see fit to make. Not a day passed in which we did not inspect at least half a dozen of the State's establishments; but travel in whatever direction we pleased it seemed impossible to find insane hospital No. 97. Every evening we trudged homeward to our dormitory, disappointed, only to take up the hunt with renewed hope the following day.

It would be impossible to give an account of these many trips. As I write this I am impressed with the manifold phases of life, and what a monumental task it would be for any one to describe with reasonable thoroughness any system of social existence. Did I not shrink from attempting such a work, the limitations of the ordinary book would still force me to leave much unsaid. The student will, I feel, regard that which is omitted as being the more valuable, but by dwelling on those things which impressed me the most I still hope to satisfy in some measure the general desire for knowledge as to the social conditions in Atlantis.

On one of our trips of exploration, it is immaterial which, the doctor and I made a visit to the Hall of Curiosities. I shall never forget my first inspection of this remarkable place, and my narrative would be unpardonably incomplete were I to omit some account of it. In fact, the visit is to be set down as one of the most important incidents of my stay in Atlantis, and, to tell the truth, I know of no more extraordinary happening in my whole life, or one which more deeply affected my destiny.

The Hall was a considerable distance from the dormitory, and in order to reach it we availed ourselves of the rapid transit system of which I have spoken in connection with the trip to the Capitol. We had been traveling for some time with surprising speed when I happened to glance upward at the empyrean of the submerged realm, and was astonished to see that the nebulous blur, which indicated its existence over the larger part of the country, was being resolved into separate and distinct lines of radiance. Now and then I even caught a penetrating glimpse into the depth of the tangled mass which composed the thatching of the mighty roof. I looked askance at the doctor. The latter smiled at my perturbation.

"There is no reason for apprehension," said he. "The dome bends closer than it did some distance back. I have neglected to tell you that the Hall of Curiosities is not a building but a series of chambers, partly artificial and partly natural, in the wall of archæan rock which protects Atlantis on the side of the sea. We are now nearing the confines of the country, and you will notice that our sky and earth gradually approach each other the farther we go.

The sea cliff is some five hundred feet high and the dome apparently rests upon it."

We continued to speed through the semi-darkness, when suddenly I was aware of numerous crystal-like columns of fantastic shapes flying past us on both sides. These columns reflected in dazzling hues the myriad lights which marked the course of our journey, and in a short time their number so greatly increased as to remind me of a forest in fairyland.

" The stalactites," explained the doctor.

The car stopped and we alighted, continuing our journey on foot along a trail through the strange jungle, which seemed to grow denser with every step. The weirdness of the scene almost overwhelmed me. I puzzled my brain to discover how this wonderland had been produced. There was not the least indication of moisture, and the only theory that occurred to me which seemed at all plausible was that, in some distant past, molten lava had dripped from above and solidified, forming the mighty pendants, which hung threateningly overhead, and the columns and grotesque formations of glistening mineral which seemed to hem us in on all sides.

Reaching the great sea-wall at last, we entered a cave-like opening and traversed a narrow tunnel that

led for fully three hundred yards straight into the
rock. We emerged into a brilliantly-lighted chamber
with lofty ceiling and granite walls — a veritable
colosseum in size. I gazed about with astonishment,
for I had considerably underrated the museum in my
preconceived ideas concerning it.

"How many chambers are there like this?" I
asked.

"Six," replied the doctor.

"The immensity of the Hall was something I had
not looked for," I said when I had somewhat recovered
from my surprise. "I have no doubt that the relics
of antiquity make a vast collection."

"True," returned my friend. "You can spend
several months in this place without seeing everything that I know would interest you. Now, this
chamber is known as the throne-room of Bulak, being
named after one of the ancient kings. In the center
you will notice the raised dais on which are the ancient
insignia of royalty."

We approached the central portion of this remarkable subterranean amphitheater and there, as the doctor said, was a platform on which were a score
or more of ancient thrones. Canopies of gold and
purple surmounted them and their seats were rich
with carving and inlaid with jewels.

I looked on them with mingled emotions. Where once the mighty sat, there now lay the scepters and sparkling crowns, coveted no more and looked on with only passive interest in the enlightened age of democracy.

" If you cared to moralize, my friend," continued my preceptor, " you would have a most excellent subject in these tokens of barbarism. Men have committed murder, embroiled society, and involved whole nations in bloody wars to possess these baubles."

" It is a theme on which one might talk an entire day," I replied. " But what is this in these glass cases? "

" The case by which you are standing," was the reply, " contains some of the crown jewels. They are choice heirlooms of past dynasties, and illustrate forcibly the passion for finery and display which I believe is common to all uncivilized peoples."

" I doubt," I remarked, " if the crowned heads of Europe can boast of diadems more resplendent than this one." I pointed to an exquisite piece of royal headgear of conical shape incrusted with diamonds of great size and brilliancy.

But the doctor had left my side and was gazing at an assortment of spears and shields which filled a number of large cases against the wall.

"See!" he cried. "Here is the great armorial collection, and a wonderful collection it is from an historical point of view. Some of these ancient weapons, you will notice, are made of stone, crudely fashioned, indicating a low stage of intellectual development. Then there are those lances of later date made of copper and iron. Relics all of an inhuman past ——"

But I ceased to listen. In my absorption in the crown jewels I gave no attention either to the ancient weapons or the doctor's homily upon them. What were javelins and catapults compared to diadems and rings, golden goblets and jeweled breastplates? The doctor was shocked at the ecstasy with which I was regarding the display of regal magnificence before me.

"You seem to be greatly interested in those petty trinkets," he remarked somewhat testily. "I know they are beautiful in a way, but I am sure I have seen many pebbles and shells just as pleasing."

"You do not seem to appreciate diamonds," I replied.

"No, why should I?" he returned. "They are nothing but bits of clear crystal and are absolutely useless, so far as I know."

"*Sic transit gloria mundi!*" I exclaimed.

"What were you saying?" queried the doctor sharply.

"Pardon me," I replied, "I forgot that you do not know the dead languages. That is a rather hackneyed exclamation, meaning that thus the glory of the world passes away."

"Very good!" returned my friend; "and quite pertinent to this place." He looked about, and, with a sweep of his arm, continued:

"Here lie in truth the buried glories of a world that has gone. Here are the things that men worked, fought and died for when they lived for themselves alone. At least the Democracy is to be commended for eradicating from man's nature that slavish infatuation for glittering stones and shining metals which characterized the ancients and which, if I am correct, still characterizes the people on the earth's surface."

"You amaze me!" I exclaimed. "Do you mean to tell me that the mineral wealth of the ancients is stored in this place?"

"I do. The use of money ceased, you know, with the establishment of the Democracy, and as for the wearing of jewelry, it was interdicted some centuries ago. It was conclusively demonstrated that it was practically impossible to secure equality between all the subjects of the State in the matter of jewel distribution. Petty bickerings and jealousies constantly arose, especially among the women. Do what the State might, some individuals were ever thinking that the ornaments worn by others were prettier than their own. It was therefore declared that the wearing of jewelry was a barbarous custom, and all personal articles of adornment of whatever character were collected and deposited in the Hall of Curiosities. They are here to-day. Thus was the last cause of envy and jealousy removed, and these passions are now unknown in our State."

While the doctor was talking I began to hurry from case to case, finding each filled with precious stones and jeweled ornaments — pendants of pearls and diamonds, signet rings, necklaces of sparkling beads, scintillating stars and glittering crescents, crosses of hammered gold, breastpins of elaborate forms, and, in fact, jewelry of all kinds resplendent with settings of emeralds, rubies, amethysts and other precious stones to me unknown.

The sight of such vast wealth made me reel. My heart sent the blood pulsing to my temples, and I would have fallen had I not grasped a pillar for support.

"The wealth of the ancients!" I repeated to myself. The full significance of the Hall of Curiosities flashed into my mind. I had frequently noted the total absence of jewelry among the Atlantides, and the lack of a medium of exchange was ever a source of wonder to me; but strange though it seems I had not previously speculated as to what had become of the money and jewels of the departed races. The sudden solution of the mystery almost overpowered me. I stood for some moments endeavoring to comprehend the magnitude of this new-found Golconda, when the thought of its possible bearing on my own fortunes inflamed my mind.

" If it were only mine," I thought, " what could I not do with it! It would make me mightier than all the potentates in the world." Then a passionate frenzy for possession seized me.

" It is mine, it is mine! " I exclaimed; " mine by right of discovery! I am rich, I am rich! "

So fired was my brain that I was oblivious to all surroundings. The wealth was within my grasp, mine for the mere taking. No longer was I a mere vagabond to be kicked from pillar to post. The world cringed and fawned, honors were heaped on me, and my lightest wish was law. The trust barons and magnates of Wall Street — I was greater than all of them!

There is no telling how far my indiscretion would have carried me, had not the castles I was building been rudely shattered by a voice that rang in my ear.

"Come!" it said. "Have you lost your reason? Be careful!"

Startled I turned and faced the doctor.

"I am afraid," he continued somewhat grimly, "you forget that you are still in Atlantis. Now I want you to look at this stone colossus. Did you ever see anything so grotesque or ugly?"

I ran my eyes unheedingly over the savage god. Though I dimly appreciated the folly of my demeanor and had recovered some measure of mental calmness, yet nevertheless I could not summon any interest in anything except the vast array of neglected wealth. Being determined to inspect it fully, I grasped the doctor by the arm and almost by main force pulled him away from the colossi, the ivory tusks, the primitive plows, and other crude objects in which he seemingly delighted. In this wise we went through aisle after aisle of crowded cases all filled with treasure of inestimable value. Falling in at last with my humor, the doctor raised the glass covering of one of the cases and took out a diamond whose size dwarfed all the famous gems of the upper world. I seized it, rubbed

The sight was overpowering my senses. *Page 101*

it with the sleeve of my garment and held it to the light. It blazed with such internal fires that I was nearly blinded. It was too wonderful for comprehension, and I pressed my disengaged hand to my eyes to shut out a sight that was overpowering my senses. When I opened my eyes again and saw that all before me was real, I was seized with a sudden desire to hide the stone, and made a furtive movement toward the folds of my garment.

"Doctor," I said in an awed whisper, "if we had this single stone on earth we should be financial kings."

The doctor looked at me in pity and alarm. He snatched the stone from my hand and hurriedly placed it in the receptacle. "Have you forgotten again?" he asked, and then, taking me by the arm, with some force he led me away from the jewels and out of the chamber.

On entering the next room, which was nearly as large as the one we had just left, I observed bin-like structures built around the walls and in rows across the center. Looking more closely I was astounded to see that they were filled with coin which apparently had been dumped into them as coal is dumped into our cellars. The precious metal could have been reckoned in tons.

"Here," said my guide, "is the entire monetary circulation of ancient days. There are coins here of gold, electrum, silver, iron, copper and stone. By studying them you can, in a way, read the history of the ancients."

I gazed open-mouthed at the exhibit. Leaning over one of the bins I permitted myself to finger the coins. The passion for acquisition again took strong hold on me, and, plunging my arms to the elbows in the golden coins, I scooped them up and let them fall in glittering streams. I cooled my fever with the feel of the precious piles. I laughed aloud in the very glee and lust of greed.

The doctor gripped my shoulders and held me as in a vise.

"Again I warn you — the inspectors!" he whispered in my ear.

Instantly I realized my indiscretion and turned away.

"These coins," said I aloud, "are interesting relics. They much resemble old pieces of money I have seen on earth. I could not decipher the inscriptions on any of them, but the heads, which are stamped upon some, fairly portray the countenance of the brutal savage."

Apparently believing that I was only interested

scientifically in the numismatic collection, the inspectors passed on without a word. With an effort, I mastered my excitement and began to look on the wealth about me with some show of stoicism.

The doctor called my attention to a collection of comparatively modern coins, among which were English sovereigns, some American eagles, and a great quantity of Spanish doubloons and pieces of eight. I looked inquiringly at the doctor.

"These coins," he explained, "came from chests taken from the sea. They were probably the property of your friend, Captain Kidd, of whom we have spoken."

At last I had discovered the buried hoards of the pirates!

"What else was found in these chests?" I asked.

"I believe a variety of things," was the answer. "Come into the next room."

Following him I came to a place in which a number of skeletons of marine monsters were the most prominent objects.

"There must be some frightful beasts in the sea," I said as I gazed with a shudder about me.

"There are," was the laconic reply.

Going to a case the doctor pointed out some of the property of the pirates. Dirks and knives and black flags were carefully laid out for exhibition. Several blunderbusses and revolvers attracted my notice. The doctor asked me to explain their use. I found that he was entirely ignorant of gunpowder, and I promised him I would some day give an exhibition of the use of firearms, if opportunity arose and I could find the substance to make the powder.

What most interested me in this exhibition, however, was a number of small books, which upon examination proved to be New Testaments. They bore the marks of frequent fingering, and many of the pages were turned down. On the fly-leaf of one I could barely decipher the words: " From your loving mother." There were also several crucifixes and a number of crosses in the collection, showing that in some instances, at least, piety and piracy went hand in hand. Or was it that these men, despite their evil lives, still clung with desperate hope to these emblems of righteousness and salvation?

Maps of islands, with curious markings upon them, indicating perhaps the places of buried treasure; a few illegible letters, and a book or two full of writing, detailing the capture of vessels, the number of people who walked the plank and similar information of an edifying character, were things in the collection that I pored over with interest.

"Now, since you seem to be ready to think of something else besides diamonds and gold," began the doctor, interrupting my reflections, "I want to show you some samples of credit cards once used by the Democracy."

I gave a cursory glance at the cards which the doctor held for my scrutiny, and saw that they resembled the ordinary commutation tickets used in American restaurants.

"These cards," continued the doctor, "were issued in the early days. Each individual received annually an equal number of them, good for a certain amount of credit at the store-houses then conducted by the State. Theoretically, the system seemed excellent, but in practice it was found to be quite unsatisfactory. Had the early socialists given the subject deeper study they would have seen, even before adopting it, that the system would only partly remedy the so-called evils growing out of individual initiative. It effectually, it is true, checked unequal production by different individuals, for this must be the necessary result of equal compensation. But it did not reach those evils growing from untrammeled individual initiative in the matter of personal expenditures. Having a whole year's income at their immediate disposal, many were not satisfied until they had wasted it in fast liv-

ing, and each month added to the thousands who
had exhausted their credit for the current year. But
those whose constitutions demanded only a minimum
of nutriment, and who were not otherwise possessed
of extravagant tastes, found they could live within the
credit assigned them and have a remainder. The inevitable outcome was the building of a most despicable
form of tyranny, in which those who possessed fore-
sight and frugal habits lorded it over their less fortunate brothers. This they did by exacting such
terms in favors and services as they pleased, in exchange for those commodities secured on their cards
which they did not need for themselves. As the individual whose credit was exhausted could not evade
service for the State, he was compelled to devote his
time for leisure in slaving for the new species of
tyrants. Despite the laws, the latter in time acquired
a practical immunity from work of any kind, and
arrogated to themselves all the honors of government.
But the agitation for a more thorough democracy
continued unabated and at last triumphed. The card
system was abolished, public kitchens and dining-halls
were established, and individual initiative in personal
expenditure was completely done away. The principle that no individual should· enjoy a better living
than another, no matter how much he produced or

saved, was in this wise given a rigid application. A considerable saving in labor was incidentally accomplished by stopping the printing of the cards and abolishing the system of espionage necessary to prevent counterfeiting. I have forgotten just what this saving amounted to, but you will find by reading the records that there was a general rejoicing because a material reduction in the amount of daily labor was effected by the reform."

"Was the reduction in daily labor permanent?" I asked aimlessly.

"No," the doctor replied, "I can not say it was. Really, it is remarkable as well as sad how, in the sequel, the benefits of government regulation vanish into nothingness. But then no matter about that. I am now speaking from the socialistic point of view and want to add that the issuing of the cards was another illustration of the truth that avarice can be eradicated from the human heart only by doing away with everything in which the element of personal ownership enters, even in the slightest degree. No individual in Atlantis can now point to a single object and say that it belongs to himself alone. Even his clothes are the property of the State, and as one garment differs in no wise from another, no opportunity is given for a display of personal striving to outshine one another. All these gewgaws over which you have been gloating are the property of the State, and, while no one owns them in particular, no one can wear them."

"Indeed, this is a virtuous realm," I replied as I ran my hands down into a heap of diamonds which stood near the pirates' collection. "Selfishness has been absolutely crushed for the want of something to feed upon. Now, isn't that stone a beauty?"

"Come away and leave that dirt alone," urged my friend. "I wish to show you something in the next room which I know you will be interested in."

Here I found prows of ships with figureheads, kegs filled with nails, anchors and other debris of heavy weight, which had come down from the derelicts of the sea. Idols of fantastic shape, sculptured marble, ancient and curious objects made of copper and stone occupied much space. The doctor drew me before a painting of a ship in a storm at sea.

"That picture," he said, "is one of the most interesting objects in the entire Hall to me. I have stood here by the hour and gazed at it. It was found in a sea chest. Does the surface of the sea actually have that appearance?"

I explained that it did during a storm. Then I tried to tell him as best I could of the varying moods

of the sea, of the brightness of the sun and the blue
of unclouded skies. He listened as a child would to
a fairy tale. For a long time he stood absorbed in
the picture, and, in truth, the fury of the elements
which it portrayed wove a spell on us both, lifting
our minds above sordid thoughts and filling us with
awe of the eternal and majestic forces of the universe.
The doctor turned from the painting with a sigh.

"There is still another picture I wish you to see,"
he said.

It was the painting of a beautiful girl, with bright
eyes and smiling face. She stood challenging one's
admiration, in full consciousness of her power of
conquest.

"There," said the doctor, "is something worth far
more than all your diamonds. I gaze on this picture every chance I have — I can hardly realize there
are any creatures in the world so lovely."

"But there are!" I replied with enthusiasm. "The
world is full of them; they are the goddesses of the
earth above! Look at her! Note the beauty of her
adornment — the harmony of color and the sweeping
curves of her dress, the rose in her hair, the brooch at
her throat! Then look at her face — do you see any
stamp of care or despair or weariness there? No,
and why? It is because she is adorable and is

adored! Upon her is lavished a father's care, a
mother's love, and now she awaits some sweetheart to
take her and cherish her for life. Compare her to
your women of Atlantis. What have you done with
them? You have robbed them, taken from them
everything that makes life worth the living and given
them a cheerless, hopeless and barren existence. How
could you expect true womanhood to bud and flower
under your infernal laws?"

I paused almost breathless and red-hot with indig-
nation. The doctor looked about, but no one had
overheard.

"You belong to a race of idiots, Doctor," I exclaimed, "and I shall lose no time in getting away
from here with the first opportunity."

The doctor now piloted me through the remaining
rooms of this sepulcher of vanities. In one there was
a large collection of books, among which I found
copies of Shakespeare's and Cervantes' masterpieces.
There were also various nautical books, some sea
charts and a few scientific works. The records of ancient Atlantis, written on papyrus, were likewise here.
We did not stop to examine this queer library, leaving
it for future visits. In the last room I sat down exhausted and bewildered by all I had seen.

"This is certainly the most interesting place in all

Atlantis," I remarked. "I should think it would be crowded, but I notice very few people here."

"It is the place of greatest interest to me," replied the doctor, "but I do not come often because it might be seen that I liked it too well. But to the average citizen of the Democracy it seems to possess no attraction. Very few ever seek to come here, and the mass of the people are wholly indifferent about it."

"Don't they show any interest in anything?"

"Rarely — except on certain occasions."

"On what occasions, may I ask?"

The doctor hesitated and then said in a tone that had a note of bitterness in it: "You will learn in due time.

"This room in which you are now sitting," he continued, "is the one nearest to the ocean. There are a number of places in which egress to the sea is reached and this is one of them. Yonder door," he said, pointing to a great sheet of copper which appeared to be built in the wall, "is the entrance to a large air-tight chamber. The door is very massive and is operated by radium force, sliding smoothly on bearings into the wall. All that you need to do to open it is to press a button. Supposing that you have prepared yourself for the sea and gone into the chamber, you press another button and the door closes. Then, by opening the valves of several large pipes, you let in the water from the ocean until the chamber is filled. Now, by pressing a button, another sliding door is opened and you step out into the sea. When you wish to return you enter the chamber, cause the sea door to close, and open the valves of certain pipes through which the water is pumped out and conveyed to a distilling plant. There the salt is taken from it and it becomes a part of the water supply of Atlantis."

"A very simple system," I observed. "It reminds me of the locks used in our canals. I can see that it would be impossible, perhaps, to pump the water back into the sea — the pressure of the ocean at this depth must be many tons to the square inch."

"Of course," he replied, "it is hardly necessary for me to add that this system comes down to us from antiquity, as does also the reduction plant for the sewage, and the great laboratories for maintaining the purity of the air."

"Suppose," said I, "the door of that sea-lock were opened when the sea was pressing against it, what would happen?"

"It can not then be opened. Neither it nor the outer sliding door will open except when the pressure is equal on both sides. I may add that, in order to guard against accidents as well as to see that none goes into the sea who has not the proper credentials, there are inspectors constantly on duty in the hall."

"Then our prison house is well bolted and barred, after all," I exclaimed with some disgust.

"What are you thinking of?"

"I was thinking, my dear Doctor, that this store-house is convenient to the sea. We have now only to find the means for reaching the surface, and when we succeed in this we shall, with your kind permission, leave this land of equality, full-burdened with the despised wealth of the ancients!"

CHAPTER XII

The day following my first visit to the Hall of Curiosities an inspector of the Department of Miscellaneous Affairs of State made me a ceremonious call. The doctor and I were engaged in talk in a small room adjoining the laboratory, which room had become our favorite retreat, when the door was thrown open without warning and there entered an individual whose countenance was even more sallow and sphinx-like than the average in Atlantis. Without even the hint of a smile this specimen of facial petrifaction made me a formal bow and launched forth on his message, which he delivered in a monotone so remarkable that it was impossible to pick out a single syllable that received more force than another.

" Sir stranger," said he, " the department to which I belong considers those unusual matters of State that do not fall correctly within the province of other departments. Among the abstruse problems with which we have been engaged for some weeks is that of determining whether you should be admitted into citizen-

114

ship in the Social Democracy. It is, perhaps, known to you that all official acts in this land are performed in line with the letter of the statutes, and it is one of the evidences of our advanced stage of civilization that very little is left to chance or to the uncertain judgment of the human mind. But in your case we found little law that was applicable, and though, after protracted search, several precedents were discovered in the records of two hundred years ago, yet these precedents were poor guide-posts at best. In order that we may not be embarrassed in like manner in the future we have appealed to the popular assembly to devise a code to govern cases such as yours; but as it will take considerable time before this code can be promulgated, we have been compelled to reach a conclusion in this instance, and we leave it to the future to justify the wisdom of our momentous decision. It is proper for me to state that when you first arrived among us we caused a search of your apparel in the hope of finding credentials showing whence you came, but nothing of the kind was secured. We did find on you, however, an interesting document on *The Iniquities of the Capitalistic Régime,* which was a strong argument for favorable consideration in your behalf. Since then you have been closely watched, and all the reports of your conduct appear to indicate that you are thoroughly in accord with our institutions. These reasons for granting you citizenship may not be conclusive, but there seems to be an entire absence of data of an unfavorable character, and we therefore have declared that you are entitled to full citizenship and the enjoyment of all the benefits of equality under which we live."

With this he handed me a card which read as follows:

DEPARTMENT OF MISCELLANEOUS AF-
FAIRS OF STATE

THIS IS TO CERTIFY THAT THE HOLDER HAS BEEN DE-
CLARED A CITIZEN OF THE DEMOCRACY

I took the card and thanked him with great gravity. "I wish to say," I added, "that I feel honored with the consideration shown me and that I deeply appreciate this mark of confidence in my loyalty to the Democracy."

When the ambassador of the Department of Miscellaneous Affairs of State had taken his departure the doctor turned to me with a sigh.

"I suppose," he said, "that this action presages a change in our relations, which I much dread; but then we should be thankful that you have passed one great point of danger, for had they decided otherwise you might have become food for the kraken."

It seemed, however, that we had not received our only caller for that day, for we had hardly resumed our conversation when there walked into the room two men who proved to be inspectors of the Department of Vital Statistics. One of them carried a note-book and pencil and the other was armed with a tape-line and several measuring sticks. I was required to remove part of my clothing, and without useless ceremony these men began to take measurements. Very little was said during the procedure except by the individual who did the measuring, and he confined his remarks strictly to the business in hand.

"Length of head," said he, as he made the required measurement, "five karets. He belongs to Class A."

"Five karets, Class A," repeated the other as he jotted down something in his book.

"Width of head," continued the manipulator of the measuring sticks, "one obit and one karet. Subclass D."

"It is written," replied the other.

In this wise the pair of matter-of-fact gentlemen continued to place me on record. My right ear, the middle finger of my left hand, the little finger of my right, my right foot, my right forearm and my height, standing and sitting, were all duly set down in the book. When they came to taking my girth I thought I noted an unusual appearance of interest on the part of both. The man with the tape measured it several times before he announced the result, but even then he with the book declined to accept the figure given until he had himself verified it. I inferred that they considered my girth quite unusual, though I must confess I had never thought it so myself.

Having completed their measurements the men had the audacity to stand off a few paces and size me up critically, after the fashion of prospective buyers studying a horse to discover blemishes.

" I should say that he is a brunette of the third degree," said one of them.

" Yes, that is about right," replied the other judicially.

" His eyes are dark brown, he has an ugly nose, his chin is ferocious and his general cast of countenance is unprepossessing. I do not think he is entitled to more than ten per cent. for looks."

" No, he is not a beauty, that is sure," the other agreed. " I think that ten per cent. is rather liberal, but then we will let it go at that."

I was beginning to feel nettled, but before I could

shape a fitting rebuke for their conduct they turned on their heels and with a "We are through" left the room.

I gazed at the doctor and saw signs of suppressed mirth.

"Are those fellows crazy," I cried, "or were they making sport of me?

"Neither," the doctor replied, trying to speak naturally. "They were merely obtaining data for the records of the Democracy, as is their duty. They meant no offense." The doctor paused, then continued:

"I will explain. You must know that a complete record of every individual in this country is kept on the books of the Department of Vital Statistics. You will receive a number now, and these measurements and general remarks as to your looks will be placed on a card, together with your number, and filed away. The Department has a system for the classification of its cards which would certainly interest you. I take it from what I heard that your classification will be A D G C Q R B S T X Z. I may have forgotten one or two subdivisions, but I am approximately correct. For purposes of abbreviation you will be generally known as being in the A D G class."

"Your explanation needs explaining," I replied

irritably. " Why don't you string the whole alphabet together and be done with it ? "

" It is this way," the doctor went on imperturbably. " All of the citizens of this country are divided into two great classes — the long-headed class and the short-headed class. As your head is considerably longer than six and one-half inches, the average among us, you belong to class A, or the long-headed class. Class B is the short-headed class. Now each of these main classes is subdivided into narrow- and wide-headed classes. You are placed in subclass D because you have a wide head. These subclasses are then divided into two divisions, according to the length of the middle finger on the left hand. I could go on showing you the various subdivisions into which the measurements just taken have placed you, but I believe you see the principle used in the classification, and that it would be very easy to pick out your identification card in the public archives, even if you lost your card, for all it would be necessary to do would be to retake your measurements. As it is impossible for any one to change the length of his head or add to his stature, you can readily see that no citizen can hope to escape the record kept of him by the government."

When I grasped the system employed for keeping tab on the citizens of the Democracy I was filled

with admiration for its simplicity. Then the thought
came that there was something familiar about it, and
suddenly it dawned on me.

"Why, Doctor," I exclaimed. "there is nothing
new about your system! They use the same thing on
the surface of the earth in order to keep track of
convicts and criminals. Once more I find additional
resemblance between your Democracy and the government of a prison."

After a pause, the doctor not replying, it occurred
to me to ask him how it was that, in a land of equality,
it was recognized that some people had longer heads
than others.

"You now touch," said he, "on one of the great
unsolved problems of the Democracy. Many efforts
have been made to correct the too evident dissimilar-
ity between individuals in this and other respects,
but not with much success. For example, in order to
produce greater uniformity in the length of the head,
the plan has been tried of using pressure on the
heads of the children, but the results have been
sadly disappointing. It seems that the human race
has for many ages been without the salutary checks
of a beneficent system of laws, and can now be compared to a rank growth of weeds of all shapes and
sizes. Recognizing the hopelessness of immediately

eradicating inequalities inherited from thousands of
years back, modern thought has reached the conclusion
that these inequalities can be overcome only by patiently following out certain policies through several
generations. One of these policies is the strict enforcement of the rule that unlikes and not likes should
be married. For example, if it is decided that you
should marry, the State will choose as your mate the
woman among those available for marriage who least
resembles you."

"That would be very kind of the State," I interpo-
lated.

"Yes, perhaps," the doctor replied, "and if you
will permit me to describe your future bride I should
say, judging from your record, that she will have
a very small head, a very slender waist, will be considerably under stature, a pronounced blonde, and
beautiful,— according to the standards of beauty used
by the inspectors." Here the doctor smiled.

"The standards of beauty as used by the inspectors?" I echoed. "Heavens! Why, Doctor, without
being boastful, I was regarded on earth as being quite
handsome — at least, I think I can truthfully say that
I was not looked upon as ugly. Gods! If those
inspectors choose me a wife she will be a hideous
dwarf! But — the thing is not worth considering."

"Not worth considering!" exclaimed the doctor. "I should think it is decidedly worth considering. No man can hope to escape marriage in this country, and no man can do his own selecting. You are such an unusual specimen of a man that there may be some serious argument as to whether you shall be permitted to marry. It may be considered unwise to pollute the pure strain of the nation's blood, you know. But then law is law, and my guess is that it will be finally concluded that, being admitted into citizenship, you must marry."

"Are you serious? They will marry me off without consulting me?"

"I mean all I say," continued the doctor. "You will be waited on by an inspector in due time, and he will inform you when the ceremony will take place, and you will have to attend as the groom."

Then, noting the look on my face, he hastily added:

"But it will be only for three years. At the end of that time either you or your wife may demand that the bonds of wedlock be dissolved, but I warn you that, in case they are dissolved, you will again be subject to marriage unless, as in my case, you commit some crime, and as a punishment it is decreed you shall not be permitted to marry again."

"Three years? What an arrangement!" I ex-

claimed. " But, Doctor, I shall draw the line on marriage,— you may depend on that. Do you suppose I
would submit to three years of perdition? No, sir,
not while I have my wits about me or a drop of blood
in my veins! "

I began to walk up and down the room.

"Your countrymen," I went on, " are a pack of
driveling dolts! They are contemptible cowards! To
think that any race of people should become so inanely
submissive, so devoid of manliness, so spineless, that
they even allow the State to do their love-making
for them! Really, I should consider it impossible for
men to sink to such degradation, were it not for the
evidence of my own eyes. I truly have more regard
for the lowest animals in the brute creation than I
have for these counterfeit imitations of men about me.
Let them marry me off? I'll fight your whole damnable Democracy first! "

CHAPTER XIII

I FALL A VICTIM TO THE LETHE WEED

Thus far I have neglected to give any information as to the principal meal in Atlantis, and some of my readers must certainly be curious respecting it. Perhaps their sympathies may have been aroused for the people because of that diet of gruel which constituted their morning repast, and it would not be surprising if, in their generous hearts, they hope that the dinner was more pretentious. I am happy to say it was. Here is the bill of fare on the day I was made a citizen of the Democracy:

Shredded Seaweed Biscuit
Salad of Chopped Sea-horse
Choice Cuts of Sea-dog
Llianas (Sea-greens)
Boikas (Atlantian Potatoes)
Mana (Bread)
Dopum (Atlantian Coffee)

Lest the apparent lavishness of this menu should give rise to erroneous conclusions, I make haste to state that an old saying in Atlantis had it that man

can not live on gruel alone. The origin of this saying had an intimate connection with some distressing
experiences through which the nation had gone in the
past. To tell the plain truth, the feasting of the latter
part of the day was but the necessary complement of
the frugality practised in the morning; and it is not to
be taken as evidence that too much food was available
at times in Atlantis. I wish also to explain that the
dinner was served in courses, each course consisting
of a sample of food, carefully measured out and
weighed, so that no person had the fraction of an
ounce more than another. Thus were the ends of
national economy and equality carefully and rigidly
subserved.

Some comment may be occasioned by reason of the
menu savoring so largely of the sea, but the geograph-
ical location of Atlantis, I think, furnishes ample
explanation. Any nation situated as it was must
necessarily resort to the valleys of the deep for its
prey. The sea has ever been known as a good pro-
vider, and it is not strange that many sharks, krakens,
sword-fish, sea-cows, turtles, dolphins and many other
curious forms of life were found in abundance within
reasonable distance of the submerged island. This
variety in the supply of edible meats made it possible
now and then to alter somewhat the bill of fare, and

the uncertainty as to what changes would be made added an agreeable zest to the daily existence.

I should be glad to give some particulars as to the manner in which the various dishes were prepared, but, to confess the truth, I never quite mastered the mysteries of the public kitchens. I can only say that I ate everything I could obtain with much avidity. The sea-horse salad was a dainty morsel to my palate, and the sea-dog reminded me of beefsteak. The man with an abnormal appetite is a poor judge of culinary art,— a fact which is well illustrated by the eagerness with which the Parisians ate rats during the German siege, and by similar tales as to the loss of fastidiousness in taste by men overmastered by the craving for food.

I have spoken about the ends of equality being subserved, but to this statement I am in duty bound to make one reservation. I refer to the fact that some of the population were not allowed to eat when the majority did. The excuse was that a few occupations were of such a nature as to preclude their followers from enjoying a privilege open to the many. I could never reconcile in my own mind the inconsistency of this excuse with the fundamental principles of the Democracy. For example, there were the meal inspectors. Did they not have as much right as any other class of people to eat at the time the principal meal was served? I could never refrain from admiring the self-control of these men, who, stifling the pangs of hunger, watched us consume the food before us, their alert eyes ever ready to detect the least infraction of the rules as to the handling of eating utensils, the mastication of food and the other regulations contained in the interesting and voluminous Dinner Code. Perhaps these martyrs of the Democracy satisfied their longing for food at a second table, but even if they did, what must they have suffered in the agony of waiting?

When the doctor and I had finished our dinner on the day of which I am speaking, we returned to the anteroom of the laboratory, and there, having closed the door, my friend surreptitiously handed me a chunk of mana, which he said he had preserved from his share at dinner, hiding it in his robe when the inspectors were not looking. I accepted the kindness with profuse thanks, and, keeping the hard-baked crust buried in the folds of my garment, I now and then stole a nibble from it. By this flagrant disregard of the sacred Dinner Code the demands of my appetite were considerably assuaged, and I began to feel that comfortable physical sensation which craves a good cigar.

" Doctor," I said at last, giving audible expression to my desire, " I wish I had a smoke."

Now I no more expected having my wish granted than in other days I expected to become a man of money by mere virtue of saying aloud, as I frequently did, that I wished I had a thousand dollars. Imagine my surprise then when the doctor replied:

" Why, certainly you may have a smoke, or as many as you wish. You see this is the smoke-time. I do not indulge, except at rare intervals, and I had not thought that you would care to do so, or I would have introduced you to the lethe weed before this. But I must say I do not think you should smoke — or I either, for that matter."

" Oh, smoking in moderation never did any one harm, Doctor. Come, now, let me sample your weed."

The doctor with hesitation yielded to my persuasions, and, leaving the room, returned shortly with a number of cigars which looked like Pittsburg cheroots, only they were much longer and red instead of black in color. Hastily lighting one I found that it smoked freely and that the flavor was pleasant, having a faint suggestion of opium. The doctor also lighted one, and for some moments we smoked in silence.

" Why, Doctor," I said at last, " this is an excellent smoke. It is strange you have not told me about these cigars before. I hardly looked for such a luxury in Atlantis."

"It is more than a luxury," the doctor replied gloomily. "It is a curse."

"Don't be a croaker. I grant that smoking may be a vice, but how could it be a curse?"

No reply was forthcoming to this. As I continued to smoke I became conscious of a growing feeling of exhilaration. I was surprised to find that things began to appear in a new light. All my pessimism and dark forebodings disappeared, and a feeling of great content took possession of me. Life, I told myself, was not half so bad in Atlantis as I had imagined. The doctor now began to talk and I listened with heightened interest.

"I have said that smoking is a curse," he began. "I meant it; but you will judge for yourself. I can see that you are already under the influence of the weed. I, too, shall be under its influence in a short time. It affects me less quickly than you, perhaps because this is your first experience. There are millions of these cigars, as you call them, smoked in this country, and at this time of the day the whole population, male and female, banishes dull care and revels in the pleasures of a narcotic debauch."

"Narcotic debauch! You are a true doctor. The

men of your profession where I came from were for
ever inveighing against the use of tobacco, and here
you are calling a little indulgence in the weed a debauch. As you sit there smoking that cheroot you
remind me of a physician I once knew, who was
always preaching to his patients about the baneful
effects of nicotine and who at the same time was himself an inveterate smoker. You doctors are wonder-
fully consistent!"

"Well, my friend," he rejoined with a faint smile,
"I don't mind acknowledging that I am at times
something of a scold. We look at things too darkly
sometimes, and despite what I have said, smoking *is*
a great pleasure." With this he began to draw on his
cheroot with much complacency, sending little blue
rings now and then toward the ceiling. "I have no
doubt," he continued after a brief silence, "that where
you came from smoking was permitted without any
restraints whatever. At last we find one thing in
which there is an analogy between your country and
this."

"If you think there are no restraints to the tobacco
habit on the surface of the earth, you are very much
mistaken," I replied. "The government there taxes
the tobacco industry to the limit, making it possible
for only the rich to smoke what they please and as

much as they please. Then, again, in some parts it is even a prison offense to smoke cigarettes."

"You astonish me! I thought that yours was an individualistic country, where every man could do just as he pleased and where the government did not seek to oppress any industry or calling."

"And you astonish me," I rejoined, "when you intimate that the Social Democracy does not regulate the number of cigars consumed by the individual."

"How strange!" remarked the doctor after a pause. "So I was wrong in believing that there was an analogy between this country and yours, even in this smoke business. What one would think individualism would not do, it does, and what socialism might be expected to do, it does not."

"Yes, there is something rather strange about that," I said. "But, so far as individualism is concerned, its tobacco regulations prove its tyranny. Somebody says that smoking is a vice, is deleterious to the health, and then a lot of goody-good people take it up and, the first thing you know, the government is making war against the so-called evil. It is the same way with gambling, drinking and many other things. I call it offensive interference with the right of every man to enjoy himself as he pleases, and if a man is foolish enough to contract injurious habits, it's his own funeral and nobody else's. Some contend that the weakness in man's nature must be protected from temptation, and that men must be restricted from indulging too deeply in certain pleasures in order to keep others from following their example to their physical and mental detriment. But I consider such argument absurd."

"Your explanation of why the tobacco habit is restrained by your government is interesting," the doctor remarked. " Now in the Democracy, we are not worried about vices. The principle on which we act is that each individual should have all he wants of everything with the least possible expenditure of labor in return for it. In the case of food, for instance, theoretically there is no limit set to the amount of each individual's consumption, but in practice it has been found that the supply is insufficient to satisfy the desires of all and thus the necessity of laws to insure the equitable division of such supply as exists. But when it comes to smoking, the ideal aim of democracy is unobstructed by considerations as to the available supply of the smoke-weed, or, as we call it, the lethe weed. This weed grows in inexhaustible quantities in a wild state, and only a moderate amount of labor is required to gather it and convert it into cheroots. I never could understand why nature should be so nig-

gardly in regard to the necessities of life and so bounti-
ful with the smoke-weed. Perhaps it is one of her
mistakes which cry so loud for correction."

"It gives me pleasure to hear you talk with such
wisdom," I rejoined, "and I am glad to be in a land
governed by sane ideas. It occurs to me, however,
that, as there are no vexatious problems as to the
supply, your people would smoke the entire day."

"My dear sir, they would," returned my friend,
"if it were not that smoking and working do not go
well together. In order to maintain the requisite
supply of food it was found after some heartrending trials that smoking would have to be prohibited
during working hours. I do not know why nature
should throw so many obstacles in the way of a true
socialistic state, but she seems determined that man
shall not enjoy that full measure of ease and comfort
which his desires cry out for. However, the Democracy seeks to ameliorate the tyranny of nature as
much as possible, and this being the smoke-time, let
us enjoy ourselves while we may. I think that during
these last few days we must have been under some
evil spell, talking and planning as we did. It is a
mistake to worry and it is useless to complain, when
it is evident that the Democracy is handling the problems of existence in the best possible manner and with

a full regard for the equal rights of all. Listen,—
there is the lecture bell. Take another weed and come
with me. We shall mingle with our brothers and perhaps hear something that will be interesting in the
assembly-room."

CHAPTER XIV

As the doctor led the way out of the room I felt a peculiar lightness and my legs seemed a trifle unsteady. I made an effort, like a man in drink, to collect my faculties. The thought came that perhaps I was narcotized, but so agreeable were my sensations that I cared not. Better be drunk, I told myself, than sober in such a country, and the idea seemed so humorous that I laughed aloud. My mirth must have been infectious, for I could see by the facial expression of my preceptor that he, too, was near to laughing. It was good to behold the somber doctor, light-hearted and free from care. His conversation was animated, and the way he extolled the Social Democracy would have done credit to a Fourth-of-July orator in a country town.

We strolled arm in arm through several halls and at last into a large room. The place was so filled with smoke that it took some time to discern that it was well crowded with my comrades of the dormitory. The young men sat about on benches, taking their ease in all attitudes. What surprised me the most, however, was that they were actually talking to each other. The scene was so out of accord with all my previous experiences in Atlantis that I pinched myself to make sure I was not the victim of some fantasy. Being reasonably assured that it was reality I was filled with rapture. I never had been a recluse and the silent ways of the Atlantides had added much to my growing antipathy for them. But now they appeared to act like rational beings, and the hum of their voices seemed the sweetest music I had ever heard.

The doctor conducted me to the front of the hall, and, wheeling me about so that all could see my face, he said:

"Comrades, it is my pleasure to introduce you to-night to a stranger from a strange land. Though an American, this man was born with strong socialist instincts, and through the kindness of fate has been snatched from an existence of woe among savages to dwell with us in equality for the remainder of his days."

The hum of conversation ceased, and a few hand-claps followed the doctor's words. There was an embarrassing pause, when two or three voices called out:

"Welcome to Atlantis! You are welcome!"

These kind greetings made me recover my equipoise, and I said from the bottom of my heart:

"Friends and fellow citizens, I appreciate very deeply your kindly welcome. Your land is the ideal that has been in my mind for years. I little dreamed, when on earth I followed the flag inscribed, 'One for All, and All for One,' that I should live to see this ideal in existence. I have observed you well and have been filled with admiration for the great army of the Democracy of which you are members. And now that the army after its day's march, so to speak, has come to parade rest, I shall be only too happy to meet all of you personally and enjoy the amenities of the hour."

More hand-clapping followed, and I was surrounded by a number of those who had been sitting near at hand. They engaged me in pleasant conversation, congratulating me on my arrival among them and saying they were glad to make my acquaintance. It all seemed so natural, so reminiscent of old times on earth, that I was transported to the fifteenth heaven.

"I would like you to meet an old friend." It was the voice of the doctor speaking in my ear, and I turned about, to be confronted by the sea-surgeon who had rescued me. It was so much like seeing an old school chum after years of separation that I could

have hugged him. He was glad to meet me, also, and
we shook hands in hearty fashion. We were talking
together for some minutes when suddenly his mind
seemed to wander, and, casting a furtive look over
his shoulder, he said:

"You must excuse me. I see my wife nodding to
me over there and I must go. But," here he hesitated, "come with me and I will introduce you."

Nothing loath, I followed him. In the direction
we were going I saw an old woman sitting on a
bench. Coming closer, I could discern her features
through the haze of smoke, and was astounded to find
that it was the old witch who had charge of insane
hospital No. 97. The shock of this discovery almost sobered me. The vision of the beautiful girl
pleading for mercy for the youth in the court-room at
once rose before me in vivid outline, and here was
her jailer, for whom I had been looking many days.
What should I do? The occasion I knew was one
for quick decision, but as I approached her I could
not, for the life of me, determine upon any line of
action.

I gazed at the ogress, smoking a cheroot, which she
wielded like a man, and it seemed to my perturbed
brain that she was returning my look with interest.
As she took the cigar from her toothless gums I could

have sworn she was grinning at me. While hesitating as to my course I was conscious that the lethe weed was reasserting its power, and the thought insinuated itself into my mind that it was a foolish Quixotic scheme to try to rescue the maiden. What if she were beautiful and good — should I jeopardize my peace, and perhaps my life, merely on that account? Why hunt for trouble and why not let things drift as they would? Though these thoughts gained the mastery, yet I knew that only indolence and cowardice could excuse them, but the opiate with which I was drugged had unmanned me and blunted the purposes which in my normal state I held most dear.

So it was with a smirk and a bow that I greeted the old witch. She rose from her seat and before I knew what she was about she slapped me familiarly on the back. A creepy sensation went down my spine.

"I know you!" she exclaimed in her piping voice. "I've got a good memory. I saw you in the court-room. I tell you that was a plain talk I gave those judges that day." With this she laughed ghoulishly.

The sea-surgeon came up at this point and to my utter astonishment said: "I am glad to see that you know my wife. So no introduction is necessary."

"Humph! If I waited for you to present me,"

With a smirk and a bow I greeted the old witch.   *Page 140*

she said, discharging a volume of smoke through her mummified nostrils, " I never should know anybody. Where have you been so long? "

" Now, my dear wife! " replied the husband in a mollifying tone, " you know that I am to speak to-night and that arrangements had to be made." It was plain that he was afraid of her.

Turning to me she said: " I have to keep close watch on my old man. He's too good looking to leave around."

While this little comedy in connubial felicity was going on I thought to myself that I had never seen such an ill-sorted pair in all my life. The man was handsome for an Atlantide. He had a well-shaped head with a broad brow, a firm chin, a good mouth, a Roman nose and deep-set and expressive eyes. His hair was black and glossy and reached nearly to his shoulders. He was broad shouldered, tall and straight. On the other hand, his spouse, as far as pulchritude went, was his direct antithesis. She was a graceless old vixen who hobbled with a cane and inspired every one with feelings of repulsion.

Not knowing what else to say to the woman, I asked inanely how long she had been married.

" Two years to my man here," she replied. " I have been married five times, but I never got such a fine-looking man before. He's the handsomest fellow in Atlantis."

"The marriage customs in this country are the best I ever saw," I remarked suggestively.

"They are perfect, young man. I suppose where you came from good-looking people can marry one another, but here we have a regard for equal rights and do not permit any discrimination against those who are shy on looks." She paused and with a silly simper continued:

"Do you think I am pretty?"

The inability to tell a lie glibly and convincingly has been one of my lifelong failings, and the creature, who was looking at me shrewdly, suddenly began to laugh immoderately.

"You need not answer," she piped. "You think I am ugly. I am. I am the ugliest woman in the cavern and I am proud of it."

Never before having heard a woman boast of her ugliness I was speechless.

"The worse a woman looks here," she continued, "the finer man she gets. Why, all the women I meet are secretly jealous of me. I am the paragon of ugliness, the model for young girls. Now I suppose you would say that the atavar you saw in the court-room was pretty?"

She again looked shrewdly at me, but without waiting for a reply continued:

" I have tried my best to redeem that girl, but she persists in disregarding my advice and consequently if she gets a husband she will get an ugly one. Some people don't have sense enough to see what's good for them, and she is one of that kind."

I was saved from making reply by her turning to her husband. Interrupting the conversation he was having with a young man, she exclaimed:

" If you are going to speak don't forget to talk marriage as I told you. Mind what I say." There was an unpleasant sharpness in her tone, but her husband ignored it and replied that he would, of course, obey the request. He then took me by the arm and, having made our humble excuses to her ladyship, we returned to the front of the assembly-room.

The sea-surgeon, or Mr. Brine as I shall call him, that being his family name of which he told me at the time of my rescue, mounted a small rostrum and addressed the audience. He began by saying:

" Ladies and gentlemen, you will kindly take fresh cheroots and I will endeavor to speak to you about our beloved Democracy."

The cigar inspectors brought in a new supply of

the weed and after some confusion the audience quieted down to listen.

"We live in a wonderful age," the orator began again. "Never before in the history of the world has absolute equality been so nearly attained. The millennium is certainly only a few years away, and you should be proud to live during the period which will see the annihilation of the last vestiges of the system of oppression and robbery of the many by the few. (Applause.)

"Let me enumerate some of our blessings. There is, first, equality in marriage. Every person has as much right as another to marry any certain person. Formerly, when two men desired the hand of the same maiden, they settled who should get her by the duel. This barbarous custom has been uprooted by the State stepping in and deciding by scientific and equitable rules the mating of the individuals."

At this point the wife of the speaker pounded loudly on the floor with her stick.

"Then, second, there is the total absence of ostentation and display. The labor of thousands was formerly wasted in producing finery, and men made themselves miserable because they envied each other the possession of useless articles. In those days, also, there were those with the so-called esthetic or artistic temperament, who spent their time in painting, sculpture and the writing of poetry. It was only a perverted taste that called for such things, and we are now happily rid of this species of foolishness.

"Third, there is the equality in the division of food. This brings me to the consideration of the food supply, than which there is no greater problem facing the intellects of the present generation. It is easily seen that no individual has a right to expect a larger share of the food supply than another, but it is more difficult to understand why the share going to each is not larger than it is. It grieves me much to learn that one of your number recently tried to cheat the State of an extra allowance, and I hope the offense will not be repeated. Those who consider for a moment the difficulties with which the State contends, in securing each day sufficient food to meet the present allowance to each individual, will certainly appreciate the grave injustice worked on the many by any one obtaining more than his share. It is not the fault of the Democracy that food does not grow in abundance ready for the eating.

"We learn in the ancient books that when Adam sinned he was driven from the food-producing trees of Eden, and the curse was pronounced that he and his descendants should thenceforth live by the sweat of their brows. The Democracy has done much and will do more toward mitigating this curse. All useless vocations have been abolished, and no one escapes contributing his share of toil toward the production of the necessary sustenance for the nation. It stands to reason that the Democracy is able to produce much more food than a like population could in the old days. Now there are no drones, no non-producing classes, and, again, the division of the food supply in former times was characterized by great extravagance and waste among the rich, while the poor suffered from want. It is surprising that many were not continually dying of starvation in those days, and yet we do not find any record that such was the case. Either the fact was not published or else nature was more lenient to mankind in the earlier stages of intellectual development than she is now. Whatever the cause, we are to-day faced by a condition, not a theory. It is absolutely necessary for the men of this age to work from twelve to fifteen hours a day in order that they may not starve, and this despite the employment of scientific methods and the doing away with all useless labor. Were we to return to-day to the old chaotic system of individualism it would certainly mean general starvation. But the time is coming, my friends, when the Democracy will successfully solve this problem of the food supply and bring about the reduction of hours of labor which is our aim.   (Applause.)

" I should like to ask our friend here from America what the average weight of the individual is in his country."

On the spur of the moment I could not see the speaker's drift, but I replied that the average height of a man was about five feet eight inches, and that for a man of this height the average weight was about one hundred and fifty-four pounds.   I could see that my statement caused something of a sensation, as it was followed by much whispering in the audience.

" Now, citizens, you see that where our friend came from the men are considerably larger than we are. It may surprise you also that the records of the ancients go to show that even six feet was not an unusual height in those days.   It is self-evident that the bigger a man is the more food he requires, but in order to prove this statement, beyond peradventure of a doubt, I shall ask our friend what is the weight of the average daily diet considered as necessary in America for sustaining the individual."

I thought for a moment and then, remembering some of my school-knowledge, I replied that the average man requires about seven pounds of food and water a day, of which nearly a pound and a half

is dry-food substance. This statement produced even
a greater commotion than the one regarding the average weight, and the speaker, before he could proceed,
had to call for silence.

" The average height in this country," he continued,
" is five feet, the average weight one hundred and ten
pounds, and the daily allowance of food is, of dry
substances, three-quarters of a pound. What a blessing it is, my friends, that such is the case! If the
daily allowance had to be increased to one pound,
imagine the great amount of additional labor it would
entail! It would be terrific. It would simply be impossible to perform it. Consequently, the necessary
food would not be produced. Now you have to thank
the Democracy for saving you from such a dire possibility, with its frightful train of starvation and of disease. How has the Democracy performed this miracle? Simply by lessening the amount of food essential
for life. As you all know, it has been some generations since the plan of making gradual and quite im-
perceptible reductions in the food allowance was
inaugurated, and we have now reached the point
where man subsists on half the food he once required.
What if the average stature and weight have been
reduced, are not we large enough? This beneficent
process is continuing, a few grains of weight being

clipped off the daily allowance for each person each year. Who can say but that in a few generations the amount of food required will be so small as to reduce labor to a minimum? Let us, for the sake of posterity, do our part toward hastening this millennium. Let us be patient. Our civilization is the highest now in all the universe, but to say that we can not solve the problem of the food supply is to say that our civilization is a failure, and to say that our civilization is a failure is to deny the veracity of our sense-perceptions. (Loud applause.) I would now like to ask our friend from the upper world to make some remarks."

I was taken completely by surprise, but I endeavored to do the occasion justice. Among other things I said:

" Your speaker has greatly interested me by his remarks respecting the gradual reduction of the daily allowance of food. I regard the plan as feasible and scientific. It recalls to my mind some experiments made in the state of Missouri on a donkey, which is a beast of burden there. In order to lessen the cost of his keep the owner of the animal gave him one straw less each day, and after the course of many weeks the amount of straw given him daily was reduced from several large armfuls to as much as could be carried in one hand. The experiment was very interesting."

"Did the donkey suffer any inconvenience?" queried Mr. Brine.

"Yes," I replied, "I am sorry to say it did. In fact, it died."

Looking about I saw that my remark had made a most unfavorable impression and I hastily added:

"Of course, the case of the donkey proves nothing, except that there was too much haste in reducing the daily allowance. Had the experiment been drawn out over a number of generations of donkeys, instead of attempting to rectify the evil habit of eating in one animal alone, I believe that complete success would have been achieved." (Applause.)

CHAPTER XV

MR. BRINE'S VIEWS ON MONETARY SYSTEMS

When the speaking was over Mr. and Mrs. Brine and the doctor and myself formed a circle and engaged in a lively conversation regarding the many reforms which had been brought about by the Democracy. In this way we drifted into a long talk about the money systems of the ancients and also of America. Having been a free-silver advocate on earth I could speak voluminously on the topic, never being at a loss for a word and always being able to develop some new phase of the subject when the consideration of the one in hand began to lag. I shall not weary my readers with a reproduction of this conversation, although I must say some of it was intensely edifying.

Mr. Brine, for example, dwelt with earnest enthusiasm on the signal and remarkable achievement of the Democracy in demonetizing all kinds of metals that had been used for money. He declared it was the death-blow to plutocracy, and I was disposed to agree thoroughly with him on the point. I remember his saying: "With one mighty assertion of the people's rights, capitalism was vanquished, and the evil brood of bankers, speculators, and money-changers was driven from the Capitol and compelled to go to work. It was calculated that the army of producers was increased twenty-five per cent. by this one reform, and the burden of supporting in sumptuous idleness the moneyed aristocracy was for ever lifted from the shoulders of the common people." He was much interested in my account of the efforts being made in America to make money cheaper by monetizing cheaper substances than gold, and thought it was an indication of the ultimate triumph of the people's cause in all parts of the world.

"In time," he said, "your compatriots will begin to see that money of any kind is entirely useless. It was some centuries before the Democracy saw the full light of truth on the subject, the last substitute used for money being credit cards. When these cards were done away with, all the useless labor connected with maintaining a medium of exchange was abolished."

I was deeply impressed.

"But there is one thing," continued Mr. Brine, "that I think remains to be done, and that is the destruction of the coin and substitutes for money now collected in the Hall of Curiosities. I have always felt that we have been derelict in allowing this debris to remain there, for as long as it is in existence it is a potential temptation to coming generations."

My purpose of relieving the Democracy of its hoarded wealth came back for an instant to my mind and I exclaimed:

"I coincide with your views, Mr. Brine. I shall think about the matter and perhaps I shall be able to make some suggestions as to the best method of removing this standing temptation to the people."

The surgeon at once evinced the liveliest interest.

"You would perform a valued service should you manage to do so," he replied eagerly. "To my mind this accumulation of the money of the past is a dung-heap of iniquity, and I have a theory that any one who meddles with it will be contaminated. I do not say that you will — you have been accustomed to handling money and your chance of escaping evil in dealing with the villainous material would undoubtedly be better than that of any one else who might attempt it. Of course, you could do nothing without a law on the subject, and it might be difficult to have a law passed; but this money is an eyesore to all visitors to the Hall of Curiosities and a menace to the purity of the moral atmosphere of the Democracy."

The bell, which was the signal that the evening love-feast was over, now broke in on our conversation, and Mrs. Brine, who had shown much interest in our talk, putting in a pointed remark now and then, said it was too bad we had to adjourn.

"I think we had better take the young man home with us," she remarked to her husband.

The surgeon at once accepted the suggestion, and after scurrying around to fix it with the inspectors, it was arranged that I should spend the night with the Brines.

The doctor whispered in my ear and, excusing ourselves for a few minutes, he led me back to the laboratory, where, after carefully closing the door, he said:

"I have brought you here in order to give you a dose of a secret preparation of my own."

With this he poured from a bottle a small quantity of blackish fluid into a glass. When I had swallowed the decoction he proceeded to take a similar dose himself.

Immediately my brain became clear, the effects of the lethe weed entirely disappearing. Realizing what he had done I said:

"Thanks, Doctor, for sobering me up. That lethe weed certainly has strong properties."

" It has the merit of making people forget their troubles," he dryly remarked.

" I never cared so little whether school kept or not as I have this evening," I answered.

" I presume you mean," he replied, " that you felt very well satisfied with your physical sensations, and had no disposition to complain about anything. In other words, you were what you call drunk, or partly so, at least."

" I admire your power of diagnosis, Doctor."

" Now you can understand," he continued, " what I meant when I said that the whole nation entered nightly on a debauch. It's a way the people have of drowning their misery. During the day they go through the tasks assigned them in a weary mechanical way, and only in the evening, by the help of the lethe weed, are they aroused to any extent from their accustomed sluggishness."

" Is it really so bad? " I asked. " From what you say I infer that the Social Democracy is a nation of dope fiends."

" I do not think I exaggerate," he went on, growing more emphatic in his tone. " The lethe weed is a fearful curse. I am sure that its continued use shrivels up the brain — at least it makes its victims stupid, slothful and indifferent to their own welfare. I have often thought that if it were not for its benumbing effect on the energies and brains of the people, Social Democracy would be impossible."

The idea of a narcotic being a prerequisite to social democracy seemed exceedingly novel, and I asked:

"Were the people addicted to the vice before the establishment of the Democracy?"

"No,— that has always been a surprising fact to me," was the answer. "I learn from the records that when the people had to do their own thinking the use of the weed was considered disgraceful, and men were even arrested and imprisoned if they were addicted to it. It was some time after the Democracy was definitely founded that smoking became a popular habit."

"It was difficult for me to see," I put in, "why any nation in the possession of its faculties would deliberately take up with such a vice. My faith in human nature is vindicated, however, for, as you say, it was only after the Democracy was established, when the people were already in a semi-somnolent condition, and when their faculties had begun to be atrophied from disuse, that they took to the weed."

"Still, the weed has the effect of deadening the minds of the people to their condition," the doctor remarked thoughtfully. "But we are talking too long — you must hasten back to your appointment. I wish you good fortune."

During the course of this conversation my mind was busy recalling the events of the evening, and I was highly elated over the turn affairs were taking. Not only had I come in contact with the ogress who guarded the prison of the fair atavar, but I was actually going to the old woman's abode, which more than likely was the prison itself. I again thanked the doctor for restoring me to my normal mentality, and hurried back to the assembly-room.

CHAPTER XVI

THE PRISON OF THE ATAVARS

The Brines were waiting for me and without loss of time we made our way out of the building. Instead of heading for the overland car-lines we descended the steps leading to the street.

"Are we going to walk?" I asked.

"Yes," replied the old woman, "the hospital is only a short distance."

Her words filled me with joy. It was true, then, that they lived at the hospital, and I would surely contrive to see the girl. To think, too, that the hospital was only a short distance from the dormitory!

We proceeded slowly along the trench-like streets under the radium lights, the surgeon on one side of the dame and I on the other. My companions, I judged, were still under the effects of the weed, and I endeavored to keep them pleased by my comments on the beneficent character of the country's institutions. At last I thought it safe to venture a remark about atavars in general, and, addressing the woman, I said:

"As you are in charge of an insane asylum, I know you could tell me a great deal about those unfortunate beings who are so irrational as not to appreciate the Democracy."

The woman immediately entered on a voluminous tirade against the creatures, whom she declared to be the bane of the country.

"I could tear out the hearts of all of them!" she cried vindictively.

I could hardly hide my aversion, but said as naturally as I could:

"I should like the opportunity of seeing some of them. I should like to study them."

"Very well," she replied; "it will do you good to see what it means to be an atavar."

There was something in the look she gave me that made me feel uneasy. Could she have intended a double meaning? The idea suddenly struck me that this woman was certainly a masterful creature to be an inhabitant of Atlantis. I could not reconcile her shrewdness and independence of thought with the docility and stupidity of the average good citizen, and I mentally resolved to be wary of her.

In order to change the subject I asked the surgeon how things were in the Fishery Department.

"If you think," he replied with a smile, "that I

have rescued any more of your Americans you are mistaken. It was a rare catch when I got you. I recently secured a peculiarly-shaped object, however, and as we can make nothing of it you will probably be asked to tell us what it is."

"What is it like?" I asked.

"It is of considerable length but rather narrow in width, tapering at both ends. The substance is hard like copper. It has a keel on its under side, while on the upper side there is a cylindrical projection, in the top of which there is something which looks like a lid, but which I have not succeeded in opening."

I puzzled over the description.

"I should be pleased to see it," I said politely, though not particularly interested.

By this time we had turned several street corners, of which I made a careful note, and at last my companions came to a stop before a number of steps that led into the coral cliff or street wall. I looked for some sign to show the place was a hospital, but there was none, and so far as I could see, the steps and entrance were in no wise distinguishable from many others along the street. Even had the doctor and I passed the place in our daily excursions we would not have taken it for a hospital.

Ascending the steps we entered a small lighted hall.

On the left were two doors, leading, as it afterward appeared, to the private rooms of the Brines, while on the right were two other doors protected by heavy metal gratings and leading to the prison cells. We entered one of the doors on the left.

"Oh my! oh my!" sighed Mrs. Brine, as she sank upon a seat, "I am not what I once was. My old bones are going back on me. Now, young man, you are in a female prison, and my husband is the only man about the place and he doesn't count." She glanced around the room and began to issue commands, which the surgeon proceeded to carry out with admirable docility. I must say that he put a good deal of dignity as well as deftness in the manner in which he "policed" the apartments, as it would be termed in military circles. The rooms needed attention badly enough, as even a careless man like myself could see, and I formed a very poor opinion of the housewifery of my ill-favored hostess. While her ladyship fussed and fumed, her husband fetched and carried. What a dull and cheerless fate for the sea-surgeon! And how he bore it like a soldier!

"We have only a short time before the law compels us to go to bed," said the madam at the end of a garrulous chatter to which I had paid little heed. "So I must shake out my kinks and make the nightly round of the establishment. Would you like to see my beauties? Of course you would! I see it in your eyes. We've had a good time to-night, and we'll wind it up by showing you something. He, he, he!"

"Can't I do it for you?" said her husband.

"Not to-night. Hand me my keys."

Mr. Brine took the keys from a shelf near the door and brought them to the woman, after which she arose and hobbled out into the hall, beckoning me to follow.

She first opened the ponderous door of what she called the reception-room. It was merely a large room containing only a few benches and a table.

"You will sleep here to-night," she said.

The remaining iron door in the hall was then unlocked and entering behind her I was soon treading a long corridor with cells on either side. At last I was in the prison-house I had been seeking. I strove to appear calm and not unduly interested. The action of the old woman in bringing me with her on her inspection tour puzzled me. Now and then she cast a penetrating glance toward me. Could it be that the lethe weed had sharpened her wits and that she thought it a good opportunity to test me, while, as she supposed, I was under the influence of the stimulant?

The thought put me on my guard, and I centered

my mind on the task of continuing the rôle I had played in the assembly-room.

"I can see," I said, "that you are an able woman and it seems very fortunate for the Democracy that you serve it in such a valuable capacity. Considering the danger these atavars are to the State, it would be a calamity were they put in charge of some one incapable of managing them."

"You are remarkably astute," she replied, eying me keenly. Then, after a pause: "You are also good-looking. Some may say you are ugly, but I don't, and I warn you now not to fall in love with any of my beauties or allow them to fall in love with you."

We had reached the first cell and I looked through the interlacing bars. The place being fairly well lighted I could see a young girl, seated on the floor and bending over a stool on which a large sheet of paper was spread. On this paper she was making marks with a piece of carbon. Glancing up she disclosed a pretty, appealing face, over which there came a look of wonderment as she saw me.

"Picture sketching," said my guide laconically.

In the next cell was a girl who was apparently knitting.

"Making pretties to be burned up," scoffed the old woman. Then she continued: "In order to keep them quiet I let them draw or paint, make fancy dresses and things, read ancient books or do anything else they have a liking for, only I tell them that the more useless things they do the less their chances are for getting out. It's a sign of their queerness when they will waste their time on such things."

"I can see the wisdom of your methods of treatment," I said with what I hope will be regarded as pardonable hypocrisy. "In America the women are crazy for finery and literature and artistic fads, and their insatiate desire to beautify themselves and their surroundings make many a man scheme how to increase his fortune at the expense of his brothers. You know it was Eve who led Adam to be ambitious, and if you allowed these creatures to roam at will they would destroy the Social Democracy in the way the democracy of Eden was destroyed."

"You have a good faculty for thinking," mused the old woman in return, "but I warn you it is dangerous to think too much. Most people don't think. It comes natural to them not to think, and the few that do think must think right."

There was peculiar emphasis to the last sentence and I quickly remarked:

"I know that I am now in the presence of one, at least, who thinks and thinks right. The doctor at the dormitory, I take it, is another, and your husband still another. With three such good teachers I certainly shall not go astray."

She broke into her mirthless laugh and said: "You may have the making of a good citizen in you, but we shall see. You say I am one of those who think right. You are correct. I may be an old crone but I've got the brains, and never forget it, young man. You don't like my looks and you fear me. But you are safe as long as you obey the laws. I am a stickler for law enforcement, and I usually have my way. Mark that, young man, I usually have my way."

I was sure there was a menace in these remarks, and the uneasiness the old witch inspired grew on me. I was foolish enough to protest against her statement that I did not like her looks and that I feared her, and she laughed in my face.

But despite our talk, I looked searchingly into every cell as we continued down the corridor, and was in momentary expectation of seeing the girl whose image was ever present in my mind. Each face I gazed on increased the pity I felt for the prisoners. Here, I told myself, were the most beautiful and noblest of God's creatures, sacrificed on the altar of human folly. Evil, as personified in the witch, seemed triumphant, and the good alone were punished. But as I observed the neatness of the cells and the many feminine touches that gave them a pleasing appearance, the thought came that perhaps, after all, these poor girls were happier than their sisters in the outer world — that world which was itself nothing more than a prison. Studying their faces, I saw, too, that while they were sad, the stamp of intelligence and refinement was there, which was in marked contrast to the coarse and vacuous features of the women I had seen on the streets. The old woman continued to relieve her mind and now she cynically remarked:

"Most of these darlings made the mistake of thinking too much, or else of giving their imagination too great play. They are creatures with emotions, and they allow these emotions to dominate them with little regard for the laws. It is wonderful how many silly girls are still born in Atlantis! I suppose these girls remind you of those in America, where, no doubt, they are all silly. But the Democracy is slowly weeding out this type of female. I suppose it will interest you to know that most of the girls on this floor took it into their heads that they were in love with some young man and refused to marry the choice of the State. We also have prisons for young men who become afflicted in this way, and you see I meant something when I warned you not to fall in love with any of my pets." With this she poked me in the ribs, which I took to be an attempt at playfulness on her part, for she accompanied the act with a sample of her peculiar laughter.

"And would you think it?" she went on; "most of them will not smoke. I encourage them to use the weed, but sometimes it is a long time before they will do it. When they finally take to it we know they are recovering their reason, and in time they are released and married off. But there are cases which are hard to cure. I will show you some of them."

We came to a stairway leading downward, and this we descended until we reached another corridor similar to the one we had left. The inmates on this floor were older than those above, and I could see from their faces that they had apparently given up hope. Some of them showed signs of weeping. I trod the corridor with a heavy heart. The old woman gleefully pointed out the excellent effects of her discipline and said:

"If they do not get their sanity on the first floor they get it here. Many of these are nearly cured."

Coming to the end of the corridor we descended still another stairway to a third tier of cells.

"Here is where we have the most hardened cases," said the woman. "Look into this cell."

I saw a woman about thirty years of age reading a book. She was neatly gowned and her hair was arranged becomingly with a dainty bow of ribbon in its coils. She glanced up from her book and I was struck by the beauty of her countenance and the look of calm resignation it bore.

"Are you ready to die?" said the old woman sharply.

The face paled a little, but in a firm sweet voice the poor girl replied:

"Has the time come? Then I am glad."

The witch laughed.

"No, not yet, my darling," she said. Turning to me she added: "This is one of the incurables. She has been sentenced to be thrown to the kraken."

I shuddered involuntarily, but the doomed girl only sighed, and resumed her reading.

In the last cell, when I had about given up hope of seeing her, I found the girl I was so anxiously seeking. She was sitting with her head upon her hand, her elbow resting on a table, as though in deep reverie. Never, thought I, had I seen a picture so exquisite! I gazed entranced, for the moment forgetful of my surroundings, when the old woman with a rasping voice recalled me to my senses.

"Here is the girl I take it you want to study. I suppose you would like an introduction." The words were uttered with a sneer, and I replied with an effort at indifference:

"So this is the girl I saw the other day! I confess I do feel some interest, but you need not make us acquainted unless you wish to do so."

"Ah, but you see, I wish it," she replied.

She unlocked the cell grating and we went inside. The girl had risen and was regarding us with amazement. My heart was beating fast, and I divined that the old woman was closely observing me and finding secret enjoyment in my agitation.

"Here, my pretty one," she gleefully exclaimed, "I want you to meet a young fellow who admires you."

The insulting tone of the old woman angered me, and I felt the blood in my cheeks. Then for a moment I looked straight at the girl and gazed into the depths of her blue eyes. I tried to say something, but my emotions overmastered me and I was silent.

"How long are you two going to stand there like dumb idiots?" piped out the old woman.

A soft voice replied: "I believe I remember meeting him in the court-room when the boy was tried."

I forced myself to say:

"I am glad to see you again."

"Can't you shake hands?" called out the old dame.

We extended our hands to each other and for one blissful moment they remained clasped.

Suddenly the old woman's treble grated again in my ear as she said:

"I can stand a good deal, but I'm too tired to wait around here for two people to get their tongues untied."

Another moment of silence occurred when the witch cried out in a tone of disgust:

"Come along and lock her prettiness in. I know you will like to turn the key on her."

The girl smiled on me and made a slight nod of her head.

I followed the old dame out of the cell, closing the door after me and turning the key in the lock. Taking it out I noticed mechanically that it was one of the smallest of the bunch and red in color. Looking up at the girl I said in a low voice:

"Trust me."

A light came into her eyes.

" Good night," she sweetly replied.

I then observed that the old woman was not going back along the corridor, but was standing by a door near at hand.

" Open this door ! " she commanded. " Use the long flat key ! "

I searched among the keys for the one described, inserted and turned it in the lock. The dame pushed the door open, disclosing not another room, but the starry dome of the eternal night. I followed the woman, after shutting and locking the door.

" I did not want to go back the way we came," she explained. " You are a nice one ! " she continued with sarcasm in her tone. " You tell me you want to study the atavars, and when I give you a chance you are as stupid as a post."

I made a great effort to recover my wits and with attempted raillery said :

" Oh, but you are too exacting. You can not expect me to be as quick with the tongue as you."

" I see you used your eyes, though," she replied. " I used mine, too."

She chuckled, and I felt like choking her there in the silence and the dark. I followed meekly enough, however, and after climbing a few steps we were walking along a side street. Soon we turned a corner on to the main thoroughfare, where we ascended the steps to the hospital entrance. Arriving in the hallway I handed the keys to the woman, who placed them on a shelf just within the door of the room nearest the outer entrance. Bidding me a curt good night the old dame left me standing in the hall. I entered the reception-room where I found a bed had been arranged, and throwing myself down upon it began to think.

CHAPTER XVII

For a long time I lay thinking of the atavar, how lovely she was and how sad her fate, and I likened her to a rose, drooping and lonely in a desert. To me she seemed the one living reality in a land of social petrifaction. That was it — social petrifaction. I could think of no better term to describe the real character of the Democracy. In its infatuation for what it called equality it had taken every vestige of independence from the individual units and had made the State into a Frankenstein, which, while crushing in its grasp the souls of the people, was itself without a soul. I reflected on what I had already seen of the country, and now saw clearly why there was little of what we know as crime. Of what use was crime when no man could profit by it, when, no matter what he did, he could not have more food or more clothes or enjoy the material comforts of existence to any greater degree than another, and when, also, he could not exercise a choice as to his occupation, or even as to his wife, and when he was in no way responsible for the maintenance of his family?

To make men socially equal it had been necessary to take from them every opportunity and means for acquiring superiority over others, and the whole race had been placed on the same dead level as that which obtains in our penitentiaries. But while negative virtue was thus widely established, positive virtue had disappeared. Individual energy, ability and ambition had been discouraged and stifled by the absence of reward until they no longer existed, and sympathy, charity and self-sacrifice had become unknown, because there was no opportunity for their display. The spiritual in man had ceased to be manifested, and it was no wonder that the physical had become dominant and that the people had sunk beneath such vices as that of the lethe weed. And now behold nature, ever fighting for her rights, persistently sending beings into the world who were living protests against the soul-withering despotism of the State.

"Let them call them atavars, reversals of type, reincarnations of ancient savages or what they please," I muttered to myself. "Let them imprison, flay and murder them, as the only real criminals in the community, yet so long as there is any vitality in the race these beings must appear and in the end either they will triumph over the State or the race will die."

As I continued to execrate the folly of social equality I had constantly before my mind the beautiful girl in the cell below. How could I aid her? How could I manage to be with her? How could I enter into her life? Let me be coldly critical of my motives. It was not merely to assist a being in distress that made me so anxious to be of service to her, though Heaven knows no one could have a higher claim to the chivalry in man than she. Since first I saw her it had been my ever-present hope to find her, and now that I had found her I felt in no wise satisfied. I was filled with a craving for her presence, for, as I told myself, it was in the light of her eyes and only there I should find peace on earth. Thus was my desire to rescue her from the diabolical clutches of the State joined with promptings for my own happiness, and it is always thus that conduct, deemed good and praiseworthy, has at bottom some selfish end.

But how could I be of any true service to her, when, if I but showed a casual interest in her cause, it would be a signal for my own imprisonment, and perhaps additional punishment for her to bear? I

must make no move or utterance in her behalf,—
and what else might I do? I groaned at the thought
of my helplessness. Could I suborn the witch? No,
bribery was impossible, for even had I anything with
which to bribe, the recipient would be unable to profit
by it. But then the witch was a different creature
from the others — she had a mind of her own, an
evil mind, it was true, but along with the power of
independent thought must come some weaknesses.
Could I not find some prejudice or some softer feeling within this hardened woman on which I might
ply my wits? My judgment told me it was a hopeless task. I recalled the malevolence that shone from
her eyes and the malice in her speech — surely if
there were an evil creature out of hell it was this
woman.

And what did she mean by bringing the girl and
me together? As I recalled her conduct, I could not
but fear that some devilish motive inspired her. I
had been quietly watchful, and as I remembered the
ostentation with which she had smoked in the early
part of the evening it suddenly occurred to me that
she had not taken a second cheroot, but had managed
to make one last the evening out. So, after all, she
was not under the influence of the weed! Here was
cunning. Could it be possible that she had been

shrewd enough to detect my more than passing interest in the atavar, and had put me to the test, inviting me to the prison and bringing me face to face with her, that she might from my conduct verify her suspicion? Her actions and words seemed to lend support to this conjecture. If it were true, she had now but to lead me on to some overt act to place me in her power, and then? I saw my danger clearly and it maddened me to think that, for the girl's sake as well as my own, I dare not utter even one word of kindness to her, should the witch bring us again together. Then in my despair I thought how I myself had locked her in with the small brightly-colored key. The key? Why, it was within my reach!

I jumped from the cot, and stealthily opened the door into the hall. All was silent, and I stepped out. I listened attentively at the door of the room where the Brines slept, which was directly opposite the reception-room, and heard nothing. Then swiftly I made my way to the other door, opened it with scarcely a sound, reached up to the shelf and grasped the keys of the prison. Back I flew to my own room, closed the door and threw myself again upon my bed. Scarcely had I done so when I heard a noise as of some one walking in the hall, then the closing of a door, and again silence. I had narrowly escaped detection and breathlessly I turned the keys over in my hands. For one brief moment I entertained the wild design of throwing open all the prison doors, but a second reflection showed me that even if the girl escaped her recapture would be certain. Then an inspiration came to me. I saw that if I only had duplicates of the keys to her cell and to the lower entrance of the prison, I should have the means at all times in my possession to effect her release. Perhaps, too — oh, precious thought!— I might even manage to see her in secret! But how was I to make two duplicate keys? I dared not take the keys from the bunch, for the old witch would miss them. If I only had some wax or some clay with which to take impressions of them, perhaps the doctor would find some way of casting them. I pondered on the problem and then I thought of soap. There was none in the room, but I remembered seeing a cake of it near a trough at the entrance of the cell corridor, behind the iron grating in the hall. I determined to get it.

Once more I stole out of the room and then for full ten minutes of dread I worked with the grating, trying one key after another. At last it opened and, stepping quickly into the prison corridor, I closed the iron door behind me. Fortune favored me that night, for I had no more than closed the door before I again heard the tread of feet on the stone floor of the hall. I pressed my body against the wall next the grating, and there stood breathless, looking with strained eyes through the bars. Scarcely a moment passed before the figure of a man appeared at the door. He paused as though to try the lock of the door, and then, casting a look through the bars, turned and walked deliberately toward the outer entrance of the hall. I was greatly relieved when I saw it was not the witch, and as soon as I heard him leave the building I hurried to the trough, which was used by the prisoners for the washing of their hands and faces. There was one similar to it in the dormitory. It was, in fact, one of the necessary appurtenances of communal life, for in the regimentation of mankind there must be set times for washing, as well as for all other acts, and when many must needs cleanse themselves at one and the same time nothing short of troughs could avail for the purpose.

I took the soap and quickly made two impressions, one of the small key to the cell and the other of the long flat key with which I had, at the command of the witch, unlocked and locked the door at the lower entrance. I carefully inclosed my molds

of soap in the waist of my tunic where I could protect them from being crushed, and then, without having disturbed a single prisoner, I went out into the
hall, locking the grating after me. All was still and
I swiftly returned the keys to their shelf. I had almost reached my room again when the outer door
was opened. I made a rush and gained my room.
Then with quaking I noticed I had left the door
ajar. I threw myself upon my bed and feigned
sleep.   I heard every step the man took as with
deliberation he approached the door. Then he stopped,
and soon I saw his head as he peered into the room.
For a long time he stood, as though meditating what
to do. Then, muttering, he turned away, shutting the door as he went. I drew a deep breath of
relief and placed the molds where they would be safe
for the night.

CHAPTER XVIII

On being awakened by the morning bell I hastily arranged my toilet and went out into the hall. Here I was astonished to hear voices in bitter quarrel and still more astonished to discover that it was the amiable surgeon and his precious better-half who were thus offending the Atlantian peace. I retreated into my room, musing on the inadequacy of the comprehensive and all-powerful laws of the Democracy to enforce domestic felicity. For the surgeon I felt a certain pity, for I was convinced he was one of those enthusiasts who, for the cause to which they are attached, will sacrifice even their personal happiness. But I had no such feeling for the old witch, to whom bickering seemed only second nature.

When I was called at last to partake of food with them I observed with sympathy that my host's nose bore a bruise only recently inflicted, and it took no prophet to see that my hostess had resorted to physical force, as well as to tongue lashing, in trying conclusions with her lord and master. The circumstances were such as to make conversation difficult, even had it been in some other country than Atlantis, and the meal passed in dismal silence. But when it was finished the old woman turned on me and said:

"Her prettiness has been crying. I thought you would like to know it." There was a malicious gleam in her look. "I want to tell you, too," she continued, "that I thought you would like to study more about the atavars and I have ordered her presence in the reception-room."

We soon proceeded to the room and found the girl awaiting us. She greeted me with a little smile, and I stood lost in admiration. Her face was pale, but this I thought added to her charm. Her luxuriant hair was loosely coiled in a becoming manner, and she wore a neat-fitting gown in place of the common garb. There was an air of refinement and innocence about her conjoined with a certain reserve against which the natural impulsiveness of girlhood seemed constantly to struggle. While I continued to gaze captivated I heard the old witch exclaim:

"Don't be backward but ask her any questions you wish."

Carefully weighing my words, I said:

"Young lady, I am from a country above the waters of the sea, and your guardian, desirous that I should become familiar with the institutions of this land, has asked your presence here that I might meet one of her charges."

The girl's face lighted and in a sweet voice she exclaimed:

"Then you came from Heaven where love reigns. I have read of it in the books. Oh, I shall be so glad to talk with you!"

I was sorely puzzled as to how to proceed in the presence of the old woman. Confident, however, that the time would come when I should be able to meet the girl alone I mastered my inclinations and spoke only vaguely of America as of something afar off. During the conversation I asked her if she was an atavar from choice. It was a crude question, but I saw I must make a try at cross-examination.

"Yes," answered the girl, "I am an atavar from choice and should think you would also become one. In Atlantis it is only within prison walls that you may think and act according to your nature. Freedom in this land means the crushing of all the finer sentiments of the soul, but here in this prison I may give vent to my thoughts without constraint and partly satisfy my yearning for knowledge and for what is beautiful."

I turned to the old woman:

"Come," said I abruptly, "I have talked enough."

I could no longer trust myself to play an indiffer-ent rôle, and though the girl turned a look of inquiry and surprise on me, I strode from the room. The old dame followed and chuckled as she walked.

"So I see," she said, "you do not like to talk in my presence. I noticed, too, that you did not rebuke her sentiments when she acknowledged herself an atavar. But I suppose we must expect young men to be indulgent to pretty girls, eh? Do you know what my husband says? He says it is not right to tempt young people too far. But I know you are wise and strong and will fly from temptation." She paused and giving me a honeyed look, continued: "I have a fancy for you, young man, and I want you to come to my asylum whenever and as often as you feel disposed. You will come often, will you not?"

I answered politely that I should be pleased to visit her whenever I felt like it. With this ambiguous reply and without unnecessary ceremony I left her and returned to the dormitory.

CHAPTER XIX

I found the doctor in his laboratory and recounted to him all that had occurred at the prison. He listened with deep interest, and when I spoke of the charms of the girl he smiled indulgently and said:

"I fear, my dear friend, you have a malady for which none of my prescriptions will avail. But you may rely on me to assist you, and even though it cost me my life I am subject to your commands at any time."

It was good to feel the pressure of his hand and to know that I had found at least one true friend in the under world. I handed him my soap molds, and he there and then proceeded to make the keys I desired. I was surprised to see how well supplied he was with tools and with what dexterity he handled them.

"Doctor," I said, "for an Atlantide you are a magician. Are all the State physicians as expert?"

"I can't say they are," he replied in a regretful tone. "The most of these tools I made myself. I

got my ideas from my reading, but I venture to
say there are very few men in Atlantis who would
know what many of these things are, to say nothing of
being able to use them. I sometimes wonder I am
not accused of heresy or something as bad because
of the contents of my laboratory, but the departments
of State have found that I could be quite useful to
them at times on account of my knowledge of the
ancient books, saving them much irksome labor, and
they have been pleased to look on my experimenting as harmless. It was because of my supposed
learning that they made me your teacher respecting
the laws and institutions of the country."

"So even the Democracy," I said, "finds it handy
to have the services of a man who knows more than
is taught in the regular schools? It is a wonder
to me they do not avail themselves at times of the
ability and learning of the atavars, for, from what
I saw last night, I judge that there must be some
capable persons among them."

"Quite so," was the reply. "Once in a while,
though only when they are driven to it by some
threatened calamity, they seek counsel of the wisest
of the atavars. Some of these poor beings receive
the best of care, merely because of their known value
in cases of State emergency. But the majority either

die in prison, or their spirits are crushed into submission to the laws. The remainder become victims of capital punishment."

"I believe I begin to understand your country more thoroughly than I did," I said. "In every land the majority of men are followers and not leaders. The majority think little on their own account, and look to political leaders and public teachers for their ideas on government and morals. It is only the comparative few who have the ability to impress their thoughts and personality on the public, and when they do this they secure a following and become leaders. Here in Atlantis those who are endowed with the power of independent thought are thrown into prison and execrated as atavars, unless, forsooth, they hold their tongues as you have done, and pretend an acquiescence in the Democracy. The majority, dominated more by the physical than by the intellectual, are kept in ignorance, and with the assistance of the lethe poison become good citizens of the State. It is a remarkable system of government, and the only approach to it on the earth among civilized peoples at the present time is, I believe, the government of Russia."

"Is that a State socialism?" asked the doctor.

"No, it is an autocracy or rather a bureaucracy,

but the only difference between it and State socialism is that it is a despotism of one man and his bureaus while State socialism is an ossified despotism of laws. In both, the individual possesses no rights which the State need respect."

After a pause I added:

" I have yet to learn the method by which your laws are placed on the statute books, seeing that you do not have any elections, and all occupations, including even that of legislator, are determined by chance."

" You will learn all that in due time," replied my friend.

He continued to work at the keys. I gazed at the rows of file cases that reached to the ceiling and now remarked:

" The Democracy reduces the science of medicine to a system, I see."

" Yes," was the reply, " any one can be a doctor or a metallurgist or a civil engineer or any sort of professional man in Atlantis. It's the simplest thing in the world. For example, if you have a backache, your doctor turns to File B —'b' for backache you know — and he opens the book and runs his eye down until he comes to the paragraph on backache."

The doctor stopped his work long enough to pull

down File B and show it to me. Opposite the word backache the book said, " Prescription No. 46795."

" All you have to do now is to run your eye along the numbers in the prescription files and pull down the case which contains No. 46795."

I did as directed and soon had in my hands the prescription for backache. It named certain materials and told how to mix them.

" There the materials are," continued the doctor, pointing to some shelves of bottles. " They are all labeled. A child can fill the prescription. It is a beautiful system — it saves so much trouble in learning about the bones in the body and the nerves and muscles and arteries. I have seen some doctors who do not even imagine there are such things as livers and kidneys, and they have only the vaguest notions as to the heart and stomach. The patients, you know, have no choice as to doctors and must take their medicine whether it kills or cures. My profession is a farce, simply a farce."

He sighed and added: " But as for me I use these file-cases more as a blind than as sources of information. This laboratory is my refuge, and here I pass all the time I can, secretly experimenting with the elements of nature."

CHAPTER XX

MY SECRET MEETING WITH ASTRÆA

I was very impatient to test the value of the new-made keys, but the doctor insisted on my waiting until the smoke-time. It was true the departments of State had given us *carte blanche* to come and go as we pleased, but while this spoke highly of the confidence reposed in the doctor, it also afforded the inspectors excellent opportunities to study my characteristics. It seems I was regarded as a child, who had suddenly been called on to learn what, in the ordinary course of events, took years to absorb, and as it was necessary to note my progress in imbibing a wholesome respect for the laws, I was almost constantly under surveillance when I left the dormitory. The doctor now argued that while I might proceed in the working hours as far as the prison without molestation, yet I should certainly be arrested the moment I attempted to use the keys. But during the smoke-time, he stated, the case was different, for then the vigilance of the departments was much relaxed.

"Although there are night inspectors," he continued, "yet they are comparatively few in number and for the most part consist of the aged, the feeble, the lame and those defective in eye or ear. When the subjects of the State are immersed in the joys of the weed the likelihood of crime is reduced to a minimum, and the patroling of deserted streets is particularly looked on as a useless precaution. Those who are unfit for active work are therefore placed in a separate class, and arbitrarily assigned to this perfunctory employment."

The good man had already, in a number of instances, prevented my committing indiscretions that might have led to my condemnation as a savage unfit for the society of civilized beings, and, impressed by his argument, I now curbed my impatience and bided my time until evening. Still, I knew that the enterprise even in the smoke-time would not be without its dangers, and my mind one minute was filled with dark forebodings, while the next I was unreasonably exultant. Then I would fall into deep abstractions anticipating the pleasure of talking with the girl alone, and composing and rehearsing what I should say to her. The doctor bore kindly with my changing moods, listening with sympathetic ear to all I had to say and respecting my silence when I did not speak. When at last the time arrived for venturing forth, he volunteered to accompany me, and I accepted his companionship with thanks.

We left the dormitory ostensibly for a stroll beneath the pillared dome, but, fearing that special inspectors might have been detailed to watch us, we took the precaution of making a wide detour that we might detect their presence if any there were. The streets, however, were deserted, save for an occasional night inspector, who, with labored effort or listless gait, went on his way. It seemed as though we were pilgrims visiting some mighty sepulcher, so silent and desolate was the scene.

Satisfied at last that we were not followed, we bent our course direct to the prison. We crept into the passageway leading to the lower entrance of the place without being seen by any of the guard, and the doctor picked for himself a point of vantage where, concealed by the shadow of the wall, he could command a view of the street and also of the prison door. I took the keys from the folds of my tunic and with beating heart proceeded to the iron grating, into the lock of which I inserted the larger key. Slowly the lock responded, and with ears alert I pulled open the door, exposing to view the long and silent corridor. Quickly and noiselessly I ran to the cell of the girl. She was reading a book and I gently tapped the iron grating. She glanced up startled, but with a gesture I checked the exclamation on her lips. To unlock the cell was the work of but a moment, and I beckoned her to come. She stood for a second the picture of amazement and then, looking appealingly and searchingly into my eyes, she moved toward me, and, taking her hand, I led her from the prison, closing both the doors behind us.

When we stood in the dark passageway beneath the starry vault I felt her hand tremble, but she made no effort to withdraw it from mine. Deep emotion mastered me, and it seemed as though it was not I who was holding her hand, but she who was holding mine. Gently I did my best to reassure her:

"Do not be afraid. I have done this that we might talk together alone."

With this I lifted her hand to my lips and kissed it.

"I shall call you Astræa," I continued. "Astræa was the last goddess from Heaven to visit the earth, and you are the last goddess to come to Atlantis."

With renewed confidence she took my other hand and, standing before me with both our hands clasped together, like children, she uttered these words:

"Oh, that the State would give me you for my husband!"

I believe that there is in every man's memory some sacred chamber which he locks from the too close scrutiny of the world, and now I will drop the curtain on this, the supreme hour of my life. Many and many a time have I looked back on it in the years that have flown, and its memory has never failed to exert an influence for good over all my acts. When I have been sorely tried it has come into my thoughts to lift my mind beyond the sordid things of life, and in my triumphs it has come to chasten me. From that hour dates my better manhood, which has given me the strength to accomplish that which came to my lot to do. Truly is that man blessed who resolves to cherish and protect some worthy woman, the noblest work of God, and he that does not lives his life in vain.

It was the good doctor who brought us again to a realization of earthly affairs. He had patiently stood minute after minute, anxiously peering into the night. Twice an inspector had passed along the street within a few spaces of the passageway, and he had given no sign. But at last he began to fear that the lethe-time was nearing an end, and he gave a low whistle, a preconcerted signal. With slow re-

"Oh, that the State would give me you for my husband!"

luctance I led my Astræa back into her cell, where, kissing her in sweet farewell, I left her.

The doctor and I regained the dormitory in safety, and for once the great Democracy, with its million eyes, saw not and knew not that the most important of all its laws — that of State regulation of the affairs of the heart — had been ruthlessly set at naught.

CHAPTER XXI

ASTRÆA TELLS ME HER LIFE STORY

The next evening the doctor and I again ventured forth with the hospital as our destination. The good man remonstrated strongly against what he was pleased to term the folly of a madman. He declared that I was flying in the face of Providence, and that he had no doubt that the three of us, the girl, himself and I, would in the end be thrown to the kraken. I urged him to remain at the dormitory, as I did not wish to feel the responsibility of getting him into trouble, should such be the issue of my visits to the prison, but to this he would not listen, and, seeing I was immovable in my purpose, he put aside his fears and went with me. As a concession to his pleading I agreed to arrange with Astræa to see her every third night instead of every night. He asked that I make it once a month, but I would not think of it. I insisted that I had already gone too far by way of compromise, and with this he had to content himself.

That night I introduced him to Astræa, and she

naïvely told him she liked him much better for a chaperon than she did the old woman. He smiled and then gazing earnestly at her said:

" You remind me of a picture that hangs in the Hall of Curiosities. Our friend here knows the picture. You also remind me,"— and his voice choked as with some great emotion,—" of a girl whom I once knew and whom I met in secret, as you two are meeting now."

Astræa held out her hand to him, and he took it in one of his in a clasp of sympathy.

" And where is she now? " she softly asked.

" I do not know," he said in a trembling voice. " She is lost to me — they took her away from me and gave her to another."

We were all deeply affected.

" The State is cruel, cruel! " cried Astræa. " But you loved her, and the memory of her must be dear to you. And perhaps, who knows? — in some better world you may meet her and be happy again."

The doctor recovered himself and replied:

" Let me not cast a shadow on *your* happiness. I pray that the Supreme Spirit will guard and protect you." With that he relinquished her hand into mine and walked away to take his post as sentinel.

Astræa told me that night her history. It was a

short and pitiable story of neglect and hardship. Though she was now twenty-two years of age she had seen practically nothing of the world, having been immured in one kind of an institution or another all her life.

" I can not recall either my father or mother," she said, to my questioning, " and the earliest experiences of my childhood are associated with the public nursery."

" The public nursery?   Tell me about it."

" That's where the infants are cared for."

" I know," I said.

" They are brought there before they can walk or talk and many of them scarcely know how to eat," she continued.   " You should see them, hundreds and hundreds of them ranged in rows on long narrow beds. Once a day they are washed and their gruel is given them at stated intervals.   But the nurses waste no more attention on them than what the law requires. They are deaf to their crying and do not take them in their arms or fondle them.   I remember very little of my own nursery days.   The first recollection I have is of crying very bitterly when a woman filled my mouth with a cloth, nearly choking me.   I can still recall the harsh features of that woman's face."

When the children were seven years old they were

turned out of the nursery-hoppers, like chickens from incubators, and sent to institutions resembling our orphan asylums, only they were conducted on a much larger scale. The boys and girls were separated, but female martinets with hard countenances and harder hearts held the reins of authority over both. The institutions were in fact disciplinary mills to grind the children into docile subjects of the State. The code of rules was so elaborate that the simplest actions of the child were made to conform to fixed standards, and none could hope to escape the brutal punishments meted out for even trifling lapses in obedience. In America it has been noticed that pupils attending the same public schools frequently acquire similar mannerisms of action and speech, and the school system has been criticized for its tendency to bend the minds of the young all in the same direction. Though this tendency is more than counteracted by parental and social influences that tell for individuality, yet it indicates the effect of education and training by wholesale methods. In Atlantis, where the government was the foster parent as well as the instructor, the art of molding the future citizens all on the same pattern was developed to perfection. That the spirits of the children were crushed may be judged from some of Astræa's remarks.

"It was a dire offense to cry," she said. "We did not dare to say we were hungry. We had to go to bed at a fixed time and if we complained of being sleepy when told to get up we were made to go without breakfast. The food was often bad, and we went un-washed and our clothes were dirty and ragged. Even when the children became sick they were neglected, and many of them died. The attendants became very angry if we disturbed them. I remember that once a little girl was put into a dark closet for annoying the matron by her play. The matron forgot her and when the closet was opened several days after she was found dead. No one took the trouble to tell us stories or amuse us and we were whipped if we asked ques-tions. When I was ten years old I was sent an hour each day to a school-room in the building where I learned the alphabet and the catechism. The teacher scolded us severely and did not seem to care whether we learned anything outside the catechism."

"What was the catechism?"

"It was a large book and we were compelled to learn it by heart. Every day we were made to recite long quotations from it. I can still repeat it word for word."

Being urged she recited a number of paragraphs, among which I remember the following:

Question: What is the first and greatest requisite for citizenship?

Answer: Obedience to the State.

Question: Can the State ever be wrong?

Answer: It can not.

Question: Why should the State be obeyed?

Answer: It gives the citizen his food, and his clothing, it supplies him with a place to sleep, and it keeps him from committing error. It is his mother and his guardian through life and is ever solicitous for his well-being.

Question: Should the citizen be dissatisfied or place his judgment against that of the State?

Answer: No, and for the reason that the judgment of the individual is often faulty, while the judgment of the State, being the composite judgment of all, is the highest attainable wisdom. The reasoning of the individual is colored by selfish considerations, while that of the State is purely impersonal and dictated by considerations for the common good. It is a grave crime to criticize the State, its laws or its decisions, for in making such criticism the citizen declares himself the enemy of his brothers and must be punished accordingly.

"The catechism," said Astræa, "continued page after page to extol the State and to teach self-depreciation. The leading offenses were set forth and their punishment stated. The condition of savagery, when the individual did as he pleased and chaos existed in the relations of man, was depicted and compared to that of the present socialistic state, when equality is rigidly assured to every citizen. The effect of its teachings inspired an awe of the State, and a blind faith in its justice, beneficence and infallibility. Even I, who have no reason to love socialism, am still partly under the influence of those ideas drilled into my mind when it was in its most receptive state."

When Astræa was fourteen she was taken to a young women's dormitory, where there were several hundred girls. The rules for their government were many and strict. Every morning they were required to go to a great factory where, with thousands of others, they cut out and sewed garments for ten hours a day. Women were not regarded as citizens until they were married and the law as to the allotment of occupations did not apply to them. Being helpless wards it was easy to saddle them with work and they were whipped and humiliated if they did not labor hard and diligently.

"Did you have no enjoyments?" I asked Astræa.

"I hardly know what you mean by enjoyments,"

she replied. " We were not, except at rare intervals, allowed to go out into the city, and when we did go we had to march in pairs under the eyes of the matron and attendants. Young men were not permitted to see us, and the evenings were passed in the assembly-room, where we were encouraged to smoke. But the lethe weed always seemed vile to me, and I would not acquire the habit. I also began to pine for more freedom, and my disposition became, I fear, none of the best. I discovered that I was being closely watched, but I did not care. One day one of my companions, in whom I felt an interest, was shamefully whipped for not working fast enough. I knew she was sick, and I openly accused the overseer with cruelty. There was a scene and I was arrested and tried. All my shortcomings in the past were brought to the attention of the judge and I was declared to have symptoms of insanity. I was then removed to this hospital, where I have since remained."

" And your life in the prison? " I asked.

" I believe," she continued, "that I have been happier here than in the dormitory. When I first came I was told that if I conducted myself as others did in the world I might hope in time to be given in marriage and released from prison. At first I bewailed my lot, and tried by my conduct to prove

I was sane, but we were frequently tempted to do things which it is not considered proper for women to do. For instance, books were placed within our reach, and if we were found reading them it was counted against us, as showing the perversity of our disposition. Not knowing what else to do I yielded, and in time became much more enamored of my reading than I did of my desire for freedom. But I was not regarded as a confirmed atavar until I spoke for the boy in the court-room, and now I am an inmate of one of the cells allotted to the incurables."

She spoke as though there were nothing extraordinary in her narrative, but to me it was the worst arraignment of the State I had yet heard. I could not find language strong enough to express my opinion of a country that could be so cruel to the young. She listened to me in some amazement, but I could see she was not displeased.

"Oh," she cried, "you are a greater atavar than I!"

I told her how none but the basest on the earth would mistreat children and young women, and it seemed she would never tire of my descriptions of family life. The loving care of mother and father for their children was to her a beautiful dream, which she could hardly realize as actually existing any-

where in the world. Then I spoke about the freedom enjoyed by children and the games they played
and how they were educated to be true men and wom-
en. Many other things I talked of and no man ever
had a more eager or a more delightful listener. The
hour swiftly passed and at last, the doctor giving his
signal, we were compelled to part; but before doing
so I briefly told her of my hopes of escaping from
Atlantis and taking her with me. At this she was
transported with joy, and she said she had every
faith in my being able to find some way of carrying
out my purpose.

" I am ready," she said, " to go with you at any
time, no matter where. Even though it means our
death, yet will I go. I can not tell you how happy
I have been since you came last night. God is merciful to send you into my life, and something keeps
telling me that my happiness will prove, not like a
pleasant dream, no sooner come than gone, but like the
dawn of which you speak that is the herald of glorious
day."

The doctor was compelled to signal twice before
we parted.

CHAPTER XXII

THE DOCTOR'S HATRED FOR THE DEFUNCT FEDERATION OF LABOR

I am afraid I was a serious trial to the doctor for the next three days, but if I was he gave no sign to indicate it, except that he redoubled his zeal in watching over me, that I might not incur the suspicion of the inspectors. Meanwhile, he evinced such a sincere interest in my confidences respecting Astræa that all my natural reserve was melted and I opened my heart more to him than I ever dreamed I would to any man. But, far from being wearied with my talk, it seemed to fill him with gratitude, and the truth was, perhaps, that it was one of the deepest pleasures of his whole life to be able to converse with me as he never before dared to do with any living being. After all, was it strange he should crave an outlet for emotions and thoughts which had been pent up for years within his breast?

I remember that once he seemed to give me some hint as to how he felt when he said:

"Atlantis is dying for the want of love, of generosity, of kindly feeling one to another. The people are no longer human beings — they are beasts. Yes, worse than beasts, for the animals have hearts, and the human heart has withered up and died. The Democracy has established equality, but it has also murdered the soul — what you see about you is the equality that reigns among the dead."

Then at another time he said:

"You have told me so much about life on the earth's surface that I can realize the contrasts between existence there and here. There men are compelled to work out their own salvation, to carve their own destiny, but this is a blessing and not a hardship for them. Why do men live if not to prepare themselves for another and higher life? The struggle in which they engage, where all are free, develops those faculties of mind which lift them above the brute creation. Though some may obtain more material comfort than others, yet none starves, and the strong learn to be charitable to the weak, while those without virtue incur the contempt of their fellow beings. Here, however, where the State does all the thinking for the populace, men's souls are like those rudimentary organs in the body for which no use has been discovered. Will-power, imagination, the creative faculty — these things are unknown, and the State trains its subjects to perform certain tasks much as your horses are trained to haul wagons. On the earth it is the debased, the pervert (which in most cases means the ignorant), who are imprisoned, while here it is the good and the intelligent. Could there possibly be any more damnable folly than this Social Democracy?"

As a means of calming my restlessness the doctor took me on several excursions over the country, and on one of these we made a visit to the monument that had been erected to the Federation of Labor of Atlantis. Our car brought us close to the base of this wonder of wonders. Imagine, if you can, a pyramid of brilliancy seventy-five feet square at the base and piercing the upper air for fully five hundred feet, and you will have some idea of this marvelous work of man. So bright was its light that it was necessary to protect the eyes with smoked glasses on approaching it. In fact, it was a veritable sun, illuminating the land for miles and miles around. I found on close inspection that it was a monolith of white transparent marble, a material which I had never before met in nature. Radium had been applied to the entire surface and the effect produced was that of liquid fire.

To say that I was astounded by the spectacle but

ill expresses it. The doctor, however, shrugged his shoulders and instead of speaking in admiration, shook his fist toward it and exclaimed:

" There is the monument that commemorates our damnation. But for the Federation of Labor the Social Democracy would never have been. It was the Federation that paved the way. It passed laws providing that the State should fix wages and hours of labor. It declared what should constitute a day's work in all industries, it limited the number of men who could be permitted to learn the various trades and occupations, and it compelled employers to hire labor whether they made any profit or not. The Federation acted on the theory that the owners of capital were a curse and that if it were not for them labor could live in luxury and work only a few hours a day. It calmly argued that the less labor did the higher would be its wages. The leaders of the Federation said that there was a certain amount of work to be done in Atlantis, and that the competition among the workers for the chance to do this work made it possible for the employers to reduce wages. ' Now,' said they, ' all that needs to be done is to get rid of this competition. Let us shorten hours and let no man perform any greater share of this labor than he can possibly avoid, and then we shall have a condition in which the competition will be transferred to the employers — a condition in which the employers will bid against each other to secure men to perform the necessary work of the nation. This will result in the enrichment of the masses instead of the few, as is now the case.' "

The doctor paused, and I made the remark that the same doctrine was believed in by some millions of men on the earth.

At this he became much excited.

" If that is so," he declared with vehemence, " then your institutions of individual freedom are in danger. The argument that the less men do the more they will get is one of the most dangerous vaporings of ignorance. Let me tell you briefly what happened when it became the cardinal principle of the dominating political economy of Atlantis. The popular assembly at first passed laws reducing the hours of labor to eight, then to six and then to five. At the same time, wages failing to advance, many strikes occurred and, the government falling completely under the control of the Federation, the fixing of wages was declared to be a State function. Bills were thereupon immediately enacted, raising them from twenty-five to fifty per cent. While all this was going on the unions took care to see that no ' scabs ' should work, and that the young men would not be permitted to enter the labor market. What happened? Did the workers get rich? No. It was found that prices for commodities made by labor became so exorbitant that they more than absorbed the increase in wages. A man who was earning fifty dollars a week found he could not buy nearly as much with it as he formerly bought when his wages were only twenty dollars. There was but one thing left to be done and that was for the State to fix prices. The government began to take up this work, and immediately there was a strike of all the employers in the nation. The employers claimed that it was difficult to make a profit, even at the high prices current in the market. They claimed that they had never fixed either wages or prices and that government should not seek to do so. They insisted that they could not be compelled to turn out goods at a loss, and that when wages were arbitrarily raised and hours of labor reduced, the cost of production was so increased as to make higher prices imperative. It was true, they said, that the demand was limited at the higher range of values, and that consequently production had been greatly curtailed, thus making it impossible for many of the people to have their needs supplied. But they did not consider themselves responsible for the situation, and, while they thought that if any one wished to play the philanthropist and make goods at a loss he was welcome to do so, yet as for themselves they had no ambitions in that direction and would insist on shutting down business entirely rather than permit the government to fix the prices on their products.

" But the labor leaders ridiculed the arguments of the employers. They declared that the high prices were due to their rapacity and greed and they loudly called for the extinction of the whole tribe of capitalists. For a while there was pandemonium and anarchy, but the government, being in the hands of the Federation, remained firm against the employers. Many of the latter were thrown into prison and their plants confiscated. Then the entire capital of the nation was declared to belong to the State, and the employers were invited to go to work or go to jail, some choosing one alternative and the rest the other. It was announced that the Golden Era had at last dawned, and the people were urged to be patient until the State could get the factories and farms and fisheries in condition, when it was promised there would be universal leisure and luxury. But alas! after many centuries the people are still waiting for the fulfilment of these glittering promises. I do not doubt that the labor leaders did their best, but under their management the industries of the country woefully failed to turn out enough commodities to supply the demand at the prices fixed. Something was wrong and it was decided that the medium of exchange, that is money, was the root of the trouble; so money was abolished and credit cards were issued to the workers instead.

"About this time the principle was established that no man should have more of the products of labor than another, and a host of enactments were put into force regarding the use of the cards. Then all occupations considered as unnecessary were abolished and the workers were divided into regiments. Still the goal of luxury seemed as far removed as ever. The men in charge of the factories were not only incapable, but they could exercise no discipline over the men, since the latter believed they were as good as their bosses and were entitled to judge for themselves as to the amount of work they should do. This condition could not last. Those controlling the government finally saw that before the needs of the people could be supplied the commodities must be actually produced, and they also saw that unless the people worked it would be impossible to produce the commodities. Accordingly, the government resorted to the expedient of increasing the forces of the walking delegates. This move not only strengthened the power of the government, but it also provided the instrument for compelling the people to labor. The term 'walking delegate' was dropped and that of 'inspector' substituted. It was then carefully figured out by the inspectors how many shoes, how much clothing, and so forth, must be produced to supply the needs of the country, and calculations also were made as to how much work each man would have to do, in order that the needed product be created. These figures were laid before the nation, and at the same time it was also announced that if any man did not perform the work required of him he would be severely dealt with. There was a great hue and cry, but it was found that the government was too strong to be easily overturned. Serious resistance to its will was easily crushed, and the people were forced to work under the lash of the inspectors. Thus did the ignorance of the Federation beget socialism, and thus, instead of leisure and luxury, did it bring forth slavery, poverty and vice. Do you wonder then that I should curse that great organization, which, while standing for the sacred cause of the masses, propagated those false ideas that led to universal misery and damnation? Yonder monument represents the triumph of the fiends of hell, and if I could but destroy it I would not count my life as having been lived in vain."

I was surprised at the feeling displayed by the doctor, but on reflection I realized it was not without good cause. I could not forbear thinking, however, that an employer on earth would be considered highly intemperate, did he speak half as strongly about the unions there. Then I wondered if the doctor really would carry his vindictive feeling to such an extent as to destroy the monument. So I said to him:

"Doctor, if you are so bent on destroying it, why don't you do it?"

He gave me a puzzled look.

"I don't know how," he said.

"You surprise me," I replied. "There are plenty of substances that will do the work. There is gunpowder, for example; also guncotton, nitroglycerin, picric acid and many other explosives."

"But we have nothing of the kind in Atlantis."

"Then make them," I said.

"We have lost the art of making explosives. Their manufacture was interdicted centuries ago as a matter of self-preservation on the part of the State."

"But you have a laboratory," I suggested.

The doctor gazed at me and a wild look came into his eyes.

" You know how to make them! You shall show me!"

With that he became greatly excited, shaking his clenched hand at the monument and declaring he would wreak his vengeance on it.

What contrasts there are in the character of every man! I should never have dreamed that one so gentle and good as the doctor would harbor in his heart so bitter a hatred as that which he now manifested.

CHAPTER XXIII

THE INDUSTRIAL MILLENNIUM

The monument served a useful as well as a sentimental purpose. As I have previously said, radium rays had many of the properties of sunlight and were essential to the development of plant life in Atlantis. The shining obelisk naturally became the center of a rich agricultural section in which large quantities of grain and vegetables were raised. Fields stretched away on all sides of it. Some of these were lying fallow, others were ready for the harvest, while still others had only recently been planted. There were no seasons in Atlantis, no cold waves or hot waves,— just the same mild equable temperature the year around, and this made it possible to grow crops at any time. During our inspection of the monument and the doctor's outbreak against the Federation we were alone, but now several inspectors approached, and we turned to walk through the fields. After a time we came in sight of a number of men, who were deployed in two ranks across a section of plowed land.

"You will now see socialism in operation," the doctor said. "Those men are planting. Observe them."

Coming closer I saw in the front rank about fifty men stretched out in one long line, like a company of soldiers on skirmish duty. They maintained a stooping posture, except at rare intervals, and their advance across the field was slow. Hanging from the shoulder of each was a bag, containing seed. Every now and then each man would thrust his right hand into his bag and drawing it out would puncture the earth with his fingers and move on. It was evident they were planting, but who were these men in the rear rank and what were their duties? They were fewer in number than those in front, but they walked erect and each one brandished a weapon that resembled the medieval morning-star, an instrument consisting of a small metal ball set with spikes and attached by a chain to an iron rod which served as the handle. There was one of these men to every three who did the planting. On the extreme right of the line was an individual who walked along in a very leisurely manner with neither seed-bag nor morning-star.

"Halt!" cried out this man, and his command was echoed across the field by the men in the rear rank.

Those in the front rank immediately stopped, stood erect and stretched their arms and backs.

"Advance!" The order was repeated down the line and immediately the men with the bags bent double at their task and slowly moved forward as they pushed the seed into the ground. Now and then some of them would go a little too fast or too slow, causing a sag in the line, and the general would yell out:

"Right dress!"

If the order was not promptly obeyed the morning-stars swished threateningly through the air. Occasionally some laggard felt the prongs upon his thigh or back. I fear that this occurred only too often, for those who wielded the weapons appeared to vie with each other in "teasing their comrades," as it was called.

The sight was revolting and I turned my eyes to the doctor.

"I have always understood," I said, "that under socialism men would require no higher incentive to labor than the common good."

The doctor looked at me quizzically, but he said, seriously enough:

"The disinclination to work is natural to men, and it is only their necessities that drive them to it. When

men are dependent on their own efforts for their livelihood, and when they know that their needs and desires will be satisfied only in proportion to the amount
of energy and intelligence they bring to their labor,
the highest possible incentive is given them to exert
themselves. It is then they test their endurance to the
limit and burn the midnight oil to improve their minds.
But was there ever a man who labored from pure love
of it? I imagine that men may become deeply interested in their work and take a pride in their ability to
create, but this can be possible, I should judge, only
after they have acquired the habit for work and the
knowledge that makes them proficient in it. I can
understand how in such cases they may continue to
work even when want does not press them. But under
socialism there is no pride in personal attainment, and
no answering reward in public approbation. Before
the army of inspectors received orders to compel people to work, dawdling was reduced to a science. The
fear of hunger was remote, and while every one
vaguely realized that the common stock of food and
clothing could not be maintained unless some labor
was performed, no one was anxious to contribute
more labor than his neighbor. The average man was
slow in getting down to work, and after he did he
would stop every few seconds to look around to see

"Advance!" The men with the bags bent double. *Page 219*

if everybody else was working. He wanted to be constantly praised for everything he did, and he was always ready to flatter his neighbor if the latter would only work hard. Gradually, but inevitably, the pace was set by the most indolent and inefficient, and the State was hard-pressed to keep national starvation away. Socialism could not perform miracles, and as there was no longer a sufficient incentive to make the individual work voluntarily, it became necessary to make him work involuntarily."

I listened to this lengthy statement with much interest and remarked:

" More and more I am impressed with the resemblance between your country and our prisons, where the convicts are forced to work. What a loss of productive power has been sustained in Atlantis by the exchange of a voluntary system of labor for an involuntary one! But tell me one thing more, why is it you have no farm machinery for planting?"

" The reason is simple. The Federation of Labor in the old days placed nearly all machinery under the ban. True to their theory that the less each man did the more labor there would be left for others to do, they declared that machinery was far worse than energetic habits on the part of the individual. Is it not true, they asked, that a great many more men would be employed if the product turned out by machinery were made by hand? Of course it was true, replied the nation. So when the Federation seized control of the government nearly all labor-saving devices were destroyed, and it became unlawful for any one to make or invent new ones. Machinery was declared to be a devilish device of the capitalist to rid himself of the necessity of employing labor, and the orators drew many dark pictures of the time when all commodities would be turned out by machines and human labor would be compelled to fold its arms in idleness and starvation."

"What did they think would become of the commodities which the machines would turn out?" I asked.

"Oh, they seemed never to think about that,— at least they never tried to explain that phase of the matter. I suppose, had they been pressed to give an opinion about it, they would have said the owners of the machines would apply all the commodities to their own use or store them away or burn them or throw them into the sea."

"I have heard the same sort of argument from labor leaders on the earth reputed to be the most intelligent," I remarked. "They seemed to think the capitalists would run their machinery merely to see the wheels go round. It certainly ought to be evident to the most dense that they could have no object in piling up products to go to waste. But how about the railroads? They did not destroy them."

"No, there were some classes of machinery which they spared," was the reply. "They did not destroy the railroads, or the air machinery, or the sewage-reduction plants or the water distilleries. Hoisting machinery, foundries and a few machine-shops were preserved, but in the main, where hand labor could do what machinery did, the latter was wrecked. As for the railroads, they employed many men, and when the Federation took charge of things these men were working for the State. They had acquired a great deal of power with the government, and were so successful now and then in getting their wages raised that they constituted an object lesson of great value in proving to labor in general that if the State were the sole employer every one would be highly paid. These men insisted that their means of livelihood be not disturbed, and the Federation, under all the existing circumstances, thought it best to yield to their desires. It is due to this fact that there was not a return to primitive methods of transportation."

The doctor now suggested that we visit some of the factories, but I decided that I had seen quite enough

of the industrial side of Atlantis for the time being
and we returned to the dormitory. I devoted most of
the rest of the day to explaining to my friend the con-
stituent elements of explosives, and the method of
making them with the least danger. I found there
was plenty of saltpeter and sulphur in Atlantis, and
that the doctor had at his command all the ingredients
necessary for the making of gunpowder and guncotton.
He set to work making these two explosives and, as
he was an experienced chemist, his progress was rapid.
In fact, an unholy zeal in the carrying out of the enterprise seemed to take complete possession of him, and
it was plain, from his constant references to the subject, that he looked forward with much unseemly gusto
to the blowing up of the monument.

CHAPTER XXIV

THE DOCTOR BECOMES A BUSY MAN

About this time my desire to escape from Atlantis became so intense that, aside from Astræa, I could think of little else. I began to see that merely to meet the girl in secret now and then were to dwell only in a fool's paradise which sooner or later must end in our undoing. I refused to contemplate the possible consequences of our rashness and at the same time I became keenly sensible of my own responsibility in exposing to grave danger the only two beings in the entire land for whom I had a heartfelt interest. The doctor, I knew, appreciated fully that we were toying with fate, and yet because of his attachment for me he was ready to sacrifice himself. But Astræa, I could see, gave no thought to the possibly tragic goal toward which we were drifting. She was apparently content to enjoy the happiness of the moment as though it were to last for ever, and when, in my visits to her, I hinted at the dark shadow over our future, she would smile and show such trust in my ability to overcome all obstacles that I had not the heart to discuss with her the limitations of my power. I had seen her several times in the days following the visit to the monument I have just described, and no incident occurred to mar the blissful dream in which we lived. But on returning with the doctor to the dormitory after one of the happy evenings spent in her company, I opened my mind to him on the necessity of quickly devising a means of escape. I told him of the misgivings I felt and how I could not rest at night because I was endangering Astræa's life and his own.

"If I could only make a water balloon," I said, "then we might all three hope to reach the upper world."

The doctor listened attentively and taking me affectionately by the arm he said:

"My brother, you must not censure yourself for the ill fortune that your visits to the prison may bring to me or to Astræa. In Atlantis no true happiness is attainable without danger, and I reap such pleasure in going with you to the prison that I am only too willing to pay the cost, whatever it may be. As for Astræa, she would, I am sure, express herself in the same way, though no doubt in better words, and would count it ill in you, did you give a thought to sparing her from the consequences by ceasing to see her. Grasp your opportunity to taste of happiness while you may, for the future may never again present such a favorable chance."

I was much affected by the gentle, almost tender, manner in which the doctor spoke, as well as by the sentiments he expressed. But I persisted in my views and said:

"If we continue to visit the prison, all the greater reason exists why we should plan to escape."

"Ah, my young friend," he responded, "if it were possible to escape it might be well to think on it; but why let it disturb your present happiness, when it is clearly out of the question? Rather should you endeavor to reconcile yourself to life in Atlantis and seek to better conditions here by reforming the government."

To this I replied in some impatience that the country was not worth reforming, that Atlantis was not a fit place for human beings, anyway, that it was impossible to make silk purses from sow's ears, and much to a like effect.

"Besides," I declared, "I have no ambition to be a great reformer." I could see the doctor was hurt by my words. Nevertheless I continued to argue against his ideas of public reformation, and said:

"A people are not entitled to any better government than the one they themselves endure. Tell me the kind of government a country has and I will tell you whether its people are intelligent or ignorant, prosperous or poverty-stricken. Your country has the worst government that man ever devised, and your people are the most ignorant, the most debased and the most wretched in all the universe. It would be a blessing to them were they suddenly destroyed by some cataclysm of nature, for the good has died in them and they no longer can serve any useful end in the scheme of creation. You say it is impossible to escape. I tell you it is far more impossible to establish any reform worth while, with the material composing the masses in Atlantis. There is an old saying that I remember well,— if a people would be free they must free themselves. Liberty can not be permanent unless the body of the people understand and value it and know how to protect it."

"You discourage me," said the doctor dejectedly; "I thought that possibly we might inaugurate a revolution by destroying the monument."

I now discerned one of the reasons for his zeal in the project to destroy the symbol of the Democracy, but I said:

"Doctor, I do not like to dampen your ardor for the welfare of your people, but one man alone can not start a revolution. He must gather around him a strong following and build up public sentiment to support his plans. Could you arouse a hatred for the Democracy among a considerable number of your countrymen, and stir them up to the destruction of the monument, then there might be some hope of success in bringing about a revolution. But as it is, you will be one man against the entire nation, and you will die the death of a traitor."

"That may be true, but we shall see," he replied doggedly.

It was evident that he was not to be moved from his purpose, and he continued with unabated energy to make the explosives for carrying out his design. His laboratory was rapidly becoming a magazine, and we were both oppressed with a constant dread lest some inspector might unwittingly cause a premature explosion while visiting the place. This compelled the doctor to keep close to his workroom, guarding his bottles and receptacles as though they were sacred.

One evening during the smoke-time we made a trip to the monument for the purpose of studying how we could best place the explosive. Good fortune favored us, for we found no inspectors on guard about it. The heads of the departments had probably never imagined that any harm could come to it. We found on one side of the obelisk a narrow stairway excavated in the earth and leading to a small door in the foundation. This door was not locked and entering we discovered well in the interior a small chamber, filled with dust and dirt. The room might possibly have served in the past as sleeping quarters for a custodian, but it was plain it had not been tenanted for years. It now appeared to be made especially for our purpose. About the walls of the chamber were a number of blocks of stone, which, I saw, would serve us excellently in closing up the passageway leading to the exit, when once we had filled the room with explosives. The doctor was somewhat appalled at the quantity of powder I considered essential for the success of the undertaking, but I did not intend to chance a failure through insufficient preparation. The problem of setting off the charge was a delicate one, but we finally determined on making a slow-burning fuse, which could be lighted at the door of the monument and would give us a good half-hour to make our retreat to a place of safety. The plan now being perfected the doctor redoubled his efforts to put it into execution; and had the State been watchful when its subjects reveled in the smoke-weed it might have observed two men leaving Dormitory 457 several times a week with their garments strangely bulging,

and returning several hours later considerably ema-
ciated in appearance. But the State, over-confident
in its security, paid no heed, and the product of the
doctor's powder factory was gradually but safely
transferred to the interior of the monument. History
is full of such instances of official carelessness, and
many a proud city has fallen because of its sentries
sleeping on its walls or its garrison feasting and
carousing while its gates were opening to an invading
host.

I confess that at this time I saw little reason why
the monument should be destroyed. While I gloated
over the idea of playing a trick on the Democracy,
for to me our enterprise had no higher import than
this, yet I would willingly have abandoned the hazard-
ous undertaking, had not the doctor been so set on
it. As the sequel showed, however, we were building
better than we knew. How frequently actions,
deemed unimportant and seemingly without adequate
object, develop either to our ruin or our salvation!

While preparing our mine of powder and visiting
Astræa from time to time, I was ever busy in my
mind contriving how I might get back again to God's
country. In order to make a water balloon I required
some material lighter than water, and I knew of none
that would serve the purpose except timber. Now

this was a scarce article in the submerged island, there
being few trees and those only in places far distant
from the dormitory. Many apparently unsolvable
problems become simple, however, if they are studied
perseveringly, and by dint of hard thinking it finally
occurred to me that the wreckage of ships in the Hall
of Curiosities was just the material I needed. As it
was doubtless thoroughly dried I figured that it could
be made into a gallant raft, to which, for sails, I
could attach a number of bladders filled with air.
The wealth of the ancients would make very excellent
ballast. When all was ready the doctor, Astræa and
myself could moor the craft into the sea and bid farewell to the Social Democracy. We would have sufficient air aboard to last the voyage out, and I pictured
to myself our rising from the deep in the surging
waves of the broad Atlantic. When I unfolded this
plan to the doctor he said it was a most beautiful idea,
and that he could find no flaw in it except that we
would not be permitted to carry it out. This was
truly a serious objection, but nevertheless I was more
than encouraged to discover that escape, after all, was
not a physical impossibility, as the doctor had always
claimed, and I began to speculate as to how I could
obtain permission to make the craft.

CHAPTER XXV

I AM HONORED WITH DOUBTFUL ATTENTIONS

It will be remembered that Mrs. Brine extended me a cordial invitation to visit her, and though my detestation for her had suffered no diminution, yet I mustered up courage one day to go to see her. I had decided, in considering her invitation, that there was no reason why, if chance offered, I should not see Astræa more frequently than once in three days; and I hoped that the real motive for my call would not be fathomed by the old woman. But no sooner did she set eyes on me than she exclaimed:

"Oh, it's you! So you have decided you would like to meet that pretty atavar again, eh?"

As she said this she tried to chuckle me under the chin with her bony hand, and laughed uncannily. She continued:

"I always did like to study young folks, and I'm partial to young men. You shall see the girl, but first I want you to meet two of my best friends."

She ushered me into her apartments, and there I clapped my eyes on two of the ugliest specimens of humanity it has ever been my misfortune to meet. One was a creature who was much like Mrs. Brine, only considerably shorter in stature. I noticed with a fascinated stare that her back rose to a peak above the line of her head, the latter protruding in front of her body. The other creature was a dwarf of hideous looks. The head and face were covered with a gray shaggy mat of hair, which proclaimed the sex as masculine. His body was deformed, as could easily be seen by the hang of his garments, his left leg was shorter than the right and his arms were long, like those of a gorilla; on his right hand there was but one finger.

Mrs. Brine presented me as the young man of whom she had been talking, and she told me that I should call the "lady" —66 and the "gentleman" No. 13.

No. —66 turned her watery eyes on me and looked me up and down. She hobbled close to my side, leaning on her stick, and then she felt of my arms and even had the temerity to touch my cheeks with her skinny fingers. I stood the examination with as good grace as possible, but her gross familiarity was too much and I involuntarily took a backward step beyond her range. She chuckled at this and said:

"You're an interesting specimen."

Mrs. Brine saw something humorous in this remark, for she giggled and said:

"Ugla, I'll wager you were going to say he is handsome."

"And suppose, Ate, I did say it, who's to hinder me? Answer me that!"

"Oh, oh, so I've riled you! Maybe you'll be saying next that you would like to marry him?"

"Well, even if I should go as far as that I see nothing funny in it, that you should try to make sport of me. I might do far worse than make such a strapping big fellow my consort. You are putting ideas into my head, Ate, and I'm obliged to you for them."

"Tut, tut!" put in the dwarf.

"No, there is no 'tut, tut!' about it," said Mrs. Brine. "If I see a sister going wrong it is my duty to put her right again. Here is poor Ugla, who would have a romance while tottering on the brink of the grave. My dear Ugla, don't you know that this young man comes from a country where the man chooses first and where the woman accepts or rejects? Do you think he would let you do the love-making? It's against his training, Ugla. My poor girl, it is hard, I know, to give up such a pretty dream, but then you must."

"You would taunt me, would you?" cried Ugla

shrilly. "You, who married the sea-surgeon, your junior by forty years! Well, we shall see. If there are any pickings in this Democracy I'll have you know I've as much right to them as you." She turned her back on Mrs. Brine and addressing me, said:

"You see Ate there is a little jealous. I do believe she's afraid I'll get a finer looking husband than hers."

Her anger, which had blazed out a moment before, now vanished as suddenly as it came. With a grin meant no doubt to be ingratiating she asked me the question:

"You are a socialist, are you not?"

"Yes," I said, telling a half-truth, "I was a socialist on earth."

"Ah, my dear Ate," she continued, "you see how mistaken you are. He is a socialist and believes in our marriage laws. The State will select a wife for him, and he will gladly show his allegiance to his adopted country by obeying the will of the State. And the State,— who is the State, Ate, answer me that? Am I not as much the State as you — and our friend here?" The latter part of the sentence was uttered obviously as an afterthought.

It may well be supposed that I was astonished at this tilt between the two wretches. I was not only astonished, but also filled with apprehension. Who were these women, that they should talk in such a way? Was it really a passage-at-arms between them, or was it merely a little play enacted for my benefit, that I might think of it in my spare moments and make out of it what I pleased? Was the witch in earnest about marrying me, and could she possibly be able to control the choice of the State in selecting my wife? Perhaps she was only attempting to be witty, though there seemed to be a serious purpose behind her words. My mind was swayed by many doubts, but the impression, though vague, remained uppermost that these women had given me a hint as to their power and proposed I should marry Ugla. It was a most significant fact to me that they should have dared to address each other as Ate and Ugla, an unheard-of procedure in Atlantis, and one in direct conflict with the laws. Certainly this must have been done for a purpose, and that purpose, I told myself, could be no other than to give me an intimation of their importance in the State and to impress on me the advantages of the matrimonial alliance so delicately proposed.

The dwarf abruptly stopped further discussion of my marriage by crying out:

"You two beauties stop your nonsense! You are scandalizing the State before this young man and putting him very much out of countenance, too, at that. Let me talk to him, since you don't know how. What do you think, young man, of socialism?"

This question was directed at me in a smooth conversational tone, and though I did not like the small beady eyes turned on me, yet I was thankful for his coming to my rescue. At the same time, I was mindful that I must use my tongue with wisdom and discretion, so I said:

"Socialism is the product of the most advanced thought, and I have never ceased to wonder at its remarkable development in this country."

"I am glad to see that you are so well taken with it," he said. "But I should like to know whether you are up on the ethics of socialism. You were a socialist on earth and you perhaps know that the fundamental axiom of socialism is that might is right?"

"Yes," I said. "I gave deep study to the basic premises of socialism years ago. You have well said that its first principle is might is right. Now, on earth to-day certain rights are justly recognized as belonging to the individual, not because the individual was endowed by nature with these rights, but because the majority of the people believe in them and have the might to enforce them. At the present time those who oppose these individual rights are justly looked upon as criminals or enemies of the State, because they are in the minority and do not possess the might to make their ideas right. For example, I might cite the case of the burglar. He does not recognize the right of private ownership in property, and seeks to put his views into practice by going by stealth at night into the houses of others and robbing them of their valuables. If he is captured it does him no good to plead that he had as much right as any one else to the property he took, for such a plea is scorned as the false argument of a criminal mind and he is sent forthwith to prison. But let a majority of the people come to his way of thinking, and decide that no individual can claim exclusive ownership in property, and what do we have? Why, socialism, just and righteous socialism. The minority may be compelled to yield up their property against their will, and may even be sent to prison as being enemies of man if they offer resistance. Thus, what the burglar could not do without committing crime, becomes righteous when the majority do it. It is merely a question as to where the power is lodged. The burglar being in a minority, is weak and, therefore, is wrong; but the majority, possessing the power to enforce their mandates, can make right the same ideas previously condemned in the burglar."

"A most excellent exposition of the socialistic principle," said the dwarf patronizingly. "I believe you would make a good member of the Vorunk or popular assembly."

"I a member of the Vorunk, as you call it?" I said. "I have no training for political office."

I had no sooner uttered this remark than I saw I had made a grave mistake. Both of the witches, as well as the dwarf, frowned heavily and before the latter could speak I made haste to say:

"No, I don't mean that. I have resided so long in America that naturally now and then I lapse into the language of individualism. Of course, my real sentiments are that no vocation requires special aptitude, and there is no real choice between jobs, one being as good or bad as another. The majority could not permit the reservation of any class of positions for those who are supposed to possess ability higher than the average. The reason for this is that those making up the majority are men of only moderate mental caliber — I might even say of small mental caliber — and as they have the power it is perfectly wise and right for them to decree that the office of legislator, as well as every other position, shall be filled by lot and that men with brains shall not be shown any special favor over the brainless. When I come to think of it seriously, I feel that if I should be made a member of the Vorunk I could attend to the job as well as another. Furthermore, I am as much entitled to it as any one else."

These words met with instant approval, as I could see by the faces of all three of the interesting personages about me. The dwarf said:

" The fact is you would do very well in the Vorunk. Your ignorance of the country for which you would be called on to make laws would be of great advantage to the State. The most ignorant, I have found, make the best officials, the best judges and the best generals in the industrial army. They cling the closest to the letter of the laws. They are most tenacious in upholding the doctrine that the individual must implicitly obey the State in all things, and they have the greatest abhorence for ideas not stamped as righteous and valid by the State. What think you, Ate and Ugla, would our young friend be a good man for the Vorunk?"

" Aye, aye he would!" said Ugla.

" Perhaps what you say is wise, perhaps not," said Ate.

" Why do you say perhaps this and perhaps that?" said the dwarf testily. " Speak out,— what do you mean?"

" I mean nothing at all," the witch replied, " except that I would first like to see him tried before I would venture my opinion."

Again the thought flashed through my mind that the conversation was not the idle talk it seemed on the surface. The manner in which my marriage with Ugla had been broached and also my becoming a member of the Vorunk was suggestive of premeditation on the part of the two crones and the dwarf. If they had been astute politicians I should have been positive they were attempting to dicker with me without committing themselves; and while I had no tangible knowledge at the time to lead me to suspect that the Democracy was subjected to personal manipulation, yet it seemed possible that instead of engaging in aimless chatter I was in reality participating in a serious conference involving my future destiny.

My repugnance for the company I was in made me anxious to get away, and moreover I was growing fretful lest Astræa should be brought into our presence. I was ready to stand being gaped at by Mrs. Brine, should I meet the girl, but to have this second witch and the dwarf also staring at us with evil and cynical eyes was a little more than I had bargained for. So I said:

" I am very glad to have met such worthy citizens

of the Democracy and now I shall intrude no longer on your time. I must return to my dormitory."

But Mrs. Brine checked me and with a honeyed smile she said:

"You surely will not leave me so soon. I have just sent for one of my hardened prisoners and you must stay and see her."

I took my disappointment with as good grace as I could and endeavored to steel myself for what I felt would be a trying ordeal.

When Astræa entered the room it was as though a gleam of sunshine had suddenly illuminated the blackness of night. She slowly looked from one to the other of us and with her eyes resting on me she smiled.

Addressing no one in particular, she said: "Why have I been sent for?"

"Because, my pet," answered Mrs. Brine, "you are the prettiest one in the prison and I like to show you to my friends."

"You could not show a prettier one, that is certain," said the dwarf in his peculiar oily tone. I turned my gaze from Astræa to glance at the speaker, and I saw that he was looking at the girl, fascinated. I strongly resented such impertinence.

"Surely," continued this caricature of a man, "this

girl must be sane. Such loveliness is not the mark of disordered intellect."

"Must be sane!" cried Mrs. Brine. "She is about the worst in the whole asylum!"

"A little less hasty, Ate," went on the dwarf. "Think again, have you not seen signs of recovery in her case? Surely we must try to save her, for I never saw a creature who would be a higher ornament to wifehood."

These words produced an astonishing effect on Mrs. Brine. The old witch jumped up from her seat, and, grabbing her stick, shook it menacingly at the dwarf, while her eyes gleamed with passion.

"You, too!" she shrieked. "An ornament to wifehood! It is bad enough to hear Ugla talk nonsense, but you, you ugly reprobate — bah, you must be falling into your dotage! An ornament to wifehood! What is the State coming to when men like you get sickly sentimental over a sprig of a girl? I suppose you will next be sighing like a silly fool over her eyebrows. Now tell me, is not her skin like alabaster, her lips like red anemones, and her hair, tell me, what are her tresses like? Oh, you fool!"

"Tut, tut, tut!" broke in the dwarf, making an impatient gesture with his one-fingered hand. "You are a venomous cat when you are jealous. When I complimented the girl I did so without prejudice to yourself. Do not think me remiss in proper admiration of the paragon whom my friend, the sea-surgeon, has for his better half."

"Stop it! Stop it!" cried Ugla, stepping in between Ate and the dwarf. "You shall not quarrel in my presence!"

Mrs. Brine for an instant seemed about to explode with renewed wrath, but a change quickly came over her, and she laughed instead.

"You are an insulting wretch," she said between fits of hysterical tittering. "You're such a giddy thing, such a lady's man. Get down on your knees now like a true suitor and you will win her from her mental infirmities. Tell her if she only will smile on you she will be pronounced cured and the banns of her marriage will be announced. And tell her, too, if she refuses that she will die as her companion in the corridor of the condemned will die to-morrow!"

As she neared the end of her climax the old witch rose to her full height and spoke with the solemn sternness of an avenging Nemesis. I shuddered with horror and before I could regain the semblance of composure I heard the voice of Astræa crying out in heartrending accents:

"Alene, to die to-morrow! Poor, poor Alene!

What harm has she ever done? Tell me, what harm has she done? You are going to murder her and for what? Poor, poor Alene!"

I saw the girl sway and then fall to the floor. She had swooned. I was by her side in an instant.

"Water!" I cried out. "Some water, quick!"

"You did this maliciously, you infernal actress!" exclaimed the dwarf as he also approached the prostrate girl.

"Get out, every one of you!" shrieked the witch. "Go, there's the door!" She took up her stick and pointed to the exit.

"A nice lot of goings-on in a respectable prison," she continued. "And don't you come back until you learn how to be polite. Go, every one of you!"

"But some water!" I expostulated.

The irate woman turned on me savagely and cried:

"She's only fainted and your assistance is not wanted. All you need to worry about is your rival there."

The dwarf and Ugla had already left, muttering to themselves, and I parleyed no longer, seeing that I should be driven out if I did not go. As I left, Ate burst out laughing like a fiend.

On reaching the dormitory I hurried to find the

doctor and asked him whether there was to be a public execution the next day. He looked pained and surprised.

"Yes," he said, "to-morrow is the Festival of Kuglum. It is a public holiday, and victims are delivered to the kraken. I have said nothing about it as I wished, if possible, to keep you in ignorance of it. How do you come to know of it?"

In reply I told him of my visit to the prison. He shook his head gravely and for a long time remained in deep thought.

"Can it be possible," he said at last, "that we are not governed entirely by our laws alone? I will not hide from you that I have had grounds for suspicion before. But no, it can not be, our laws are too comprehensive, too rigid, too thorough, to admit of any exercise of personal power. Every department of the State works automatically in obedience to statutes centuries old."

"But," said I, "do not changing conditions make new laws necessary now and then?"

"Yes," he replied, "many new laws are constantly being made, but these new laws must all conform to the laws governing the making of laws. The legislator can no more exercise his personal judgment or will than the judge or doctor. If you should become a member of the Vorunk you will early learn this fact."

Despite his dismissal of the idea of individual authority in the State I could see that he was much worried, and from his close questioning and the remarks he dropped now and then it was evident his credulous faith in the government of Atlantis being a pure Democracy was considerably shaken. I interrupted his musing by declaring my intention to see Astræa that very night.

"Impossible!" said he, arousing himself. "You shall not go! The danger to-night would be increased a hundredfold. There will be many going and coming in the lower corridor of the prison and detection would be almost certain."

I begged and pleaded with him but he remained obdurate, and I was forced at last to recognize the wisdom of his position. We remained at the dormitory and I passed a sleepless night.

CHAPTER XXVI

At the sound of the morning bell I arose and mechanically prepared for breakfast. Long thinking on the terrible fate of Astræa's companion and my utter impotence to stay the ghastly carnival had benumbed my faculties so that I went through the entire day like a passive figure in a gruesome dream. I saw much with my eyes but little with my mind and I am grateful to this day that the atrocities of the Festival of Kuglum left only a vague impression in my memory, like that of some unpleasant nightmare which we gladly forget when the mind awakes.

I was dimly aware during the first hour of the day that my comrades were displaying an unwonted interest in life. They laughed aloud and talked incessantly, and though I marveled at their conduct I gave it scarce a second's thought until the doctor whispered in my ear, telling me that many of the laws had been suspended for the occasion and among them the restriction as to the amount of daily speech.

249

" How awful," I exclaimed, " that the sacrifice of helpless and innocent beings should be made the occasion of public celebration ! "

" But it is so," said the doctor, hanging his head as though in shame. " Ever since I was a child these holidays have filled me with dread and with a loathing for my fellow men. The memory of the torture and the suffering of the victims, and the horror of seeing them eaten by the monster, have stayed with me days at a time, making life hideous and sometimes well-nigh unbearable. Yet these creatures here about us, this rabble, think it huge sport and account this festival the greatest of the year. Nothing gives them greater pleasure than the agony through which others are made to pass."

At breakfast I forced myself to eat my share and then the doctor and I left the dormitory for the " festivities," as he ironically put it. In the street we were jostled by many people, all hurrying in the same direction. I had never seen such activity displayed in Atlantis. The scene reminded me of the gay throngs that my home city was wont to turn out at night to a circus. But it was not a menagerie of wild animals or acrobatic feats that these people were so eager to see — such amusement would have been too tame for them. Nothing short of a spectacle of death could have aroused them from their lethargy or animated their wooden countenances.

A short walk and we came to a long line of cars, the lights of which shone with ghostly pallor in the semi-night. Here a dense crowd was engaged in a ceaseless scramble for places aboard the trains, which, as soon as they were filled, started swiftly away. Almost before I knew what was happening there was a rush all about me, and I was pushed into a seat on one of the cars. Then came a whirl of motion and looking out I saw the giant columns of crystal rushing by in a blur of light. By and by the clanging of many gongs was heard, the car stopped and we alighted. Wedged in a crowd we walked at a snail's pace between long rows of cars, at last emerging into a highway which was fully two hundred feet in width. Before us was a high embankment running at right angles to the road, but the road dipped and pierced it with a mighty arch overhead. Beneath this arch several streams of humanity from as many directions converged, and the concourse that poured through it was like a mighty river. Arrived on the far side of the arch I beheld a spectacle never witnessed on the earth's surface.

It was that of an amphitheater of prodigious size being rapidly filled with thousands of people in scarlet garb — I might truly say with hundreds of thousands, for the doctor told me there was room for a million; and everywhere I looked I could see the surging of the crowd, even into the most distant aisles, where the people looked like insects. I gazed blankly at this astounding scene of animation. The place was simply a great pit in the earth the half of a circle in shape. A solid wall rising perpendicularly as high as the eye could reach, formed the straight side of the basin, while the curving sides sloped gradually upward, giving support to tier after tier of benches which rose one above the other to a height, according to the doctor, of three hundred feet. The arena inclosed by the semicircle was of immense dimensions and an elaborate system of illumination made the whole place as light as day.

The stream of people coming through the arch spread out like a delta on the arena, the many mouths of which poured its humanity into the various aisles. The doctor and I were carried along in a resistless swirl toward an aisle on the far side of the amphitheater. Up this we clambered, higher and higher until we were quite at the top, where we found seats. Here we had a remarkable view of the vast spectacle. Having feasted my eyes with the stirring scene below, I looked to the right and saw that the embankment through which we had come was in reality a portion of one of the sides of the colosseum and that on its summit ran a smooth highway which apparently terminated at the great wall in front. Looking to the rear over the top of the amphitheater I was astonished to find that the land stretched away practically on a level with the point where we were sitting, and I was still more surprised to see plainly in the distance the shining monument of the Federation of Labor. For a time I forgot everything else in observing the magnificent panorama about and below me and then suddenly I remembered the frightful significance of the gathering of this myriad host. Once more I became to a large degree oblivious to my surroundings.

By and by I felt the doctor touch me on the arm and I heard him say:

"Yonder is the Crystalline Wall and behind it is the sea."

I looked blankly at the great wall, which the multitude faced, and idly noted how the light was reflected from its surface as though it were glass.

"So you call it the Crystalline Wall!" I said with an effort at conversation. "I can see that it is very smooth and glossy. One can almost imagine it to be a great curtain to some mighty stage."

" And in a way it is," said the doctor.

He continued to speak, but I did not hear him; for at that moment, while looking at the wall, it seemed to vanish suddenly and I gazed not on opaque rock but on the green waters of the deep!

" Great God! " I exclaimed. " The sea! "

At the same moment a mighty yell went up from the multitude, and I grabbed the doctor, panic-stricken.

" Don't be afraid! " he cried in my ear.

Then I saw that the waters remained stationary, suspended, as it were, in mid air, as the waters of the Red Sea were suspended when the Israelites crossed over dry-shod to the wilderness. I quickly recovered from my nervous shock, and heard the doctor say:

" The program has begun. I thought you knew the wall was transparent. It is made of marble of the same character as that of the monument. The turning on of the lights in the sea is the signal for the opening of the festivities."

At last I understood. There in that great aquarium of the ocean on which the myriads gazed, must lurk the monster which was about to be fed with human lives!

The mighty sheet of green extended upward and to right and left as far as my vision reached. Though

some distance from it, I could make out that the sea
was illuminated to a considerable depth. I could see
the tops of the spear-like vegetation at the ocean's
bottom and higher up the moving forms of many fish.
Now and then some phosphorescent species shone
like fireflies in the far depths and then a larger fish
would sweep down before the arena and seize its
prey. The multitude yelled its delight in one in-
cessant din. But strain my eyes as I would I could
not see as yet any signs of the monster which was to
enact a leading part in the day's events.

A sound like that of beating tom-toms in the distance now smote upon my ear. The noise grew
steadily in volume, rising weirdly above the shouting
of the multitude. The doctor pointed to the entrance
of the great arch, and after some minutes of ex-
pectant watching I saw the head of a procession enter
the arena. First there came a company of decrepit
men and women, many of whom leaned forward upon
their sticks. They were dressed in black, and at their
head was a dwarf holding a black flag. It was difficult for me to see because of the distance, but before
this leader reached the part of the arena nearest me I
saw that he was the dwarf whom I had met the day
before. The old witch, Ate, I was sure, was also in
that motley crew, though I could not distinguish her

from the rest. The tom-toms ceased to beat, and as the black-robed column slowly emerged from the arch and wound about the arena it set up a chant, discordant and unearthly. The vast assemblage was suddenly hushed into silence, as though fear had entered all hearts, or was it that the horrid noise to these people was like that of the sacred songs of the processional? The black train stretched nearly the length of one side of the arena before its end had appeared through the arch, and was followed by three or four hundred creatures costumed in yellow and carrying drums of ancient style. After these came some fifty figures in grotesque garb like masqueraders. Some of them looked like devils, some like clowns, and others like the painted Indians of the plains. Next came a second company arrayed in black, but, unlike the first dressed in this fashion, these wore cowls which hid their faces.

Previous to the appearance of these creatures nothing but the horrid shrieking of the chant was heard, but now the whole multitude burst out in a savage yell. At the same time those with the drums or tom-toms set furiously to work, and pandemonium prevailed. In the midst of this outburst there entered beneath the arch a score of white-clad figures, and in their front rank was a girl with long tresses hanging down her back. Some of them walked with heads erect while others seemed to falter as though about to fall, but the girl kept her face turned upward as if she were gazing into eternity. These were the victims, and it was in honor of their entrance that the demonstration was made. Behind them came more figures in cowls and another detachment of tom-tom beaters. The whole procession now marched about the arena, the tom-toms keeping time, and the weird chant rising and falling in dismal cadence. I kept my eyes on the figures in the white robes and as they came closer I saw that the girl with flowing hair was Alene, the prison-mate of Astræa. She had said she did not fear to die, and now with a brave heart she was marching to her awful doom. There she was, the central figure amid a million fiends, and to her no helping hand could be extended.

The black-garbed battalion in front, which the doctor whispered to me contained the heads and staffs of all the departments of State, had made one entire circuit of the arena and was marching close beside the great green wall, when another immense shout burst from the multitude and the entire assemblage with one accord arose, stamping its feet and yelling.

"What now?" I cried out to the doctor.

"The kraken!" said the doctor pointing to the sea.

I looked quickly and at that moment an incredible monster seemed to dash itself at the amphitheater. I saw two immense eyes, a cavernous mouth and a dozen great arms or tentacles all flattened against the transparent wall. A more horrible sight I have never witnessed. Though I knew it could not reach me, yet my blood ran cold and terror gripped my heart. In an instant the creature had gone and a second later it came again. I thought I could hear the impact of its dash against the wall. I now saw that its body was as large as a whale's and covered with scales that glistened in the light. Its arms reached apparently a hundred feet in length and seemed as large around as a man's body. But most terrifying were its eyes, which looked like concave lenses about five feet in diameter, and the mouth, capacious as a hogshead, which contained teeth like those of a crocodile. I never before knew there were such creatures in all nature, but it must be remembered that the scientists have not yet obtained specimens of the larger animal life at the bottom of the sea.

The repeated rushes and attacks of the monster against the great wall made the vast assemblage frantic with delight. The procession stopped, and in the midst of the furor the white-garbed victims were marched close to the green wall. Thankful I am that

The attacks of the monster made the vast assemblage frantic with delight.
Page 258

I could not see their faces to mark the blanched cheeks and the terror in their eyes. I could see, however, that some of them fell as though they had fainted, but Alene — beautiful Alene — still stood like a statue with face turned upward.

"What are they doing now?" I gasped.

"It is the preliminary ceremony of offering the victims to the monster," was the doctor's reply. "There, you can see them lifting one of them up to a niche, which was hollowed out in the wall for this purpose."

I strained my eyes and saw two of the black cowls lift a white-robed figure four or five feet, and stand it in a small cavity in the wall which I had not before noticed. The monster made an instant dive for the poor creature and in its rage at being balked, struck fiercely at the wall with its huge tentacles. The white figure swayed and was caught by the creatures in black, while the assemblage yelled demoniacally.

Then another figure was placed in the niche and still another, and finally it was Alene's turn. She stood the ordeal, apparently unmindful of her surroundings, and, despite the lunges of the frightful beast in the sea, continued to gaze upward as if in prayer.

The procession once more began to move about the

arena, and then out through the arch. The doctor
pointed to the summit of the opposite embankment,
and in a short time I saw the dwarf and his black
cohort appear over the crest and advance along the
highway at the top. The tom-toms beat and the weird
line stretched itself along the height. When the head
of the procession reached the great wall it broke into
two reviewing columns while through the center
marched the victims accompanied by the creatures in
the black cowls. A silence fell on the multitude and
all eyes were turned to catch the next move on the
program. Then two figures in black, with one in
white between them, began to walk slowly athwart the
green sea-wall, or so it seemed, but, as the doctor explained, they were traversing a narrow ledge which
was not apparent from where we sat. On they went
until they arrived opposite to the center of the amphitheater and about a hundred feet above the arena. As
they stood facing the crowd it looked as if they were
surrounded by the waters of the sea and would fall
easy prey to the monster. But the wall still protected
them, and the plunging of the kraken was without
effect.

"You can not see it very well," said the doctor,
"but over the head of the victim there is a transparent hood, impervious to water. Do you see the

large bag upon his back? That is a bladder filled with air which is slowly supplied to the hood, so that the victim will not suffocate in the water before the monster seizes him. There is also a light in the hood to illuminate the features. It is a devilish device to enable the people to see the horror on the face of the condemned as he is about to be swallowed by the monster."

While the doctor was talking the three had receded somewhat into the wall.

"They are now in the sea-chamber," he explained. "It is a small compartment that fills rapidly with water. Those in black have now put on their breathing apparatus. But look! They are already opening the small sea-door."

The amphitheater was now silent as the tomb, so intense was the interest. Looking fascinated at the three figures suspended there between sea and air, I now saw the ones in black seize the victim in white and hurl him apparently out into the sea. The white figure fell head-first some fifty feet and then its arms frantically beat the water. At this instant the monster appeared and a huge tentacle reached out for the struggling victim and grasped it. I was spellbound with horror. I tried to turn my eyes away, but could not. The illuminated hood shone brightly on the darker background of the sea, but happily I could not see the agony on the face because of the distance.   There was a swaying motion of the gigantic arm and the body in its grasp was lashed rapidly through the water first one way and then the other. Then came a longer swing, the bright spot shot through the sea and in a twinkling disappeared, swallowed by the yawning mouth,— the dreadful scene was over.

The assemblage had been wrought up to the highest pitch of excitement, and now that the tension was relieved it yelled like a million demons. I closed my ears with my hands to keep out the hideous noise. There is no more frightful sound than that of a mob frenzied with joy over the taking of human life and the diabolic ingenuity of the execution just consummated magnified the heinousness of its wild transports a hundredfold.

There was one atavar the less to threaten the permanency of the Democracy, but the eyes of the monster still shone with appetite unappeased. On the height the tom-toms beat and the chant was sung, while below in the arena there reappeared the figures in grotesque garb, who began to circle round and round in single file, giving vent to a monotonous refrain as they glided rhythmically along. Faster and

faster they went and louder and louder grew the refrain. It was the dance of the savage tribe over again.
I gazed heart-sick on the scene and turning to the
doctor said:

"Yonder savage dance — this fiendish multitude —
do you know what it all proves to me? It proves that
there is reversal of type in Atlantis, a return to the
traits of ancient ancestry; but it is the multitude that
are the atavars and not those poor wretches that are
being fed to the monster. Come, can we get away
from this? I am sick, I can stand no more!"

"I, too, have seen more than I cared to look on,"
he said; and glancing behind him he continued: "Let
us climb over the edge of the amphitheater — there
is the level land only a few feet below."

This we did and encircling the upper rim of the
great caldron of humanity we made our way down the
farther embankment and lost ourselves in a crowd that
could not find room within the amphitheater. The
last glimpse I had of the atrocious spectacle was
Alene, poor innocent, beautiful Alene, walking between two black figures along the ledge of the wall.
Her face was still turned upward as though she saw
something above that gave her fortitude and hope.

"Great God," I muttered, "let Thy curse rest upon
this people!" And the doctor responded "Amen!"

CHAPTER XXVII

I AM MADE A MEMBER OF THE VORUNK

On the day following the Festival of Kuglum, Atlantis returned to its humdrum existence as though nothing had occurred to interrupt its profound placidity. My comrades of the dormitory went to their tasks with their characteristic stolidity and hopelessness, thinking, I presume, if they thought at all, of the evening when they might smoke the weed and drug their decadent sensibilities into a false glow of enthusiasm over the virtue of working each for all and all for each. Poor miserable dupes of the beautiful dream of socialism, who never knew the pride of possession, the glory of attainment, the sharpening of wits against wits, the joy of true friendship or the tender yearnings of love, who were clamped as in a vise in one unending, dreary, damnable round, wretched slaves in a mighty treadmill,— who could but pity them?

Deprive men of individual independent participation in that struggle which characterizes nature, and you take from them all that makes life worth the living and they become as walking dead men. Even had Atlantis been filled with milk and honey, and labor had been unnecessary, yet would her people have been worthy of great commiseration, for no system of socialism can be devised or dreamed of which does not take away that great incentive to mental development which individual responsibility for one's own destiny imposes. Unless men are forced to think from hour to hour and day to day, they will neglect to think and inevitably in the end they will lose the power to think, and when men are no longer thinking animals they will be savages and possibly apes again. When " You must " takes the place of " I will " in the government of mankind, then the race will become refuse on the shores of eternity. May the Angel Gabriel proclaim the day of judgment before that fate overwhelms it!

The doctor was doggedly at work making explosives, and I was giving vent to some of the thoughts I have just expressed, when we were honored with a call from an emissary of the Department of Vocations. This individual looked about the laboratory inquiringly and, addressing me, said:

"I have come, stranger from another land, to announce to you that citizenship No. 489 A D G has been conferred on you, by which number you will hereafter be known. I am also to inform you that it has been determined by lot that you shall be a member of the Vorunk. Your duties will begin to-morrow."

"A member of the Vorunk!" I exclaimed, the memory of my conversation with the dwarf rushing back into my mind.

"Yes," continued the inspector politely, "I regret that such is the case. The position is not one that is generally looked on as desirable, if it can be said that one position is more desirable than another. The hours are long, being from eight in the morning until nine in the evening, with an hour for dinner, and the work is laborious, as you will be required to read many documents and construct bills. I know of no more painful task than that of exercising the brain in reading and composition, but then there is a necessity for this work which can not be avoided and some one must do it. You are merely unfortunate in that lottery of chance to which all must submit when the time comes for the selection of the work they shall perform for our beloved Democracy."

"I wish I knew more about that lottery of chance of which you speak," I returned with nonchalance.

The inspector became patronizing in his manner and said:

"It is my duty to give any information that you may desire, providing it is not contrary to the interests

of the nation. You see, No. 489, the Department of
Vocations has a great wheel which revolves on a
pivot and which absolutely assures equality in the
distribution of jobs. On the rim of this wheel are
the names of all the occupations in Atlantis, each
occupation receiving a certain space depending on
its numerical importance. By careful computation it
has been ascertained that, approximately speaking,
one-fourth of the workers are required to perform the
duties of inspectorship, and therefore one-fourth of
the rim of the wheel is allotted to that occupation.
Agricultural pursuits require another fourth and hence
are given a corresponding space on the wheel, while
the remaining half of the rim is largely taken up by
such vocations as those in the mines, the fisheries,
the factories, the public kitchens, and so on. Only a
small segment remains for a variety of occupations
such as the judgeships, the generals of the industrial
army, the heads of departments and the members of
the Vorunk,— the latter, indeed, being so few in number, receive a mere dot on the wheel's circumference.
When the occupation of a citizen is to be determined,
the wheel is revolved rapidly, and when it stops the
part of the rim opposite a stationary pointer indicates
the kind of work he shall do. Do you understand
my explanation?"

" Perfectly, perfectly," I replied with feigned admiration. " You have described to me what on earth
is known as a wheel of fortune, only I hope your
wheel is better than some I have heard of, which exhibit a remarkable persistency in winning all the large
bets and losing only the small ones."

" I hardly understand your allusion," rejoined
the extraordinarily polite inspector, " but you know
that what is is; and fate, as expressed in the wheel,
has willed you to be a member of the Vorunk." He
made a deprecatory gesture with his hand, and, turning to the doctor, said:

" It is stated you keep very close to your laboratory
these days. What, may I ask, are you now experimenting on ? "

The doctor had the appearance of a man struck
dumb with astonishment during the conversation between the inspector and myself, but now a slight flush
suffused his brow. I was anxious as to what he would
say, but he rose to the occasion.

" I am hunting," he said slowly and hesitatingly,
" for the elixir of life; but it is very elusive and foils
me just when I think I am on the brink of success."

The inspector, aroused almost to the point of enthusiasm, picked up some of the gunpowder and
crushing it between his fingers, said:

"It is very interesting and I hope you will succeed, for I know of some to whom your success would be very welcome news.   But now I must bid you both good day, as I have many others to call on."

When the inspector bowed himself out and the door was closed the doctor began to pace up and down his little room like a caged animal.

As for myself I must acknowledge that I was filled with despair and bitterness.   Would not this call to the Vorunk be followed by orders for my marriage to Ugla, and would not Astræa be handed over to his majesty, the dwarf?   I saw the web closing in about me and pictured both myself and Astræa walking the ledge of the great green wall.   In the midst of this somber meditation the doctor queried:

"It can not be a coincidence that the wheel should have stopped with the pointer on the dot making you a member of the assembly?"

"No," I replied, "coincidence in this case is impossible.   My suspicions have been confirmed.   They deliberately showed me where the power in the State lies and they relied on my judgment to see that it would be to my interest to serve them.   If I should not accept their terms including my marriage to Ugla, they have only to order my execution.   There are more atavars in Atlantis than you have dreamed of, and they are not all to be found behind prison bars either, I can assure you."

"What a fool I have been!" exclaimed the doctor, shaking his head. "I agree with you — your experience conclusively proves that the powers of the State have been usurped by individuals. While I have been searching all my life for good atavars, behold, the evil ones have been using me as a tool! But to think that we should be governed by blear-eyed hags and dwarfs, who never had a wholesome thought in all their miserable lives! Oh, it is terrible, terrible!"

"Your Democracy," I remarked after a pause, "is only an illustration of the impossibility of equalizing the powers of government among all the people. Authority must be lodged somewhere. Nowhere in nature do we find community life without some governing head. Take the bees — they have their queens, and the ants their slaves. As for man, never in all history has there been a nation which did not have its leaders and rulers. The powers of sovereignty, restrict them as you will, must be wielded by individuals. There is but one course to be pursued now, and that is to show a seeming compliance to the will of the powers that be while we pursue our efforts to escape; and if, after doing all in our power to escape, we fail, then we can go to our doom resigned to our fate."

CHAPTER XXVIII

THE DWARF FURNISHES INFORMATION ABOUT THE VORUNK

The next morning found me in the Capitol of Atlantis, that elaborate structure of stone with innumerable offices and many floors and corridors of which I have spoken. The hall of the Vorunk, the scene of my future labors, was in a remote and ill-ventilated portion of the building, being on the fifth or bottom floor of the basement and about a mile's walk from the main entrance. Had I looked on my tenure of office as anything more than temporary I should have been much chagrined because of the ill-favored locality of the chamber, which I thought could have been put to a more proper use as a burial-place for musty documents. As it was I did not care whether the Vorunk met near the center of the earth or on top of the brilliant monument of the Federation of Labor.

Nevertheless, I entered the dismal crypt with all the humility that becomes a new member, and was met by his smiling lordship, the dwarf, who piloted me to a seat in the midst of the august assembly. Glancing about I found that the august assembly consisted of a score of solemn-looking men, mostly gray-headed, and all garbed in the plain democratic habiliments of the common people. I noticed particularly that the brows of all except those of the dwarf were corrugated with horizontal wrinkles as though they were all afflicted with severe headaches, superinduced, I surmised, by heavy thinking. The dwarf's presence did not surprise me — in fact, I should have been disappointed had I not met him. Neither was I surprised when I learned that he was the chairman of the committee to which all bills were referred. It seemed a little queer that one committee sufficed for a national parliament, but then it was a queer parliament. The dwarf had me take the customary oath to obey the laws, and then escorted me into an anteroom, leaving one of my colleagues reading something about the acts as to kissing in the year one after the deluge. Having shown me to a seat the hideous creature was good enough to put me at ease by saying he hoped I was well and would like my employment. Then in the manner of a man proud of his country's institutions he asked me how I liked it.

"Like what?" I asked imperturbably.

"The Vorunk, of course," he replied.

"Oh," I said, "it does pretty well. I see you have hidden it away as far as possible. That's a splendid

idea. I have seen some other legislative bodies in my time that it would have been well to have buried like this one. You have no idea how insufferable are some of the legislators in my land — they are for ever flaunting themselves before the people as possessors of supernatural wisdom — it is very disgusting, I assure you. Socialism, I see, has found the remedy. I don't suppose any one ever cares to come here to hear the silver-tongued oratory of the members, now do they?"

"No," said the dwarf with undisturbed equanimity. "It is not a matter of common interest what the honorable members have to say. No one ever comes to hear them, and only their brother members are required to listen to their eloquence."

"This is very interesting," I rejoined, "and incidentally just as it should be. But it seems to me you are failing to make use of a ready means of punishment if you do not provide that certain offenders should be sentenced to listen to the debates."

"You have an acute intellect," he remarked in turn. "I shall make a note of your suggestion, or, better still, you might draw up a bill amending the punitive code."

"I do not suppose, judging from what I have already learned, that there could possibly be such a thing as a shorthand report being made of the proceedings?" I now asked.

"Oh, no, that would be useless labor. Only copies of the laws passed are put in the record."

"Excellent!" I remarked. "You have no idea of the amount of printing wasted in America in making official reports of proceedings. Thousands of volumes are constantly issued which nobody ever thinks of reading. I also infer, from what you have told me, that the members of the Vorunk do not become public characters, courted and looked up to when they go out among the people?" I propounded this question rather anxiously.

"Such a thing would be quite unsocialistic," the dwarf replied with the suggestion of a smile. "The member of the Vorunk is necessarily very limited in his acquaintances and as for the general public it can not tell him from any one else, and, if it could, it would have no more regard for him than for any one else."

"And there is no publication heralding the doings of the members?"

"None."

I drew a long breath.

"It is well," I said. "What is fame, after all, but empty nothingness? It is queer how men on the earth will sweat and stew for what they all in their saner moments deride as hollow mockery. How thoughtful it is of the Democracy to keep men from following after strange gods — what an immense amount of human energy is prevented from going to waste!"

The conversation continued in this pleasant strain for some time and at last drifted into a discussion of the uselessness of elections. The dwarf seemed to have the theme very much at heart.

"Even in the old days of barbarian government," said he, "the elective system was found to be a poor means of ascertaining the will of the majority. The political machinery had a way of falling into the hands of a small minority, and only occasionally could the majority, by extraordinary efforts, break the machines. After the principle was recognized that the majority possessed rights superior to any the individual might claim, it became absolutely necessary that a better method than that of the ballot-box be found in order to assure the permanent supremacy of the majority. In fact it was found that the elective system was thoroughly and completely inconsistent with socialism. No sooner would the majority elect representatives to form the government than these representatives would become a minority, and a minority, too, with power to make the majority obey it.

"Although it became the fashion to confiscate the property of the members of a defeated party and even convert them into slaves of the members of the successful party, and although there were many official appointments of profit and many special privileges to be granted, yet it was utterly impossible for any administration to satisfy the demands of all its adherents. Far from succeeding in doing this, every new set of officials incurred the common fate of their predecessors in being charged with base ingratitude by the larger portion of their following, long before their terms of office expired. You may well imagine that a condition of considerable instability resulted,— a condition which was by no stretch of the imagination to be considered as serving the ends of equality. At last it came about that a majority determined to abolish the elective system entirely. Certain fundamental laws were adopted which could never be repealed and among these laws were those providing for equal compensation, the allotment of occupations by means of the wheel and the regulation of marriage by the State."

"The genesis of the automatic impersonal system of government is remarkable," I ventured to remark.

" The mechanical geniuses on the earth have long dreamed of perpetual motion, and I little thought when living there that I should ever see anything resembling it in actual operation. I am surprised that there should be anything for the Vorunk to do."

" In that you are mistaken," he rejoined. " Here is a set of rules for the guidance of the Vorunk and you should carefully consider them."

He handed me a printed card that looked like the notice tacked on the doors of hotel bedrooms. It read as follows:

READ CAREFULLY

RULES FOR THE MAKING OF LAWS

1. No laws shall be passed that are in conflict with the organic laws of the Social Democracy.

2. The test that every proposed law should stand is: Does it aim for more complete uniformity as to the food, sleeping accommodations, attire, speech, opinions, actions, personal appearance and methods of working of the individuals composing the State? In order that complete equality exist it should be the constant effort of the Vorunk to remedy any defects in the present laws under which any individual may in any wise possess characteristics distinguishing him from others or enjoy favors not enjoyed by all. Acts that do not meet with the requirements of this rule are null and void.

3. As the greatest crime that can be committed is that of

disobedience to the State it is the high prerogative of the Vorunk to determine on the proper punishments for the various grades of disloyalty and treason, and in fulfilling this duty it should be remembered that laws of this character can not be too drastic.

4. Any member of the Vorunk who shall propose laws that are unsocialistic shall be thrown to the kraken.

Having read this document I volunteered the remark that after some centuries of continuous labor on the part of the Vorunk there ought to be very little left to be done in the way of passing laws to correct minor inequalities.

"I must confess," replied the dwarf, "that the field of possible enactments to perfect equality has been narrowed very greatly, but human activity has a wide range, and it is surprising, when you come to study into the subject, how many things the individual may yet do independent of State guidance. The Vorunk must engage in much research and study existing conditions carefully, to see how these matters that have so far escaped legislation may be grappled with. Again, all the departments of State make reports to the body, and it is necessary to digest these reports and adopt measures now and then that will prevent overlapping in the work of the bureaus, eliminating unnecessary employments and providing for the adequate carrying out of that which necessity imposes. There is enough to keep you well engaged, my friend."

CHAPTER XXIX

Several weeks now passed, weeks full of anxiety and bitterness, with intermittent periods of hope and self-assurance. They were also weeks of strenuous work, for I threw myself into my duties as a legislator as though I had a reputation to make, and in truth I had, for I wished to stand well with the powers that were and disarm their suspicions, if any they had. Then, too, there was the enterprise to blow up the monument. All the preparations for the final act, even to the lighting of the fuse, were fortunately completed without discovery. Lastly, and needless to say the most important of all, these weeks were rendered blessed in my memory by my secret visits to Astræa, when she and I would for a few fleeting hours drink deep of happiness made all the more precious by the perils which surrounded us. These visits never failed to lift me from despondency and imbue me with new determination to escape the clutches of the Democracy. When I told Astræa of my fears as to the designs of the State to marry her to the dwarf she simply said:

" I shall never marry any one but you, even though I suffer the fate of Alene."

She was ever looking into the future with faith in my power to triumph over all obstacles and yet I could see that the death of Alene had affected her deeply, that to her Alene was a saint whose example had inspired her with strength and resignation. The brave girl endeavored to show me that she did not fear to die, as though to prepare me against the coming of the worst.

In the Vorunk I had introduced several measures which the dwarf, as chairman of the only committee of that body, reported on favorably and commented on very kindly. These measures were by their titles as follows:

A Bill to Regulate the Trimming of Finger Nails.

A Bill Requiring the Use of the Left Arm as Much as the Right.

A Bill Providing for the Equal Use of the Maxillary Muscles on Both Sides of the Mouth in the Act of Masticating Food.

A Bill Requiring Every Individual to Laugh Aloud Once Every Hour, and Providing Inspectors for the Enforcement of the Act.

A Bill to Abolish Snoring at Night in Dormitories.

A Bill Providing for the Removal of the Wealth of the Ancients beyond the Temptation of Future Generations.

Perhaps the titles of these bills are sufficiently illuminating as to their nature, but I will, nevertheless, make a few remarks concerning them. From the very inception of my legislative career I was oppressed by the apparent impossibility of devising new ways to limit the freedom of the individual, and it took much study to devise the measures here spoken of. I had my first inspiration when I noticed the great irregularity in the way my comrades cut their finger nails, and in drawing up this, my first bill, I incorporated a suggestion of the dwarf's, providing that those who cut their nails straight across instead of round should be compelled to listen to the debates in the Vorunk for certain specified times according as it was the first, second or third offense. In order to make sure that they listened I provided that offenders should pass an examination as to what they learned from the debates.

Regarding the left-arm bill I observed that the muscles in the right arms of my comrades were much more developed than those in the left, that in point of fact many left arms were little more than skin and bones. Being naturally solicitous for the welfare of the country I hastened to rectify a condition so palpably at variance with proper ideas as to true equality. I also used the argument very effectively with my colleagues that, whereas a certain amount of work was being performed with the right arm alone, almost double the work could surely be expected from the employment of the left arm as well. The maxillary-muscle bill arose from a minute examination of the Dinner Code in the effort to find some defect which others had not seen. Although the code was well-nigh perfect as to the amount of food to be inserted in the mouth at a time, the manner in which the eating utensils should be handled, the nature of the noises permitted and not permitted with the lips, and so on *ad infinitum,* yet I happily discovered that the entire subject of mastication was left untouched. Therefore, with the zeal of a new legislator, I drew up a bill requiring that food should be chewed nine times on the right side of the jaw and nine times on the left side, after which it could be swallowed.

I do not see the need of commenting on the anti-snoring bill, the fact that I slept in the same ward with many others being sufficient, I take it, to show the origin of the measure in my own mind. I really extracted more pleasure in being the father of this law than I did of the others I have mentioned, for it was the only one in which I succeeded in turning my power as a Vorunkian to my personal profit. I provided for capital punishment for the offense.

The laughing bill was a humanitarian measure, based on the principle that whereas happy thoughts caused the muscular actions known as laughter, these muscular actions, if forcibly carried out, would in turn by reflex action produce happy thoughts. The need for gaiety in the daily affairs of life was painfully apparent, and the measure had the additional merit of providing equality in merriment. This bill was truly a happy stroke of genius, although, I regret to say, I was among its first victims. On the second day after it went into effect I was hauled up before a judge by an observant inspector who noted my failure to laugh in accordance with the provisions. I pleaded to the judge that I was the author of the measure and was absent-minded by reason of my thinking on new measures for the good of the Democracy; but he was obdurate and sentenced me to one day in prison, without food, the minimum punishment. Thus I had good opportunity to marvel on the insignificance of a member of the Vorunk, and the impartial character in which the laws were administered. But I was in a measure recompensed by having a genuine laugh to myself when I recalled how the honorable Court, while sentencing me, had to stop to comply with the act himself, which he did with a loud guffaw.

The bill providing for the removal of the wealth of

the ancients beyond the temptation of future generations was the result of the conversation I had with the sea-surgeon on the occasion of my first experience with the lethe weed. It provided that a committee of one member of the Vorunk should be appointed to examine into the possibility of removing the coin and jewels in the Hall of Curiosities to some place beyond the reach of human hands, and gave this committee the right to make any preliminary arrangements which, in its judgment, would subserve the end desired. It was an innocent-looking bill, and I congratulated myself that the suspicious nose of even the dwarf did not detect any ulterior motive behind it. In behalf of the measure I used the excellent argument of the sea-surgeon that while the wealth was an eyesore to the present generation, there was no telling but that it might be the means of sore temptation to posterity, and that in order to save posterity from any possibility of incurring the misery which the money and gewgaws had inflicted upon the forefathers of the country, it would be an act of true patriotism to remove the stuff out of human sight and reach for ever and ever. I did not bring forward this bill until after I had acquired a certain prestige in the chamber by reason of the other measures I have mentioned and I pretended only a passing interest in

it, but the debate brought out so many questions that
I was induced to talk at length upon the advisability
of the proposed undertaking, and I am pleased to state
that I spoke with such effect that it passed unanimously. I was warmly congratulated and much lauded by
my fellow members, as being the author of what they
declared was the most important measure adopted in a
generation. They insisted that, as a matter of course,
I should be appointed the committee of one; but this
honor was qualified by the stipulation that because of
my invaluable services to the Vorunk during its ses-
sions I should contrive to carry on my investigations
after eight o'clock in the evening.

"This is a remarkable measure," said the dwarf in
private to me after the bill passed, "and I am much
interested to see what you propose to do, for I have
no doubt you have some plan in view."

"I hardly know as yet," I replied with composure,
"what I shall do, unless it be to construct some kind
of a vehicle in which the coin and jewels can be placed
and taken out to sea and lost among the rocks."

"And why should you put yourself to all that
trouble?" he quietly asked.

"Why? For the good of the Democracy, sir, of
course," I said.

"Of course, of course!" he replied, bowing gravely.

There was nothing in the way he spoke which seemed objectionable, but there was a queer glint in his eyes and his lips had a cynical twist, which caused me some uneasiness, but only for a moment. Had not the dwarf allowed the bill to pass, and was this not sufficient evidence that he did not question my motives? I told myself that I should not be over-suspicious, and I awaited the adjournment of the session with ill-constrained impatience.

CHAPTER XXX

MY HOPES ARE RAISED AND THEN DASHED

By the time I reached the doctor's laboratory that evening I was bubbling over with jubilant spirits. At last I was making headway toward escape and the more I meditated on the details of my plan the more sanguine I grew of ultimate success. All the dread of the fearful future which threatened Astræa and myself fell from me and in the reaction I could hardly keep from dancing a hornpipe.

"Doctor," I said exultantly, "we are going to escape! Behold me, the authorized representative of the State to build a vehicle for the removal of the gold from the Hall of Curiosities! We shall now construct a raft as fast as we can saw the timbers and drive the nails. Then some pleasant evening, during the smoke-time, we shall take French leave of the Democracy, you and Astræa and I."

But the doctor only shook his head dismally. He was not impressed and I was piqued by his unresponsive demeanor.

"You are over-confident," he said slowly. "You

are not yet out of Atlantis, and you must remember that. Still I am ready to assist you, though in this matter I do it reluctantly, feeling, as I do, that it will come to naught." He paused for a moment and then, like a man who suddenly remembers something, he exclaimed:

"How about the monument?"

I laughed gleefully.

"The monument, to be sure!" I echoed. "We certainly will not forget that. We will touch it off as our farewell message to the Democracy. It will be a grand leave-taking!"

"But I would like to be here when it explodes," said the doctor, crestfallen.

I saw what ailed my friend. To him the destruction of the monument meant an event like that of the fall of the Bastille, and not to participate in the stirring events which it was to precipitate would be a lifelong disappointment to him. I tried to reconcile him to my way of thinking.

"It will not do," I said, "to be here when the monument falls, unless you wish to lose your head. As for me, I want to be as far away as possible, and you must not forget Astræa."

My reference to Astræa had its effect.

"If she can be rescued," he said with emphasis,

"then it is our duty to sacrifice everything else to that end. The monument can wait."

"You are a trump, Doctor," I exclaimed, shaking him by the hand. "And now let us hasten to the Hall of Curiosities."

Arriving at the great repository of wealth and relics I presented my credentials to the inspectors, and we were allowed perfect freedom to do as we pleased. For a considerable time I gloated covetously over the sparkling jewels and diamonds exposed in profusion all about, and I resolved to make the raft amply large to carry considerable ballast. For several hours I figured extensively on specific gravities, and measured carefully the old hulks of ships stored in the place, in order to ascertain the maximum of timber suited for the structure. The result was very disappointing as compared to my desires. Figure how I might, I saw it would be impossible to convey more than approximately a million dollars of precious cargo, and this would make no appreciable effect on the vast collection! I looked greedily at the bins of yellow metal, and was filled with vexation and grief that I should be forced to abandon them. But the thought that I was about to recover my liberty and to take with me to the land of the sun the most lovable girl in the universe made me execrate myself for my avarice, and

I became resigned to the limitations of the raft it was possible to make, though I must confess it was not without some lingering regrets.

When we were about to retire that night I said triumphantly to the doctor:

"It's going to be the easiest thing in the world. Such a simple plan, too. It only shows how readily a man from the upper world can outwit the most wide-awake statesmen the Democracy possesses. That cunning old fox, the dwarf, has met his match at last. I'd give something to observe his beady eyes when he finds we are gone."

But the next day I had all of my self-conceit plucked out of me to the last feather, and I was plunged into despair blacker than I had yet experienced. The dwarf did it very adroitly. The Vorunk was in session and I was called on to make a partial report on my project to remove the gold. I at once gave a full account of how a raft could be made, the objectionable material loaded upon it and towed out to sea.

"How long will it take to make this raft?" asked the dwarf.

"About two weeks," I replied.

Nothing more was said, but when the committee, the sole mysterious adjunct of the distinguished body, made its report in the last hour of the session it handed down a bill making it unlawful for any foreign-born citizen of Atlantis to attempt to return to his mother country, and, continued the bill, " if any such citizen should be convicted of such an attempt, he shall be publicly thrown to the monster."

During the reading of the measure I clenched my fists so hard that my nails were driven into the palms of my hands. The disappointment was great, and yet I realized that the moment was fraught with peril and that I must appear unconcerned at all costs. When the reading was over I arose to my feet and indicating by my manner I regarded the bill with indifference, I said:

" Gentlemen, I know of no foreign-born citizen of the Democracy other than myself, and, therefore, it seems specially appropriate that I should be the one to urge the adoption of this bill, and thus set at rest once and for all any suspicions as to my future intentions." (I bowed to the dwarf.) " I hope the measure will be passed unanimously."

There was a semblance of applause at my words, something very unusual, and I thanked my colleagues. One of them arose and said that he was positive the bill was not intended as a reflection on the junior member of the body, and if the junior member had thought that it was a reflection he would record his vote against it.

"But," he added, "since he urges the passage of the measure himself, I can not do less than yield to his wishes and accordingly I vote aye."

I felt grateful for the expression of the member that under certain contingencies he would have voted against the bill, but at the same time I was cognizant of the invariable custom of the Vorunk to vote unanimously on all measures as they came from the committee and in full accord with the nature of the committee's report. How fortunate that my colleague was not called on to alter the time-honored customs of the body! The bill passed unanimously.

I returned to the dormitory that night with leaden feet. It was clear that I was engaged in a hopeless task. The doctor was right — I should never be permitted to escape. I was doomed. Astræa was doomed. There was nothing left but to await the end.

CHAPTER XXXI

A GIFT FROM THE SEA

When the doctor saw me he was startled.

"What's the matter?" he exclaimed. "You look like a ghost."

"The plan to escape is wrecked. All is lost!" I made the announcement stoically.

"Infernal Beelzebub!" he ejaculated. My friend had a queer choice of expletives on occasion.

"No, it was the dwarf," I replied.

The doctor poured a little liquid into a glass and made me drink it. Its effect was stimulating, and then I told him how, if I attempted to escape, I was destined by the Vorunk to become a sacrifice to the monster for the edification of the multitudes. He listened with the deepest sympathy, and allowed me to vent my bitterness at length.

"What do you propose to do?" he asked.

"Do?" I exclaimed. "Fight, of course! There's nothing else to do. You must make more gunpowder, Doctor, you must make more gunpowder!"

"What will you do with it?"

" We will mine the amphitheater."

The doctor stared at me as though he thought **me** mad.

I laughed grimly and said:

" You must not look at me so. I am perfectly sane. The plan is feasible. It is desperate, but then I am desperate, and we are in a desperate plight."

The doctor did not have the chance to reply, for just as he was about to speak a knock came at the door.

" Calm yourself," he entreated, and then aloud he called out: " Come in."

The door opened and there walked in, as affable as you please, our mutual friend, the sea-surgeon. His handsome face wore a smile and his eyes shone with unusual brightness. He grasped us both by the hands and said gaily:

" So both of you are cooped up in this cubbyhole like two hermits! But I'm glad you are, for I wanted to see you the very worst kind. I have heard of your great success," addressing me, " and that is what has brought me. You have accomplished a glorious deed for the Democracy, and please permit me to congratulate you. I little supposed, when I gave you my opinions as to the contaminating influence of the gold, that you would so soon become the instrument to remove it beyond the temptation of our children and our children's children. So, you see, I feel as if I had a personal interest in this patriotic undertaking of yours, and I wanted to know whether I could not accompany you to the Hall of Curiosities to-night and tender you my assistance."

"Your company and also your assistance are thrice welcome," I said, smiling despite myself. "We were just about to start."

Previous to the arrival of the surgeon I had quite forgotten about the raft, but now I saw that I must go through with the enterprise as though my interest in it had in no wise abated.

The surgeon proved exceptionally good company that evening. He was so elated over the stupendous undertaking, as he called it, that he babbled about it like a brook, and I had to supply him with the minutest details of my plan. In answer to one of his queries I told him I estimated it would take almost three hundred trips with the raft to dispose of all the coin.

"It's a task worthy of a giant!" he exclaimed.

I thought so myself, and I began to wonder whether I could not transfer the major part of the job to him.

But despite his interest in the enterprise he took

up about an hour's time at the Hall, examining different coins and telling us their history and the amount of alloy they contained. He was an expert on money, and had it not been for the doctor I believe we would have wasted the entire evening in idle talk. He was speaking volubly on the theme that money was the root of all evil, when the doctor, with some testiness, suggested that we get to work. We had hardly begun to attack the wreckage of an old frigate, however, when the surgeon suddenly stopped us by saying:

"Bless me, if I had not almost forgotten! Do you remember my telling you about a curious object we found at sea?"

I dimly recalled his having said something of the kind and told him so.

"Well, sir," he continued, "it is here. We hauled the thing into the sea-chamber of the Hall, meaning to place it in this room, but the inner door of the chamber was too low to admit it. We are now in a quandary to know whether to demolish it, that is, if we can, which I much doubt, seeing that it is made of solid iron, or whether we shall take it back into the sea. Come and have a look at it. Perhaps you can give us some advice about it."

The doctor and I followed him to the door of

the sea-chamber, which began to open upon the pressure of a button. As the great sheet of copper moved slowly into its groove I looked carelessly into the chamber, and there I saw a cigar-shaped object of considerable size. My heart gave a great throb. The object looked like a boat, a boat made of iron and shaped like a fish!

I rushed into the chamber, extremely agitated. I had a hammer in one hand and I began to run up and down the sides of the object, tapping it to test whether it was hollow. Then suddenly I recalled a conversation I once had with a fellow member of a socialist club in New York. He was employed by an inventor at the time I knew him, and he often told me of his work. Once under strict confidence he gave me an account of a curious boat his employer was making which would navigate the under waters. This information, which at the time made a deep impression on me, now vividly returned to my mind.

"Surely," I said to myself, as I continued my examination, "this thing tallies with his description of the boat!"

Becoming satisfied now that it really was a boat, I was on the point of blurting out the fact when I caught myself in time. Why could I not make it the means of escape! The idea dazzled me. Then I became as secretive and crafty as a miser, for I realized that once it was known it was a contrivance that would navigate the sea, I would not be permitted to come near it except under close surveillance.

I continued to tap the steel with my hammer, and in a few minutes had examined the entire exterior of the vessel. It was about seventy feet in length and about twelve in width. At one end were two rudders, one vertical and the other horizontal, and also a propeller screw. On top of the boat amidship was a round tower, part of which was made of heavy glass. Examining this tower closely I saw that on its upper side was the lid of a hatchway.

" What do you think of it?" said the surgeon, who had been patiently waiting for me to speak.

" I never saw anything like this before," I replied glibly. " I wonder what it can be?"

" It resembles a whale," said the doctor. " Maybe it is some kind of boat."

" There are many different kinds of boats on the surface," I said. " Probably, after all, it is an ordinary vessel which has met the ordinary fate."

I now climbed upon the cylindrical tower I have just mentioned, where, giving the hatch-lid a few blows with the hammer, I reached down and lifted it.

There was a rush of noxious gases from the interior of the boat and so terrible was the stench that I made a jump and landed by the sea-surgeon, who was gaping at me open-mouthed.

"How did you do it?" he exclaimed.

I did not reply, but climbed back to the tower, when, finding that the odor was nearly gone, I began to lower myself into the manhole. But going down a few rounds of a ladder my feet suddenly touched water. I stopped and looked about. Though the light came dimly through the opening I could see that the interior was a mass of pipes and machinery which went down into the water, showing that the boat was at least half flooded. I knew that some accident had occurred, which had admitted the sea and caused the vessel to sink to the ocean's bottom. As to the nature of this accident I could only surmise. It was clear there was no leak in the hull or the water would have run out into the sea-chamber. Perhaps the hatch-lid had been open when the ship was awash, and a great wave had struck it, sending the boat downward and letting in tons of water, and perhaps the rushing water closed the lid again when it was too late. This was the only theory that seemed reasonable. I lowered myself to the waist in water, and then reascended.

"Get a pump," I said to my wondering friends, "the thing is half-full of water."

An old ship's pump was brought out of the storehouse of relics and we set manfully to work, enlisting in our service several of the inspectors who stood about. After an hour or thereabouts, we had covered the floor of the sea-chamber with water to the depth of three or four inches. I now stopped the work and went below. I saw that the boat had been nearly emptied, but as I stepped from the last rung of the ladder to the flooring my foot struck something soft. The thought had been running through my mind that perhaps I would find some bodies in the interior, but nevertheless the object there in the dark beneath my feet unnerved me. After a minute's effort to master my fears I reached down with my hand. It came in contact with the stiff cold muscles of a dead man's face. I sprang up the ladder and out of the hole, trembling violently.

"Bring a light," I gasped, "there are dead bodies below."

The doctor and the surgeon were horror-stricken by the intelligence, but in a short time one of the inspectors brought a rude lantern containing a tallow candle, and then a solemn procession wended its way down the hatchway. I was in the lead with the flickering light. Reaching the bottom of the ladder I stepped over the body and stood in a small compartment, while the others silently grouped themselves about me. Then I approached the body with the lantern. The light shone ghastly on the features of a face convulsed with agony, testifying to the horrible death the man had undergone. The body, too, was bloated to twice its natural size.

"Let's remove it," I said.

The sea-surgeon and an inspector took hold of it, and with the assistance of others got it up the ladder and through the manhole.

The doctor alone remained with me. I looked the compartment over carefully but found no other bodies. In my search my eyes fell on a belt hanging on a wall to which were attached a number of cartridges and two holsters containing pistols. I stared blankly at the object a moment, then swiftly removing my tunic, I girded the belt about my waist and again donned my outer garment. The doctor was looking at me with surprise.

"These things may come in handy," said I, "and you must keep silent about them."

I now proceeded aft, followed by my friend. We found two small compartments here, in the first of which there was nothing except water and dripping machinery, but in the second we looked upon a ghastly sight. Five bodies lay huddled together, with their eyes open and their features horribly distorted.

"I have seen terrible things, but nothing quite so gruesome and uncanny as this," whispered the doctor.

Closely examining the faces of the dead with the lantern I suddenly shrank back.

"Good God!" I exclaimed.

I had recognized one of the bodies as that of my young friend of the socialist club!

The boat was, after all, the very one he had talked to me so enthusiastically about. Poor boy! It had been to him only a death-trap, an iron coffin at the sea's bottom.

How strange are the workings of fate! The sea had brought him to me to bury and at the same time, it had given me as a gift this strange craft,— a helping hand from Heaven reaching downward to rescue Astræa and me from living death!

CHAPTER XXXII

THE SCORPION BECOMES AN ARGOSY

The next day at the meeting of the Vorunk the dwarf profusely thanked me for the service I had rendered in recovering the bodies from the queer derelict.

" Perhaps you can throw some light on what manner of vessel it is? " he inquired.

" I can not," I replied deliberately, " it is a mystery to me as well as to you."

" Suppose you give it further examination and make a report," he said quietly.

" I will do so if you will permit my absence for half a day from the Vorunk."

" Very well."

The dwarf seemed specially gracious, having, I surmised, satisfied himself that he had nipped in the bud any possible notion of escape on my part and was now desirous of mollifying my disappointment.

Ever since I first laid eyes on the submarine I had been constantly studying how I might make it serve my purpose. In the night, when others were sleeping, my mind had been busy with the problem, and now, while pretending to listen to the proceedings of the Vorunk, I still wrestled with the enigma, searching for a solution that was seemingly impossible to find. The likelihood of being able to elude the ubiquitous inspectors and the watchfulness of the dwarf was so remote that at times I was oppressed with a feeling of utter hopelessness, and at last I was forced to realize that, unless chance favored me, the craft would avail me nothing.

In my agony of mind lest this last hope should be snatched away I had recourse to the philosophy of the fatalist. I counted it a good augury that at the moment when I had about resigned myself to the thought that I could never escape, the mysterious boat had been placed within my reach. It had come like a pardon to a man condemned, and surely it had not come in vain — surely it had not been sent to raise new hope only to mock me and make more poignant my despair. If it were to be my deliverer, then it would be. Let me be on the alert and seize every advantage chance should offer, and perhaps — well, as long as there was a shred of hope remaining I would cling to it like a drowning man to a straw.

When the day was half over, armed with the credentials of the dwarf, I sought out the doctor, and we repaired to the Hall of Curiosities. We set to work on the submarine, removing the remainder of the water, wiping the machinery and oiling it. Thanks to the information my young friend had given me several years before, I had a general idea of the complicated apparatus. There were two motors, one electric and the other gasoline. I located the tanks for water, gasoline and compressed air. In the fore part of the vessel was the torpedo tube, which contained a missile ready to be sent on its death-dealing mission. Two other torpedoes were lying near at hand. While looking at them I conceived the idea of removing them, in order to lighten the craft as much as possible. Calling a number of inspectors to our assistance we managed with some exertion to take them out and lay them on the floor of the sea-chamber, where they were permitted to remain. The torpedo in the tube I did not touch. Telling the inspectors that we had no further need of their services they left us, apparently unconcerned about the boat. I now continued to study the machinery, explaining everything to the doctor as best I could. Being well versed in mechanics for an Atlantide, my co-worker was quick in comprehending, and in a short time was more competent to handle the craft than I ever could hope to be. Getting everything in shape we set the gasoline engine going, restored the supply of compressed air and recharged the batteries. The water-tanks, I found, were empty, having probably been blown out by the men in their descent through the sea. The electric motor had not dried sufficiently during the night to permit of its being used, but we satisfied ourselves that there was nothing radically wrong. The entire apparatus, in fact, seemed in good condition, save for the wetting it had received. I noticed particularly the way in which the vessel had been strengthened by numerous steel girders running from side to side and from bottom to top, enabling it to resist the frightful pressure of the water at the sea's bottom.

"It is a fish," exclaimed the doctor enthusiastically, "with machinery for entrails."

As he spoke, I happened to be looking at the dials and mechanism in the conning-tower, and my eye fell on a small copper plate on which were the words: *The Sea Scorpion.*

Calling the doctor's attention to the inscription I exclaimed:

"It *is* a fish — a mechanical fish — but it is more than that; it is a fish that stings."

While we were at work the thought struck me

that escape would never be easier than at that very time. Here was the boat in the sea-chamber, like a coach at the door ready to take us where we willed. It only required the closing of the inner door of the chamber, the letting-in of the water, the opening of the sea-door and the closing of the hatchway with the doctor and myself aboard. What if the electric motor could not yet be used — we could risk the gasoline motor for a few turns of the propeller, and once out in the open sea, the boat could be depended on to rise of its own buoyancy. But the idea had no sooner insinuated itself in my mind than I spurned it. What! Leave Astræa! Rather would I remain behind and die! If only she were with us, nothing could induce me to forgo the chance for flight so temptingly presented. Why not then get her that very evening? The idea intoxicated me. I sprang for the ladder.

"Come," I cried, "to-night is the chosen moment for escape! Let us hasten to the prison to bring Astræa."

I felt the doctor's detaining hand forcibly on my arm.

"Restrain yourself!" he pleaded; "to-morrow will be time enough."

"To-morrow!" I exclaimed wrathfully. "To-

morrow may find us all in prison.   Now is the chance,
and there is no time to waste."

I hurried swiftly from the boat, followed closely
by my friend.   I heard him say:

"Remember the monument!"

I turned on him.

"Do you think I would let the blowing up of the
monument hazard our escape?"

I spoke harshly, but glancing backward at him as
I ran I saw, despite my self-absorption, that he was
deeply grieved and dejected.   I relented at once and
said:

"We can blow it up to-night and escape too!"

We had now reached the first chamber of the Hall,
and looking about saw not a living soul.   The vast
cavern was as silent as the tomb, and the figures of
the idols and colossi looked down on us, inscrutable
and ghost-like from shadowy walls.

"Where are the inspectors?" I whispered appre-
hensively.

"Gone!" said the doctor, perplexed.   "Can it be
possible that this is the smoke-time?"

We hastily traversed the various chambers of the
immense cave, and found no one.   The silence and
gloom were appalling.   I had a feeling that I was
treading the charnel-house of ancient kings where,

reposing with their bones, were all the trappings and insignia of their vanished glory. My eyes swept round the rooms, taking in the empty thrones, the suits of shining armor, the immense array of spears, javelins and battle-axes; then, drawn by irresistible attraction, they glanced downward at the cases of shining stones and golden jewelry. The sight of these objects scintillating in the radium light caused a new idea to spring into my mind. As I made for the outer entrance of the Hall, I checked my pace, then halted altogether. The idea became a mastering passion. My brain was on fire and the chilling somberness of the place lost its spell. I started forward toward the cases containing the crown jewels, but again I hesitated. Was this the time to falter, to be swerved aside from the main purpose? I thought of Astræa in the prison cell, waiting patiently for her deliverance, and here was the chance, the golden, precious chance to escape — only a fool would juggle so with fate! I stood, swayed by conflicting thoughts. Had I been left to wrestle it out myself I would doubtless have put temptation behind me and fled from the place. But just at the critical moment the doctor spoke.

"It is too late to go to the prison — it would be useless, it would be madness. For aught we know the smoke-time is already passed. We had better hasten to the dormitory."

Was it too late? Should I be compelled to postpone our flight until to-morrow? If I left the Hall now, and found I could not go to the prison, then I should doubly lose. Better to act on a certainty than to take doubtful chances on an uncertainty. My mind was quickly made up. I fairly sprang for the jewels.

"To work, Doctor, to work!" I cried. "Let us fill the boat — this is our chance!"

I looked about for something in which to carry the jewels, but I saw nothing. So I pulled off my tunic, spread it on the floor and quickly emptied the contents of several cases upon it. Then I gathered the ends together and throwing the load over my shoulders made for the boat. In my haste I had paid no attention to the doctor, but now I looked toward him and saw him regarding me as though he thought I had gone daft.

"Hasten!" I exclaimed impatiently; "seize a load! It will make us rich when we reach the surface. Rich, man, fabulously rich,— don't you understand?"

"It is folly, folly!" replied the doctor plaintively. "For the sake of this trash you risk everything. Don't you know some one is likely to come in?"

I looked at him, I fear, somewhat contemptuously, and retorted harshly:

" This is no time to argue. While there is no one here I mean to carry all the diamonds and gold to the boat that I can. If you will not help, then stand by and see me do it."

With this I marched away with my load and carried it down the conning-tower of the craft, dumping it into one of the compartments aft. On emerging from the manhole I had the satisfaction of seeing the doctor approaching reluctantly with a burden on his back.

" That's the way to do it, Doctor!" I cried out exultantly from the conning-tower. " Hand your load up and get another."

He lifted up his precious burden and while he went again into the storehouse I emptied it beside the first pile. Again and again he returned with a load from the inexhaustible Golconda. I instructed him to bring diamonds in preference to all else, and soon the floor of the submarine was covered as with rocks and gravel. As last I began to fear that the argosy would be overloaded, that its reserve buoyancy would be offset, but I calculated that the torpedoes that had been removed and the empty water-chambers would allow for considerable ballast. Besides, the crew would be short-handed, and men weighed something. So I loaded the compartments until there was scant room in which to turn about and work the machinery. I even partly filled the water-chambers between the two skins of the vessel. This seemed a foolish thing to do, but why leave behind any wealth that it might be possible to carry to the surface?

When at last I called a halt from sheer certainty that the boat contained all it would carry, we obtained old boards from the relics of ships and placed them on top of the jewels and diamonds with the idea of hiding the treasure from any casual visitor. Of course, it would be useless to try to guard against investigation — the only thing to do was to hope there would be no investigation. But was there any way in which the risk could be minimized? I cudgeled my brain, and then I thought of shutting the hatch-lid — the inspectors could not open it before, perhaps they would not even try it again. So as I left the boat I closed the lid with a bang. I then tried to reopen it, and for a few moments I was filled with consternation, for lift as I might it would not yield. Then I got a hammer and began to pound the handle and the edge of the cover, as I had the day before. I found that the handle moved slightly under the blows. The explanation was at once apparent — there was a hasp or a small bolt on the inside, and a slight turning of the handle was necessary. I now opened it with ease and once more slammed it shut.

Now that the work was done I gave a thought to our condition. Both the doctor and myself were covered from head to foot with dirt and grease and perspiration. We washed our hands and faces in the water on the floor of the sea-chamber, and departed slowly, with aching limbs, through the vast and silent chambers of the Hall. For hours we had both been undergoing such excitement as to be wholly oblivious to tired muscles and empty stomachs, but now the reaction had come. Too wearied to talk or think we made our way to the dormitory. On going through the treasure-rooms, however, I glanced about and saw that our raid upon it had made no appreciable difference in its appearance — so inexhaustible was the hoard of wealth. We found two guards outside the entrance of the Hall, but after examining our credentials they let us pass without a word. When we arrived at the dormitory we found that the smoke-time had long passed, and that all had retired. We threw ourselves down on our beds and slept the sleep of exhaustion.

CHAPTER XXXIII

With the opening of the Vorunk the next morning I was in my customary seat, prepared to perform what I intended should be my last service for the Democracy. But because of the nervous excitement under which I labored, I found it difficult to feign calmness. I could not concentrate my mind on the proceedings, it was hard to remain quiet in my seat, and when I talked my tongue ran away from me. One thought kept reiterating itself in my consciousness — the intoxicated, maddening thought that I was going to escape — that Astræa and I would in a few hours be in the upper world, where the sun shone, where liberty and happiness and life were, where the black dungeon of Atlantis, with its tyrannical laws, its dehumanized people and its cold, cheerless, inane and monotonous existence would no longer be able to throttle our lives and keep us dangling on the brink of fearful death.

I had come to this sea-covered purgatory in a mad effort to escape from freedom. In my ignorance

I had cried out for socialism and had plunged beneath the waters in search of death rather than assume the responsibility of making my own living.
Instead of dying, my prayer for socialism had been
answered.   Instead of dwelling in a land where the
law was that the world owed no man a living, I
had been suddenly transported to a country where
the world owed every man a living, but I had found
that it was a mighty poor living, and I had also
found that while I had escaped working for my own
livelihood I had not escaped working for the livelihood of others.   I had learned a bitter lesson.   Between working for one's self, which is selfish labor,
and working one for all and all for each, which is
socialistic, unselfish and humanitarian labor, I had
found a great gulf fixed.   I now knew that working
for one's self spelled Liberty and working for mankind in general and no one in particular spelled
Slavery.

I had found that when the individual was free and
planned and worked for his own benefit, he benefited
all his brother men, as well as himself, and that
when he worked, not for his own benefit but for the
benefit of the entire State, he injured, not only himself, but also all his brother men.   It had required
severe experience for me to see the inexorable logic

behind this paradox. The trouble with me had been that I had never used my brain. I had never really studied the problems of social life. I had taken the Golden Rule to my heart and had given it a meaning in conflict with the laws of the Creator. I had not seen that socialism was only a superficial dream and, as all superficial things are likely to be, was utterly false and delusive. The picture of paradise, in which there would be no labor and only lazy contentment, had affected me, and I had not realized that mind and muscle were given men to be used, and that if not used existence would be marked by insufferable ennui and the warping of manhood. I had not realized that men were compelled to labor in order to force their mental and physical development, and that it was the natural law for the individual to labor primarily for himself, because only by his own voluntary exertion could his faculties, his soul, be developed. I had not seen that personal reward was the highest incentive to make the individual struggle to the full extent of his strength, that unless he could enjoy the tangible fruits of achievement, be it wealth, fame, learning or what not, he would not try to achieve.

I had not appreciated the truth that as the units are so will be the whole; that if social conditions

develop energetic, independent, self-thinking, masterful men the whole state will be progressive, prosperous and enlightened, and that if conditions tend to
make the units dependent, slothful, ignorant and weak
the whole state will become steeped in misery, poverty, depravity and intellectual darkness. I had not
discerned that the Golden Rule was a guide for free
men and not for slaves, that it was meant to teach
men in their *voluntary* conduct to have regard for
others, to be charitable and just to those whom they
have it in *their power* to injure. It was a Rule for
the strong to obey, and as they obeyed so would they
reap the reward of their own self-respect as well as
the approbation of others. Besides, it was a Rule
which could not be flagrantly disregarded, for it was,
in fact, the law of equal rights; and where equal
rights were recognized there were statutes to punish
those who infringed on them. The Golden Rule
was thus the law of liberty and not of socialistic
slavery. If socialism had always existed, there would
never have been a Golden Rule, for if men were not
free agents but mere automata, such a rule would
be a meaningless collocation of words.

The important thing in life is, not that men should
each have exactly the same number of loaves of
bread, but that they should possess souls capable of

being just, charitable, and self-sacrificing of their own volition; this is impossible in socialism, where no man, do what he will, can have more loaves or other labor-produced wealth than another. All this I now clearly saw, and as I sat in the hall of the Vorunk that day I was feverish with the joyful anticipation of escaping from a nation that, with marvelous fatuity, was seeking to reverse the plain purposes of man's creation. I was about to be liberated from a Stygian cesspool that was stifling me, and I could hardly restrain my impatience for the evening.

In order to divert my mind, I resorted to the only expedient I could think of. This was the framing of a bill, which I could leave as my final contribution to the legal lore which bolstered up the equality of the State. I cast about in my mind to see what remained that might be legislated upon, and I finally determined on a measure to limit to ten inches the length of the step in walking or running. I had observed that, owing to the varying lengths of the legs of different individuals, some would cover a much greater distance in one step than others, and this certainly did not seem in accord with complete equality. Surely no man should be able to cover more ground than another with a like exertion.

Having come to the conclusion that a law on the

matter would be in consonance with the principles of the State, I next pondered as to what should be the proper length of a legal step. My decision was governed by merciful considerations. I had observed that a number of my comrades did not advance more than ten inches at a time, and it might be that it was a physical impossibility for them to take a greater step. Therefore, out of compassion for them, and also incidentally out of respect for that immutable rule of the Democracy that the pace must be set by the slowest, I fixed the length of the step thereafter to be taken by all the loyal citizens of the nation at ten inches.

While putting my idea into writing, I happened to notice the dwarf as he walked across the room and saw that, while one of his legs was shorter than the other, he nevertheless covered fully two feet in every stride. This only made me the more enamored of my measure, and, with some pardonable *éclat,* I read it to my colleagues. I glanced at the dwarf and saw him regarding me with a cold malignant stare. When he saw my eyes rest on him, he assumed his usual friendly mask and rising, said:

" The member has introduced a very good bill and the committee will give it early consideration."

" Will it be reported on to-day? " I asked.

"I can not say. The committee has a good deal of work before it, but you may expect an early report."

The cold, incisive way in which he spoke was plainly an indication of anger, but what did I care? I only wished I knew how I could still further exasperate him, without incurring the risk of being arrested. It went against the grain to have the last bill of which I should be the father hung up in committee, merely because the chairman of the committee could not conveniently comply with its provisions. I had no doubt that if the measure had provided that every man should limp, or stride not less than two feet, the committee would have been favorably impressed. Perhaps I might make a speech, I thought, demonstrating so clearly the correctness of the bill in principle that even the committee would not be able to find a plausible excuse for turning it down. I was about to attempt this, when it occurred to me that it would be more politic to effect a compromise with the committee. I thought very hard, and in a few minutes asked the privilege of introducing an amendment to the bill. Permission being granted, I said:

"Since drawing up my measure I have thought that the bill would work an unnecessary hardship on those among us who have only one leg, or one leg shorter than the other, or legs so twisted that it is a physical impossibility to take ten-inch steps. Hence I wish to amend my bill by exempting such persons on their passing a proper examination and receiving a special certificate from the new department created by the bill."

The dwarf smiled on me and followed me in addressing the assembly. He spoke as follows:

" I believe the amendment makes the bill as nearly perfect as it can be made, and with the permission of the Vorunk I would suggest, in consideration of the evident desire of the author of the measure that action be taken immediately, that it now be put on its passage."

The bill was accordingly passed unanimously, and it was quite refreshing to note the mincing steps which my colleagues thereafter took in moving about the chamber. I was greatly edified, and in my mind's eye I could see the whole nation going about as though every man wore invisible hobbles.

I was studying how I might further leave my impress on the Democracy, when an inspector entered the chamber and coming up to me said:

" You are 489 A D G I believe?"

" Yes."

"I am an inspector of the Department of Marriages," he continued, "and it is my privilege to inform you that the State has taken note of your being without a wife although of marriageable age, and has now made up for the deficiency by selecting —66 to be your better half."

I gasped, but quickly replied:

"The State, I am sure, is kind."

The expected had happened. I remembered that —66 was Ugla, the amorous old witch who had made me the apple of her eye. I laughed to myself at the good joke I was about to play by leaving the fair bride bereft on the eve of her marriage. It would have been very disappointing to bid farewell to the country before the official cards were issued for the marriage.

"As you are perhaps not aware of the rules governing courtship and marriage," continued the inspector, "it is my duty to hand you these printed regulations." He handed me a paper. "You can read them at your leisure," he continued. "The date for the wedding will be four days hence. I have the honor to bid you good day."

Leaving me he then approached the dwarf, and I cast my eye over the paper he had given me. It was very lengthy and began in this wise:

"The bride and groom shall take their first view

of each other under the chaperonage of two inspectors of the Department of Marriage. On this occasion the contracting parties shall be seated at least ten feet apart and shall gaze at each other intently for five minutes without speaking. Respect for the marriage institutions of the Democracy demands that both display evidences of pleasure on their countenances. They shall, in fact, manifest intense longing in their eyes. The inspectors are strictly enjoined to report any looks of dislike or scorn and any indications of shrinking or aversion. Dissatisfaction with the marital partner selected by the State is proof of insincere citizenship, ingratitude for favors bestowed and disordered mentality. The initial inspection being over the happy couple shall rise from their seats and advance toward each other. The groom shall seize the hand of the bride and say that he takes her for his wife. He shall say this ardently. The inspectors shall report fully as to the earnestness and force he puts into his voice. The bride shall now whisper that the marriage is agreeable to her. Having thus plighted their troth it is imperative that they seal it with a kiss. This ends the first meeting."

I tried to imagine my going through this set performance with the blear-eyed Ugla. It was too frightful to contemplate. As I was about to read the next paragraph the dwarf interrupted me by remarking in my ear:

"I see that you and I are both about to become benedicts. I presume mutual congratulations are in order."

It suddenly flashed on my mind that Astræa's marriage with the dwarf had also been commanded. I was consumed with anger, but I choked my resentment by thinking how this engagement would also add interest to our sudden departure. I looked up at the dwarf and said:

"Congratulations must be in order, if you also have been provided with a wife."

"I am to marry," he responded, smiling, "a girl who is still in prison as an atavar but who has been pronounced cured."

"Lucky dog!" I exclaimed.

"Spare your compliments!" he cried, bristling up.

I replied calmly: "I meant to say that you are fortunate in that she is no longer insane. I am to marry Ugla, the friend of Ate and your Highness." As I spoke the last words I made a profound courtesy.

"Speak lower," he whispered, much mollified, "do not give me titles in the presence of others. I am glad to see you are so tractable. We fully understand each other, I am sure. I shall take much pleasure in welcoming you into the inner circle of the Democracy."

"My advancement is very rapid," I whispered in return. "I shall not hide from you that I understand the meaning of my marriage with Ugla. I shall endeavor to requite you fully for the unmerited trust you have reposed in me."

"I foresee," he whispered in a burst of confidence, "that we shall be able to do much for our mutual interests in the future."

"You possess the power," I remarked calmly, "but you are only beginning to seize the emoluments."

I looked at him meaningly and he returned my look with interest. Then he remarked gravely:

"I see that you thoroughly understand, and you may depend on it I need and shall value highly your assistance and advice."

He left me, casting furtive glances my way, like a conspirator who is not altogether sure he has not gone too far. I maintained a sober countenance, however, and endeavored to live up to my part. It was not the easiest of rôles to play, for the temptation to laugh was strong upon me.

"The old fool!" I said to myself.

When later in the day I was asked about the boat, I replied that my examination of it was not completed and requested an exoneration from the Vorunk for working overtime the evening before and missing my dinner.

"The boat is not provided with a bell," I explained, "and I was not informed of the time to eat or of the time to leave the Hall for the night. The result was that I was astounded on reaching the dormitory to find that all had retired."

On motion of the dwarf a special dispensation was granted, relieving me from punishment for my inadvertent infraction of the rules as to eating and going to bed.

CHAPTER XXXIV

MY PLANS ARE FRUSTRATED

The day dragged itself to a close and the doctor and I were at last alone in the laboratory, going over our plans for the night. These were simple enough. We were first to proceed to the prison to release Astræa, and then the three of us would go to the monument, light the fuse, take a car for the Hall and lose no time in boarding the boat and getting away. We were rapidly making our small preparations when some one knocked at the door.

"Visitors!" I exclaimed in a panic.

The doctor opened the door and there stood before us the sea-surgeon.

"I do not want to intrude," he said with his usual smile, "but I am so interested, you know, in your enterprise."

I was in despair. I knew it would be impossible to get rid of him, and there was no time to lose. The doctor looked at me helplessly.

"We were just about to start," I said at last. "Would you like to go with us again?" I spoke rather ungraciously, but the surgeon was wholly oblivious to the coolness.

"Gladly, gladly!" he replied, his countenance beaming.

I was nonplussed. Should we take him with us in the boat? Suppose he refused to go? I had it. We would say nothing to him of our intentions until the last moment, and then, if he declined to enter the boat, we would bind and gag him. But we could not take him to the prison or to the monument! This was a disconcerting thought. There was only one other thing to do. The doctor would have to take him to the Hall while I went for Astræa alone.

"My dear surgeon," I said, "could you not go and get us a few cigars?"

"Certainly!" he replied, leaving the room with alacrity.

I rapidly explained to the doctor my plan. He demurred greatly, because he would not be able to light the fuse of the monument himself, but I gave him my solemn assurance that I would attend to the matter faithfully.

When the surgeon returned we lighted our cigars, and for a few minutes talked on indifferent topics, the doctor and I as unconcerned as we could appear. Suddenly I arose and exclaimed:

"If I did not almost forget! I had an engagement to see the dwarf on a matter of State. I must be off immediately. You, Doctor, take our friend to the Hall, and I will join you there as soon as I can."

I hurried away as fast as I could, under the constraint placed on my progress by the "Short Step Bill," which I now thoroughly anathematized. When I reached the street I threw away the cigar I had only pretended to smoke. I had gone but a short distance when I stopped abruptly.

"My pistols!" I muttered. "Left behind at the laboratory, and this of all nights!"

The day I had taken the weapons from the submarine I gave them over to the doctor, who had hidden them in the laboratory. I had found it inadvisable to wear them constantly, because of the bulge they made about my waist, which would certainly have been noticed. But now that I was putting into execution my plans of escape it was nothing short of criminal negligence to leave them behind. I would not go back, however. Time was too precious, and, besides, how could I get them without the surgeon's knowledge?

I continued my journey to the prison, peering constantly about as I went. The night was unusually

still, and I gained the entrance way to the door of
the third corridor without seeing a single being.
Cautiously I approached the door, inserted the key,
unlocked and opened it. The cold corridor stretched
before me, deserted and still. With beating heart
I swiftly glided forward to take Astræa from her cell
for the last time. In a minute more how happy she
would be — how happy I would be! Hand in hand
we would take our flight; once we gained the start
we would laugh at all pursuit. There was a song in
my heart, the darkness was already gone and I was
entering on a future bright with love and hope and
achievement. Then suddenly I was plunged headlong into black abysmal depths.

I had reached the front of the cell and had peered
through the iron bars, expecting to see the bright
welcome on the face I adored, but instead I gazed
into the small basilisk eyes of the witch, gleaming
malignantly into mine.

A mist came before me and my knees gave way. The
moment was such as make men's hair to grow gray,
and their minds to become unhinged. In a trice I
had lost everything — bride, fortune and freedom,
and death in horrid shape awaited me. The first
glimpse of the witch's baleful gaze told me all. I
stood looking blankly into her face. Then an ago-

nized scream pierced me to the soul, and turning my
eyes from the witch I saw Astræa fall fainting to
the floor.

The strength of madness came to me. With a
kick the cell door flew open. I sprang within, and
took her in my arms. With my burden I stepped
quickly forward — I was filled with a resolve to
steal the girl from under the very eyes of her jailer!
But when I reached the door of the cell I found it
shut and locked — the witch had seized her chance
while I was leaning over the girl. I was caught and
trapped. I knew it. I drew the girl close in my
embrace and gave her one kiss, a kiss of reverence
and despair, and then gently laid her down. So constituted is the brain of man that one minute it may
be tempest-torn and the next calm and placid. As
I laid down my precious burden I felt as though I
was consigning it to the grave. I rose cool and collected, albeit hopeless. I glanced toward the witch
and said:

"What do you intend to do?"

My voice sounded strange in my ears. The witch
glowered on me, though her eyes seemed to blaze
with triumph.

"I has gone beyond me," she replied. As she
leaned on her stick I could see that she seemed to

be palsied from excitement, for her hand shook and her head wagged to and fro.

A noise at the cell door attracted me. I looked about and saw half a dozen men. The witch now fairly shrieked:

"I summoned the guards and they are here!"

Perhaps she had feared I would attack her and the relief she felt found vent in this discordant burst.

I leaned down once more and kissed the girl on her unconscious brow, for what I thought would be the last time, and walking to the cell door which now had been opened, I said to the guards who were about to seize me:

"I submit. I am your prisoner."

CHAPTER XXXV

THE DWARF HAS THE TRUTH TOLD TO HIM

I was roughly handled, my wrists were caught with handcuffs, and while the guards brandished iron weapons in front and rear I was told to march. They took me out of the prison by the way I had so often come to pay my secret visits to Astræa. The spot where she and I had spent many happy hours together drew one last lingering look from my eyes, and then I went forward stolidly, with my chin on my breast, a condemned convict of the Democracy. I was unmindful where we went; I no longer cared. Despair had at last taken me for its own,— I had given up the battle.

I have no doubt that many in my place would have struggled desperately to the end. They would doubtless have brushed the witch aside, or frightened her into opening the cell door, and then would have carried the unconscious girl out into the night and fled across the city. When pursued by the guards and overtaken, as they assuredly would have been, they would have fought until beaten into insensibility.

But as for me, I had quickly realized the futility of resistance. Had the prison been close to the Hall of Curiosities it might have been worth while to try what grit and desperate will could do, but it was miles away, and was to be reached only by the railway. It is one thing to be valorous when there is a glimmering hope of success, and quite another thing to struggle madly with the inevitable.

We had proceeded for many minutes, I know not how many — it might have been hours — when I was taken through clanging doors and along dreary corridors of stone, until finally I was thrown into a dungeon where my legs were fettered in irons. They left me. I heard their steps retreating in the corridor, and silence settled like a pall. I lay on the bare floor, stunned with a sense of irremedial loss, heedless of the passage of time and barely conscious of my surroundings. I could see that the dungeon was small, and without furniture of any sort, that its door was made of solid iron, that the walls were stone and barely visible in the dim light which came through the iron grating of a small opening connecting with the corridor. But these things caused scarce a passing thought. What matters it to the condemned what manner of dungeon he inhabits?

The minutes had probably run into hours when my

ears caught the tread of approaching feet. Nearer and nearer came the sounds, until they ceased outside my cell. Then came the noise of opening the lock, and the door flew back on its hinges. I glanced up to see who might be my visitor, and saw not without some interest that it was his Highness, the dwarf, come to pay a call to his new lieutenant!

"Are you there, No. 489?" he asked as he peered into the dungeon, his eyes as yet unable to see through the darkness.

"How could I be elsewhere, your gracious Majesty?" I replied, taking a grim satisfaction in baiting him.

"I presume you mean to be facetious," he replied sternly. "It is out of place in one in your present straits."

He strode into the dungeon.

"I can not see why," I said quietly. "Your Highness knows that when a man has reached the end of his tether he does not restrain his tongue, unless, forsooth, he is gagged. Surely you have not so soon changed your fancy as to titles of royalty?"

The dwarf made a deprecatory gesture with his hand,— the hand of the one repellent digit.

"I did not come to bandy words," he said testily. "I came to ask you a question, to which I want a positive answer. Will you or will you not marry Ugla?"

"Suppose I said yes, what then?"

"You will be released and your recent escapade will be forgotten."

There was a note of anxiety in his tone which caught my attention. I remained silent and he continued:

"Think well of what I have said. You know what this chance for liberty means to you. It means an enviable position in the State. You may even count upon enjoying privileges not accorded others. Ugla will make you a good wife, though you may not now think it. You will be a member of the inner circle, and I will go far in advancing your fortunes. Be advised. Do not, like a headstrong youth, rush to your death."

I was still silent.

"You know my power. For some years I have held the destiny of the Democracy in my own hands. The time is growing ripe for me to reach out and grasp the substance of authority as well as the shadow. There is none that dares oppose me. Be tractable in this one matter,— it is not much to ask, — and I will promise you on my sacred honor that you shall have all the slaves and all the food and

adornment and all the power that you may crave, next
my own. What more can I offer you?"

He strode up and down the cell, waiting for my
answer. His person was hideous and repugnant, but
association with him had moderated my dislike and
I was beginning to admire him for his masterful
ability. Had he desired to marry some one other
than Astræa I would, very likely, have thrown myself on his mercy, urged him to cancel the command for my marriage to Ugla and give me Astræa
as my wife. Then I would have promised him faith-
ful service, but for no other price would I have sold
myself to the devil; for well I knew that is what the
compact would have meant.

I studied his demeanor as he walked to and fro, and
wondered at his urgent desire that I should marry
Ugla. Could it be possible that he had made a secret
visit to my cell in the dead of night, merely because of
a desire to save me and gain for himself a useful
coadjutor in his schemes? The more I thought of it
the more suspicious I grew of his motives. There
must be a stronger reason for his visit than appeared
on the surface. He was too confident of his own
power to feel the need of my assistance — that was
merely an excuse, the subtle flattery of which was calculated to allay my suspicions as to the true grounds

of his anxiety. What did the man really want? He wanted to marry Astræa. That was it! In some way his visit related to that. Could it be that she had been interrogated and had refused to marry him? It was possible. It was also possible when he saw she was fixed in her decision that he had formed the idea of inducing me to wed Ugla, believing that if I yielded the girl could in turn be induced to wed him. I was satisfied in my own mind that I had now guessed the correct reason for his visit, and raising myself up from the ground I faced him that I might lend emphasis to my words.

"You stunted toad!" I said between my teeth, "you miserable misshapen botch of a human being, you viper, you cowardly scoundrel and cur, get out of my reach, or, by God, I will crush you into pulp and grind your bones to powder!"

The creature quailed and shrank before me like a craven. My hand itched for his throat, the blood was surging to my brain and in an instant more I would have brought my manacles crashing down upon his head. But with a cry he precipitately slunk beyond my reach and out of the door, clanging it shut behind him with all the force of one panic-stricken with terror. I laughed. I had given him my answer, but not with titles so pleasing to his ear as that of his Highness or

With a cry he slunk beyond my reach. *Page 338*

his gracious Majesty. I sank down again upon the floor, and felt relieved as if I had unburdened myself of a load.

CHAPTER XXXVI

Hours passed. For a long period I must have lain in a half-stupor. I had no control over my thoughts. Ideas and fantasies surged in endless procession through my mind. One moment Astræa was crying bitterly in my arms, the next I was frantically shoveling gold, then the faces of the dwarf and the witches appeared fiendishly distorted. The doctor, the sea-surgeon, and men whom I had met would suddenly come and depart; I would now be addressing the Vorunk and the next instant I was gazing at the monument. It was all a jumble unrestrained, unending and unrebuked.

But no matter what might be in the foreground of my mind, in the background was something horrible which I was ever seeking to keep there. Every now and then I would catch a glimpse of what this was, and a cold perspiration would break out on me as I strove to take my eyes away and think of something else. What was this thing that filled me with terror? I gathered up my courage and looked at it boldly —

it was the monster of the sea! How fearful its eyes! How they kept looking steadily at me, drawing me nearer and nearer! My God! could anything save me? I cried out and rose to a sitting posture. I rubbed my eyes, stood up and now, thoroughly awake, wondered whether I had been dreaming or only thinking.

The dungeon looked as it did when I first entered it. The silence was as absolute as ever. The light came as dimly as before through the ventilator above the door. How long had I been there? I could not tell, but it seemed ages. I lay down on the floor once more, determined to keep the mastery over my mind. I began to speculate deliberately about the doctor and the surgeon. I wondered how long they stayed at the Hall before they gave up my coming. What did they do at the Hall, and how did the doctor feel when at last he learned the cause of my absence? Would he act discreetly? How fortunate it was that he had not been with me when I went to the prison to meet Astræa — as it was, if he kept silent he could not be implicated in my acts. What a kindly man he was, and how out of harmony with his race and country! What would he do about the monument?

I reviewed the whole length of our intercourse, and came to the conclusion that he would light the fuse himself, if not immediately, then later on. I told myself that he could not resist doing it, and it was interesting to speculate as to the time he would select for the deed. While thinking of the past with him I suddenly remembered the pellet he had given me one day in the laboratory. I recalled the solemn manner in which he had said it would bring instantaneous death, and how he urged me to keep it, on the plea that some day it might stand me in good stead. Had that day now come? Despite my manacles, I managed to search the small pocket in which I had placed it, and there I found it incrusted in lint and dirt. I rubbed it clean, and holding it in the palm of my hand looked at it steadily for I knew not how long.

Once before I had contemplated suicide, and had actually tried to die — and would have died had it not been for the inscrutable ways of Providence. Should I now try again? I remembered that when I pushed myself to the brink of the pier it was in a spirit of some bravado. I had been supported in my purpose by a fierce hatred of the world as it existed, and it seemed in some queer way that I was performing a noble and valorous act in leaving it. But since then I had changed. Though measured in months and days the time had not been long, yet measured by experience it had been years in length. My youthful ardor had become moderated and I had grown more philosophic, more prone to weigh the whys and wherefores, more cold and calculating. Should I take the deadly pellet? Was there any possibility that I might yet be able to circumvent the Democracy? No, none,— I was sure of it. If I could only think of some means of resistance that would make my death costly to the Democracy, it might be well to see the play out to the end. But seeing none should I permit myself to become a helpless sacrifice for the amusement of the nation? Better to cheat them of their pleasure. But there was Astræa. Might I not be able to console and strengthen her in the last hour of dread? That was a serious consideration, and yet how unlikely it was that I should ever be able to speak to her — in all probability I should never see her again. I hesitated. The pellet lay temptingly in my hand.

How enraged the dwarf would be when — I started nervously. Had I heard a noise or was it merely imagination? I strained my ears. There was something at the door! I heard a low, scratching sound, then the lock turned, and the door began to open slowly. Who could be coming so stealthily and mysteriously? My nerves were tense, and I waited for I knew not what. At last a figure pressed itself into the cell and I saw — the sea-surgeon! My heart gave a throb of joy — the first sensation of the kind that I had felt for hours.

"A friend!" I exclaimed in the first moments of violent mental reaction.

The surgeon shook his hand frantically.

"Silence!" he whispered.

He turned and closed the door softly behind him. This done he began to talk rapidly.

"I have ventured here," he said, "unknown to any one. I could not help it. I have only a few minutes to stay — it would be dangerous for me to tarry longer. But I want you to know that I am deeply grieved over this, and I also want you to know that I would be extremely glad could I do something for you."

I realized instantly from his simple speech that he had risked much to come to me, and I felt deep gratitude for this unexpected demonstration of friendship.

"I'm glad you've come!" I said from the bottom of my heart. "I value this act of yours more than I can tell you."

"The doctor is terribly disconcerted by this," he continued, disregarding my words. "From remarks he dropped it seems that you and he have some mutual affairs which remain unfinished. I do not know what they are, but could I serve you in any way? Could I take a message to him?"

"I know of nothing you can do, my dear surgeon. You might say to the doctor for me, though, that I love him and that I shall be with him in the spirit."

"Is that all?"

"I fear it is — but tell me, has my fate been determined, and how long have I been here, do you know?"

The surgeon looked at me sorrowfully and said:

"It has been a full twenty-four hours since your arrest. Has no one been here to see you?"

"No one except the dwarf," I replied carelessly.

"Ah, the dwarf! He is angered at your deed."

"Well he might be!" I returned with a grim laugh.

"You crossed him? Now I understand the energy of his hate."

"What has he done?"

"I do not like to bear ill news."

"Come!" I exclaimed with an attempt at animation. "Do not take my situation so seriously. I care not, why should you? Do you think I could continue to live as I have — acting a daily lie? I hate your Democracy, its atmosphere is stifling, it parches my blood, crushes my vitality, offends my eyes and is driving me mad."

"Hush, hush!" he cried, interrupting me and holding his hands to his ears as though to keep out my words.

But I continued, putting more earnestness in my tone as I proceeded.

"I do not wish to shock you," I said. "You are a good man among rogues and devils. Your Democracy might be all right were men all angels and specially created to live under such a system, but as it is — well, my dear surgeon, as it is, the socialistic state seems a hell to me, and if death is the only avenue of escape, then I crave death."

My visitor regarded me fixedly, his countenance drawn as with anguish.

"I can see how it is," he said in a voice tense and low. "You are mad. The discovery of your attachment for the girl, your arrest and your hunger have combined to unsettle your mind. Poor man! I hoped much from you, and it has come to this. Better by far had I never rescued you."

"Think me mad if you wish," I replied calmly; "but I am saner now than ever before. You were going to say something, however, about the dwarf. Tell me. Whatever it is, it can not make my burden heavier."

He made several ineffectual attempts to speak, and at last succeeded, pouring out his words rapidly as if he wished to have it over as quickly as possible.

"I have need of haste," he began. "Let me say then that the dwarf in a most bitter and vindictive speech attacked you in the Vorunk to-day, declaring that your breaking into the jail and meeting with the girl was the worst crime in all the history of the Democracy and called for condign punishment which should be immediate and exemplary. By his suggestion a bill was passed denying you trial by judge and ordering your public execution to take place —"

He stopped, unable to proceed.

" Out with it — when? " I cried a little sharply.

" May the gods have mercy — to-morrow! " As he said this his head dropped to his breast and he hid his face in his hands.

" My dear man," I said consolingly, " do not take it so hard. You have only confirmed my own expectations. I am ready — do you understand? — ready and waiting for them to do their worst. But how about the girl — the atavar? Do you know I have named her Astræa? How does she fare at their merciful hands? "

" Alas, she, too, is to die — she is included in the bill. She will be given to the monster at the same time."

" May God damn them all! " I cried, the bitterness welling within me again.

" A public holiday has been proclaimed," he continued bitterly.

"So?" I said, partly regaining my composure. "The dwarf carries his venom far. We are to serve as the prime attraction — for the multitude!" I gave a disdainful laugh.

The surgeon started up and looked anxiously at the door.

"I must be hurrying," he said. "Think again now, is there anything I might do for you? I would be thankful could I perform some service, however small."

He was so earnest in his desire that I began to think how I might impose some small errand on him.

"Tell me!" I exclaimed, "was there no other charge made against me except that of secretly meeting Astræa?"

"None!"

"And no suspicion attaches to the doctor because of my offense?"

"None that I know of. The doctor is suffering grievously, although he hides it as best he can. But his face is haggard and his eyes are red, and that is why I know."

So my plans for escape had not been suspected! If I could yet reach the boat! An idea possessed me. Suppose the surgeon could bring me the pistols!

"Make haste!" said the surgeon.

"Have you paper and pencil?" I asked.

He ran his hand down into his tunic and pulled out a sheet and some carbon.

Meanwhile my idea was undergoing development. I studied a few moments and then as rapidly as my shackles would permit I wrote a few lines, folded the paper and returned it to the surgeon.

"Can you carry this note to the doctor?" I asked excitedly.

"I will!" he replied.

"Can you bring back what he sends me?"

"I will do my best."

"My dear friend!" I said, scanning him anxiously in the face, "I want you to make me a solemn promise, that under no circumstances will you permit any one other than the doctor to read this note. If there is any danger of its falling into the hands of others destroy it without hesitation."

"I will carry out your desires to the letter," he replied in a voice which showed he was deeply moved.

"Good! I know of no words which can express my gratitude."

The surgeon took my hand and pressed it hard; then hastening to the door of the dungeon, he turned and said with deep emotion:

"We may never meet again. Good-by!"

There were tears in his eyes.

The door was closed, the lock sprang in its place and he was gone. Again the silence settled over all. But how different it seemed! I took the pellet out of my pocket where I had placed it and ground it under my foot. It would never again tempt me, and I would accept my fate whatever it might be, like a man. Would the surgeon be able to deliver the note, and would the doctor do as I had instructed him? The next few hours alone could tell.

CHAPTER XXXVII

THE DEATH MARCH BEGINS

"Come, wake up, wake up!" The voice sounded as though coming from a distance. A sharp blow across the bottom of my feet gave me a shock of bodily pain. I rose quickly to a sitting posture, wide-awake. Before me was a man, holding a basket in his left hand, while his right grasped an iron rod or club frequently carried by prison guards and attendants.

"I have brought you food," said the individual roughly. "Hold up your hands so that I can unfasten your wrists."

My hands had been gyved so that they were only eight or ten inches apart, and glad I was to have them freed. While the man whom I took to be a guard was performing this office I ventured to question him as to the time of day, but he rebuffed me with a curt reply that he could tell me nothing. He departed, locking the door and leaving the basket within my reach.

I was famished as a man will be when he has eaten nothing for many hours, and I attacked the food ravenously with scarcely a thought of my execution, which might be, as far as I could tell, only a few hours away. I meditated grimly that the State fed its victims to prevent their being too weak to walk. To throw creatures to the beast who were already half-dead from starvation would certainly be to make the entertainment needlessly tame. So I felt no gratitude to the functionaries for their tardy remembrance of my needs. I had scarcely taken the edge off my appetite, however, before it struck me that the basket was remarkably well laden, and I began to set out its contents on the floor. I had about half emptied it when my hand encountered something too hard to be food. It felt like leather to the touch, and in a tremor of excitement I jerked it out. It was the pistol belt! There it was, revolvers, cartridges and all! My joy was unbounded.

I took the weapons from their holsters, examined them critically, took out their loads, aimed at imaginary spots on the walls and pulled the triggers. The clicking of the hammers afforded me peculiar pleasure. I reloaded them carefully, examined all the cartridges in the belt one by one, and at last strapped the girdle around my waist beneath the tunic, after which I tucked my garments about it in such a manner as seemed most likely to allay suspicions respecting my appearance. I felt a deep gratitude toward the

surgeon and the doctor, and marveled at their ingenuity. Thanks to them, I was no longer a helpless,
despairing and unresisting victim, but an adversary,
alert and dangerous. I finished my meal, eating all
the food to the last crumb, and sat down to wait.

Minutes went by, merging into hours. I stared at
the walls, drummed with my fingers, performed mental calculations — and waited. There is nothing so
trying as suspense. To be for hours in momentary
expectation of some event fraught with peril, and to
have no distraction for the mind is torture. How
long I endured the agony of inaction I do not know,
but footsteps approaching in the corridor finally put
an end to what seemed endless.

"At last!" I muttered in relief.

The door of the cell opened, and this time it was
the old witch, Ate, who stood peering into the darkness
that surrounded me. I regarded her disdainfully, and
waited for her to speak. Either from stiffness in her
joints or rheumatism in her limbs she had difficulty
in getting through the door, but finally she stood bending over her stick and looking on me with her baleful eyes.

"You didn't expect to receive a call from me, now
did you?" she began with a simper.

I kept silent.

She continued unabashed and devoid of feeling:

" I have come a little in advance of the others. I wanted to have a little talk with you alone. I expect you would prefer the girl to me, but now it's my turn. It does my old bones so much good to see you there, ironed to the floor. Have you been tearing your hair? But no matter, you will do so soon enough. We shall see you quail and cringe before the day is over."

She paused and I still held my peace.

" You don't seem very sociable this morning," she kept on, growing a little shriller in her tone. " But this is one of those occasions in which I can overlook bad manners. I must say that I am proud of you, because you didn't disappoint me. It would have been a bitter moment with me had you married Ugla. I have had a good deal of experience with foolish swains and lassies, and I have never yet had my expectations go wrong. It is my whim to pander to their love-sick madness, and when the disease takes fast hold on them I extract pleasure from the dull routine of life in handing them over to the law."

She paused, expecting me to make answer. She then proceeded:

" I saw from the start you fancied her. You ought to have worn a mask, for you do your thinking with your face. You did not accept my invitation to come to see me as you should have done, but then you made up for your unkindly treatment in the end, and I can not say I have any fault to find with the way you did it. The dwarf and Ugla laughed at me for a jealous fool when I told them long ago the truth, but now I am vindicated." She wagged her head from side to side, chuckling.

"You came down here to goad me," I now put in, "but you waste your feeble breath. I care no more for you than I do for a snake. You are an ugly carcass of skin and bones with venom in your withered veins instead of blood, but I am beyond your sting. I quickly saw you were an atavar, and that if you had your just deserts you would yourself soon fill the monster's maw, though I have no doubt the beast would spit you out, seeing that you are so bitter."

"You would berate me with your tongue, would you?" she rejoined in her highest treble. "There is no love lost, I assure you. I am an atavar, I own that to you, who are so soon to die. Die! Did you hear me say it? I came to tell you so. You are to be fed to the kraken, and that within the next few hours! The people are already gathering and there's to be a grand holiday with you as the chief actor, though many would say that she is the chief actor,— for she, too, is to die. You know whom I mean. I wish it were not so dark — I would like to see the pallor on your cheeks. What would life be in Atlantis, were it not for the pretty and the sentimental that hate us and our laws and keep us busy cramming them down the mouth of the monster? Are you trembling? does not the horror of where you will sleep to-night paralyze your tongue and cause your eyeballs to bulge? Oh, I wish my old eyes could see as once they could! But you are silent and this bespeaks the wretch abject with terror and I am satisfied."

I laughed loud and long.

The witch stood as though amazed. Her head began to wag and her hands to wabble. Then, muttering words that seemed like imprecations, she hobbled out of the dungeon.

Almost immediately there entered a creature dressed entirely in black and wearing a cowl that hid the features. His robe was long like that of a monk and was girdled at the waist. He carried in one arm a white bundle and in the other was an iron club. He addressed me in a deep and solemn voice, saying:

"No. 489 A D G, you have been condemned to death, and now is the hour of your execution. I will unfetter you, but before I do so I will ask you if you mean to go peaceably or rebelliously?"

"I will go peaceably," I said.

"It is well," he continued. "But understand there is absolutely no hope for your escape. You will be placed in the center of a guard of forty men, all armed with these weapons "— he brandished his club before me — "and if you make one false step you will be beaten until you submit."

With that he laid down his bundle and unfastened the irons that bound me. Then he handed me the bundle and said:

"Here is the garb you are to wear. Stand there in the corner, remove your tunic and put it on."

A qualm of dread went through me. I had not counted on changing my garment. But knowing that hesitation might be fatal I instantly took the bundle and unwrapped it. It was the white robe worn by the victims. I went over into the darkest corner, and as I pulled my right arm out of my tunic I inserted it into the right arm of the robe, and so manœuvred that, thanks to the darkness and the man's inattention, I was new-garbed without disclosing the pistol-belt about my waist. There was a girdle to the robe and when I had drawn and fastened it I was pleased to note that I had no longer need to fear detection of my hidden weapons.

"Are you ready?" asked the man in black.

"I am ready," I replied in a calm voice. He looked me over and said:

"Follow me!"

When we stepped from the dungeon I saw the corridor filled with creatures in black. Among them was the witch surrounded by a retinue of ill-favored hags like herself, though in truth none seemed to come quite up to her despicable standard. My appearance seemed to be a signal, for immediately they drew on their cowls and began the horrid chant with which I was already familiar, though there in the corridor its unearthly hideousness was magnified a hundredfold.

I was quickly surrounded by a number of guards, dressed in black like the rest. The death march had begun.

CHAPTER XXXVIII

THE DOCTOR DOES NOT FAIL ME

I will hasten over the details of the dreadful journey to the amphitheater. When we emerged from the prison into the lighted thoroughfare the escort was reinforced by several hundred black cowls who set up a screeching wail at my approach, stretching their right arms toward me with their forefingers extended as though in derision. It was here that the dwarf placed himself on my right and assumed command. He bowed superciliously and in return I gave him a look of contempt. The witch Ate came close up and snapped her fingers in my face, but I laughed at her for her pains. Then I heard some one fairly hiss words of derision and hate in my ear. I looked about me and saw Ugla, my State-affianced bride, whom I had scorned. Her face showed all the malice her wounded heart could summon and she tried to assail me with her long bony talons, but the guards pushed her back.

I walked boldly, pressing my arm against the pistols at my side, and looking neither to the right nor left, but with my senses all acute. For several miles we swept along, keeping step to the monotonous droning of the witches, until we reached an open plain which proved to be the rendezvous for the gathering horde. Here awaiting us were the regiments of inspectors and heads of departments, my colleagues of the august Vorunk, the tom-tom beaters, the grotesque dancers and more detachments of black cowls, all of whom greeted me with vociferous hoots and insulting grimaces. There was one figure which commanded my attention more than any of the rest. It was that of a cadaverous creature with sunken cheeks and deep-set eyes who, with the aid of paint, looked like a living skeleton. This figure was brought up and introduced to me as Death, with whom I should speedily be better acquainted.

While being made the recipient of these fantastic attentions there appeared in the distance, beneath the distant lights, another black-hooded column which soon drew the eyes of the entire host. As it came closer I saw in its midst a white-robed figure, and I knew immediately it was Astræa. My gaze remained fixed on her, and I saw that her face was turned in my direction. Nearer and nearer she came, until at last we stood only a few yards apart, separated by the guards that surrounded us. How beautiful she was!

How placid, how calm, how unmindful of the deafening din and the insolent indignities of the mob! Had she conquered the dread of death, or did her woman's pride sustain her in this fearful hour? Perhaps it was the remembrance of Alene that made her brave; perhaps she wished to save me the pain of seeing that she suffered. But whether these conjectures were right or wrong, certain it was that her eyes conveyed one message and only one, and that was the message of love, love that rises transcendent above all earthly things and stands forth in full radiance in the shadow of death. How I wished then that I might whisper a word to her, telling her there was yet hope of life! But this could not be. I gave her a reassuring look, to which she smiled sweetly and yet I thought wonderingly in return.

The dwarf now called out in sharp command, the tom-toms beat and the procession resumed its march. Those surrounding Astræa moved first while my body-guard followed a short distance in her rear. From my position in the line I could see her constantly, and a picture remains vividly in my mind of a white figure with head well-poised, walking serenely amid a swirl of swaying and screaming ghouls in black. It is a picture of an angelic spirit being swept along by a brood of demons in the realms of darkness.

We reached the neighborhood of the amphitheater. The highways were packed with people seeking to get a glimpse of the victims and raising up their voices in mad jeers as we passed. Every minute the pandemonium seemed to increase. Now we turned beneath the great arch, and then out into the vast arena. The insane frenzy of the thousands that banked the amphitheater as with a sea of faces filled me with a sudden panic, so that for some moments I lost the power of thought. But a few blows of a club across my shoulders brought back my scattering senses and I set my teeth and gripped my pistols with my arms. I glanced at Astræa who was some paces ahead and I saw her sway and reel in a jostling mass of the taunting harpies. To get to her side would be impossible, but a few quick steps put me close enough for her to hear and I cried out:

" Courage, Astræa! Courage! "

My guards jerked me back and struck me fiercely with their weapons.

We now marched about the arena, and while the frightful din continued I swept my eyes over the frantic multitude. I saw that the lower portions of the amphitheater, those directly in my line of vision, were choked with scarlet masses of humanity that seemed in a constant and violent state of upheaval. The cause was self-apparent — it was merely a struggle for the best points of view. There they were, those citizens of the most advanced form of government in or on earth, fighting for the best positions for gratifying their lust for cruelty. The bull fight of the medieval Spaniard, the slaughter of the Christians in the Colosseum of decadent Rome, the pow-pow of the savage tribe around the victim burning at the stake, were but faint reflections of the beastly passions of men compared to the feeding of the atavars to the monster in the amphitheater of Atlantis. The faces that I gazed on were those of the brute, bereft of every lineament of human reason and compassion. Civilization had been swept away and only the howling ape remained.

The procession continued on its round and now we faced the great wall with its depths of still green water stretching back into the mystery of the sea. As we came closer and closer I could mark the schools of fish swimming before the arena and looked with wonder on the phosphorescent species that like torch-bearers illume the deep. The monster had not yet appeared but I had nerved myself against its coming, and when at last its frightful bulk was hurled like a gigantic catapult against the wall I looked on stolidly, while maddened frenzy reigned about. I saw at close range its mighty mouth, its huge saucer-shaped eyes and its monstrous tentacles that looked like hairy serpents of enormous girth.   I quickly withdrew my eyes, and looked steadily at Astræa.   She continued to walk bravely erect, and I breathed a prayer of deep gratitude.

But now the time had come when we must mount the niche against the very body of the beast.   How would she stand this terror-inspiring ordeal?   I had not long to wonder.   As fortune had it they chose me as the first to be presented to the monster.   I was suddenly seized by the arms and hurried forward to the wall.   Around me gathered a semicircle of the cowled figures.   Silence fell on the multitude.   Then the dwarf made an obeisance to the monster and, pointing to me, uttered an incantation in a strange tongue.   My arms folded, I looked at him steadily. As soon as he ended his adjuration the cracked-voiced choristers once more set up their screeching, and I was again grasped by the arms and fairly thrown upon the narrow cleft in the wall, where before all the multitude I stood within apparently a few inches of the cavernous mouth of the kraken.   I stood erect, and without once looking at the monster I had the temerity to wave my hand at the amphitheater and then at the beast.   In some way I seemed to spoil the scene, to make ludicrous what was designed as a choice feature of the program. I was jerked down amid derisive jeers. Then came Astræa's turn. I looked at her for one moment with a smile, and she went through the performance coolly and bravely.

When we resumed our march I saw the dwarf was regarding me with intense hatred. Things were evidently not going the way he had planned. Meanwhile, I had to struggle to keep myself calm, for now the critical moment was near at hand when I should know whether the doctor had followed my instructions, those instructions I had written him in the note carried by the surgeon. "He can not fail! He can not fail!" I kept muttering to myself, and yet the thought would steal into my mind now and then that possibly some hitch might occur — some fatal hitch — and then? My plans were all thought out contingent on his success. I struck my pistols with my elbows — if events fell foul of my design I would at least make every cartridge count. I knew I had one great advantage — the lost knowledge of firearms among the Atlantides. If I should shoot the dwarf it would probably be like an earthquake to the minds of the mob.

So preoccupied was I that I reached the highway cresting the embankment before I realized it. From the commanding height we had now attained

I cast one searching look toward the horizon where stood the monument. I saw it shining in majestic splendor, and a vast expanse of empty land, save for the pillars of the dome, stretched as far as eye could reach. But what I anxiously scanned the distance for I could not find.

Now the column wheeled and all heads were turned toward the green wall, the final destination of the marching throng. I dared not turn about to look again. On and on we went. The bellowing of the human pit ascended from our left, the tom-toms beat and the weird chant rent the air. As we approached the end of the highway it seemed as if we were about to march into the sea which stretched in one mighty sheet far down on our left and right and high up toward the dome. I now saw the ledge in the transparent rock extending like a faint line out over the arena and along which three persons could walk abreast, the victim in the middle and a guard on either side. I asked myself, as I viewed the fatal road, whether Astræa and I would ever walk it, and I vowed in my heart we never would! Here at the end of the highway, hard by the wall, I would take my stand, and if my plans went awry then here would we die and not yonder in the deep.

At last we halted, and without arousing suspicion I

could again search the horizon. My eyes swept carefully over all the distance between the monument and the amphitheater, but, strain them as I might, I could not see that for which I looked. My heart began to sink. In a few minutes, at the most, I must begin to act if act I would. Although I kept my eyes fixed on the distance I felt that the transparent hoods were being made ready, and that at any instant they would be clapping them on our heads. " Courage! courage! " I kept muttering to myself. I continued to risk the last few moments of possible freedom of my arms. At last, just as I was about to withdraw my gaze from the monument, I saw between an avenue of columns a speck of light. I riveted my eyes on it. It was growing larger — it was moving! It was coming toward the amphitheater! Hope rose like a tide in my heart. Now my rigid gaze made certain that the speck was whirling in a circle — Praise be to God, it was the signal! The doctor had not failed me.

I turned triumphant to face the devilish vultures near at hand, and none too soon. Two creatures were in the very act of placing a hood on Astræa. I gave one sweeping glance about me, saw that all eyes were on the girl, and with one bound I gained the wall, placing it at my back. At the same time I drew my pistols. A quick aim and an explosion, and one of the wretches fell headlong to the ground, carrying with him the transparent hood.

It was all done so quickly that not a hand was lifted to deter me. In an instant I had turned the tables. From being a passive victim I had suddenly terminated the ceremonies at their most important point. But this was not a case of merely a youth outraging the majesty of the State — it was the case of a desperate man fighting for his life and for the life of one he loved. Not in long centuries had Atlantis had such an emergency to meet, and though the official program had been abruptly abandoned there would, very likely, be entertainment enough for the myriads before the day was done.

The effects of the first shot were overwhelming. Amazement clutched each creature by the throat and held him rooted to the spot where he stood. Hushed as by enchantment were the tom-toms and the singing. The dwarf gazed at me awe-stricken. Quick as thought I ran forward, seized Astræa by the hand, pulled her back with me to the wall, and placed between us and the nearest wretch fifty good feet of open space.

Brandishing my weapons above my head I cried in a loud voice: " Run, you devils, or I'll kill you all ! "

The creatures still stood like wooden posts, gaping blankly at me.

"Run for your lives!" I cried again.

At this the dwarf on whom I had kept an eye made a movement as if to dash upon me. I hesitated not an instant, and the uncrowned master of them all sank groaning to the ground. Panic now seized on the rest, and the mob turned upon its heels and like scared dogs ran madly down the highway. But some remained looking at their chief. A score or more they numbered, and I saw I would have to give them battle. They surrounded the dwarf, and lifted him to his feet. I had not killed him, but his left arm hung limp. He stood for a moment holding his injured member with his right hand, and then began to speak rapidly to the remnant of his followers that stood about. The effect on them was plainly apparent. Should I begin to shoot them down? It seemed unwise, for it might precipitate the entire number of these braver spirits upon me.

I glanced in the direction of the monument and saw a man — no doubt the doctor — running toward the amphitheater, while in one hand he madly waved a lantern. Then I glanced at Astræa by my side and saw that she was standing with her hands clasped, regarding me with a look that, whatever of hope and confidence and wonder it expressed, showed absolutely no fear. From the amphitheater came a mighty roar.

" Whatever happens," I said quickly to her, " be not afraid."

The men in front seemed about to execute some move, and I resolved to temporize. Time was the stake I played for.

" I have drawn a dead line fifty feet from where I stand," I shouted, " and any man that crosses it shall die."

The dwarf was standing to the rear of his men but I could see that he quickly measured the distance between us with his eye and looked malignantly at me. His followers stretched themselves out in a long line, and suddenly a number of them sent their clubs hurling through the air. The weapons fell short of their mark. I held my pistols ready for action. A man now dashed forward with his club held poised to throw. I fired and he bit the ground. The rest, as if stunned by some sudden mystery, stood stock-still, looking at their fallen comrade. The dwarf, however, with wild gesticulations and loud commands ran back and forth rallying them, and now, confirming my fears, they were massing themselves preparatory for a desperate charge. I glanced anxiously toward the

monument. It still shone resplendent in the distance.
Would it never happen? I must still bid for time.

"Let us parley," I called out.

The dwarf showed his misshapen figure between two
of the men.

"Hand over your weapons," he cried, "or you'll get
no quarter!"

"A one-sided parley," I rejoined. "Let the girl and
me go our way without interference and no more lives
will be lost."

"Think you the State can acknowledge itself beaten
by such as you?" he sneered in return.

My God! Would it never happen!

"If that is your final answer, listen!" I cried at the
top of my voice. "The moment you rush upon us, I
shall cause an earthquake to shatter yonder monument
into a million fragments and shake Atlantis to its
foundations. I have spoken! Beware!"

The dwarf looked at the monument and then at me.
For a moment he seemed to give my words serious
thought. Then breaking into a contemptuous laugh he
gave the order:

"Rush upon him!"

I thought the end had come. I could not disable
more than half a dozen of the scoundrels before the
weapons would be snatched from my grasp. But

the command was not quickly obeyed. The men hesitated, and in that moment of hesitation I was saved.

"Look!" I cried with arm outstretched toward the monument. I fired my pistol into the air.

"Look!" I repeated, still pointing.

Even as I spoke there came a great flash of light. A volcanic eruption had belched forth where stood the monument. The pillar of brilliancy tottered and fell, swallowed up in an immense cloud of smoke that enveloped in inky darkness the entire horizon. All this in but a moment of time. Then came the report of the explosion, so terrible in its intensity that it threw Astræa and myself to the ground. The earth shook and the wall swayed where we lay. The first thunderous shock was but the prelude to a continuous cannonading of frightful sounds. There was not one but a whole series of explosions. Was the entire universe going to fearful wrack? I jumped to my feet in blank dismay. I saw to the left a great section of rock from off the sea wall go crashing down, and now an avalanche of material from the empyrean fell in an awful thud upon the arena. Was this the end? Would the sea come bursting through some new-made vent in the protecting cliff? Was I gazing on dreadful devastation and death? Had an entire nation been sent to its doom? But already the recurrent

The earth shook and the wall swayed where we **lay.** *Page 372*

waves of sound had moderated, the great wall stood firm, the sea did not enter. The explosive reports subsided and died away in rumbling reverberations in the distance. I now understood. There had been only one explosion, but its echo had resounded back and forth within the confines of the dome and sides of the mighty cavern.

I turned to Astræa. I stroked her hands smartly and shouted in her ears. It took but a moment to bring her back to consciousness, thank God! and then with her hand in mine we ran down the highway.

"Our chance of liberty!" I kept shouting to her.

CHAPTER XXXIX

FLIGHT AND PURSUIT

We sprang over the bodies of our enemies lying prostrate on the ground, and raced on. The immense pit of humanity was strangely silent. The lights in the dome had been blotted out by the smoke while those on the distant columns were dim and red. But the illumination of the amphitheater and of the highway continued to shine in all its cold brilliancy. On and on we went. We reached the foot of the embankment. The ground was thickly covered with bodies, but here and there a few creatures were standing either dazed or bewildered. I knew there was no time to lose. Soon the whole mob might rise up and rend us limb from limb. I stopped and looked hurriedly about. Where was the doctor? It was here I should have met him. I now saw some fifty yards away a small knot of people and among them some one was shouting earnestly. I rushed toward the spot, taking Astræa with me. It was he. As I came up he was holding a lantern in one hand while with the other he

374

was making fierce gestures as he poured forth a torrent of words:

"The revolution is at hand! Strike, slaves, for your lost liberties! It is the hour to overthrow the Democracy. Heaven has smitten the monument, and Atlantis has been convulsed! Tyranny is dead! Awake! Rise up and shake off your chains! Down with despotism and drudgery and starvation! Up with freedom, reason and hope! Are you dumb beasts? If not, then listen!"

For an instant I regarded the men about him. Most of them stood as if their senses had departed, but a few were hostile in their attitude. I dropped Astræa's hand for a moment and grasped the orator by the arm.

"Come!" I shouted.

Just then a man struck the doctor in the face with his fist. I whirled upon the dog and shot him in his tracks. There was no time now for hesitation. It was life or death for the three of us, and again grasping Astræa by the hand we fairly flew. Directly behind came the doctor, crying out his presence, while at his heels were half a dozen creatures, who, seeing us in flight, had taken the courage to pursue. Rising shouts in the rear told me the populace was waking from its trance. I was not running at random,

however. Thanks to my previous visit to the amphitheater I knew where stood the cars that went to the
Hall of Curiosities. It was for them that I now
headed.

Between long trains standing upon the terminal
tracks we sprinted at top speed. Astræa, brave girl,
seemed all agility and swiftness. The noise in our
rear was increasing. The doctor was crying out to
hurry faster. At last the end of the long line of cars
was reached. I jumped aboard the last one, pulling
Astræa after me. The doctor sprang to my side, and
we threw the astonished motorman from the car. The
doctor grasped the lever, and the car bounded forth
just in time, for the cries of our baffled pursuers came
from only a few feet behind. We sat down panting on
the seats.

" We are saved, we are saved! " I exclaimed between
breaths.

" Listen! " cried the doctor.

The gigantic columns were whirling by us in a blur,
but we could hear nothing save the slight noise of the
speeding car.

" I heard a gong! " said the doctor.

We listened again and this time we caught a peculiar
sound. The car now made a curve, giving us command for a few minutes of a considerable stretch of

track over which we had come.   A car was swiftly cut-
ting the air in pursuit!

"Give her the last notch of power!" I cried.

It was a beautiful race.   We had about a mile the
best of it, but what was a mile to the radium energy of
these vehicles?   It did not represent half a minute —
it was a mere bagatelle.   Our pursuers had lost little
time.   Could we reach the Hall in time to give us a
fair start on foot?   The doctor applied all his attention to the mechanism at his command.   He understood thoroughly the art of motoring — he knew just
when to slacken power and when to turn it on full
speed.   Now he had become a very daredevil.   Down
grade and up grade we went faster than the wind.
The car rocked violently at the curves.   I never
traveled so fast before and I hope I may never travel
so fast again.   There was a hurricane swish to the
air, and momently I expected we would be sent
flying in all directions.   Now and then we caught a
glimpse of our pursuers.   They seemed neither to gain
nor to lose.   The same power that supplied us supplied
them.   Much depended on the man in charge, but it
was evident the enemy was as reckless and determined
as the doctor.   On and on through the semi-night of
the Atlantian solitudes the two cars flew on their wild
career.   We were quickly beyond the region affected

by the explosion and no smoke now obscured the lights of the dome. Perhaps ten minutes had passed when we saw these lights growing preceptibly closer. I took advantage of the chance to reload the empty chambers of my pistol.

"We are nearly there," shouted the doctor, "hold fast!"

The car began to slacken and suddenly it stopped with a frightful shock which pitched us forward over the seats. The doctor had applied the brakes the moment he dared, and he dared much. As we alighted the other car was on us. I gave it one hurried glance, and saw on the motorman's seat the dwarf! The determined character of our pursuit was explained.

The doctor took one of Astræa's hands and I the other, and the three of us ran along the defile that led through the stalactites to the entrance of the Hall. It was mostly uphill and Astræa was fairly carried for a large part of the distance. We had covered perhaps thirty yards when we heard the oncoming of the pack behind. "I can go no farther," cried Astræa. "Save yourselves!" With superhuman strength I took her up in my arms and hurried on. The noises in the rear increased — they were gaining on us. We came in sight of the tunnel opening, and I saw a guard barring the way. Pausing a moment to free my arm I

quickly fired and he fell. Astræa with renewed
strength disengaged herself from my arms and ran on
ahead. We reached the spot nearly spent and dragged
ourselves into the cave with the enemy not fifty feet
away. For just a second I thought of standing there
at bay, but though we panted for breath I still revolted
from shooting down the hounds save as a last resort
and on we went. We left the tunnel and traversed the
throne room of Bulak. Here, despite the dangers
that pressed about, I stopped to seize the great diamond
and gave it to Astræa. This act nearly cost us dear,
for as we pushed forward again a man came rushing
toward us from behind. I turned and shot him as he
ran. We now hurried as best we could through chamber after chamber of the mighty Hall, the rabble entering each room by one entrance as we left it at the other.
In some of the rooms we encountered inspectors, but
they were so taken by surprise that they did not have
the wit to stop us. Still they reinforced the ranks
of the enemy, and, being in good wind, became our
most dangerous pursuers. At last we gained the final
chamber, the one next the sea compartment, where lay
the submersible.

Once in the sea-chamber with the door closed the
victory was ours. Events now came swiftly, one on
top of the other, and to this day I have only a vague

idea of their succession. I noticed as I ran that the
door to the sea-chamber was open and my heart
bounded with joy as I saw the boat — the object of our
flight — looking just as it did the night the doctor and
I loaded it with wealth. Then I looked up at the great
copper sheet that formed the door, and remembered
with a flash that it closed slowly. Should we go
through the opening there was nothing to prevent the
pack at our heels from coming pell-mell upon us.
That would mean a fight at close quarters in the sea-
chamber with the odds against us. I dropped Astræa's
hand on the instant, and halting, turned swiftly about
so that I faced at an angle the door through which we
had come. As I did this I pulled the second pistol
from my belt and stood with both weapons pointed
ready for action. Here I would make a stand.

"Take Astræa into the chamber," I cried to the
doctor. "Press the button that closes the door and
tell me when it is nearly shut!"

I had no sooner said this than two figures came
rushing through the entrance on which my pistols
were trained. I fired relentlessly and the creatures
pitched forward into the room. But behind them came
a pushing mass. My weapons belched forth a continuous fire until nearly every chamber was empty. Then
there came a respite — no more heads appeared. But

it was a bloody piece of work. The bodies lay in a mound that barred the entrance. Perhaps, had I stood directly in front of the door so that those coming on behind could have seen what fate awaited them, there would have been less slaughter, but as it was they saw too late to retreat. Pushed forward from behind, they came within the zone of fire and died. Now the pile of bodies told its tale to the thinned ranks of the enemy, and I heard them taking counsel of themselves beyond the door. I mounted the human rampart and cried:

"Come on, you wolves!"

And thereupon I brandished my nearly-emptied weapons in their sight and jumped down beyond their view. While hastily reloading a pistol I glanced at the door and saw that it had hardly begun to slide in its groove. Astræa was standing just beyond the opening, but the doctor was on the side next to me and holding a crowbar in his hands. My sweeping glance also fell upon the figure of a man I had not before observed. Although in a state of mind in which one feels surprised at nothing I gazed astounded. It was the sea-surgeon! He stood within a few yards of me, gaping as one who had been struck dumb.

"You here?" I cried.

He did not answer.

But this was no time for explanation and I turned my attention to the enemy. My eyes fell on the figure of the old witch, Ate, framed in the doorway beyond the pile of the dead. Her face was livid with hate and baffled rage.

"My husband, too!" she screamed. Then turning her batteries on the stupefied man she shrieked:

"You ingrate! You two-faced fool! If you are not a traitor seize those murderers!"

"Silence!" I cried out threateningly. "You forget, my beauty, that with your husband it is a case of one against two while with you and your friends it is a case of a whole mob against two! Come on, I defy you all!"

"The door is closing!" shouted the doctor warningly.

I slowly backed toward it, holding my weapons pointed at the witch. She made no attempt to follow, for she was wise in her day and generation. Had she ventured one inch too far I must have shot her, and had I done so my conscience would have acquitted me, for a more vindictive, heartless and sexless old creature I know has never lived. She now saw herself utterly defeated and foiled, and in her bitter chagrin she burst forth in a stream of disgusting billingsgate. As I retreated, the dwarf to complete the picture appeared

"Come on!" I cried. "I defy you all." *Page 382*

at her side, shooting venomous fire from his eyes. I now spoke out rapidly to the surgeon.

"Choose quickly, my friend!" I said. "Yonder hag or us. Stay and you will play the victim to the monster in our stead. Come with us and you shall live in freedom in a new land. You are too good for this wretched country, and it would give me joy to rescue you from its horrors as it did you to rescue me from the sea. Only a moment remains! Which shall it be? Choose and be quick!"

I reached the closing door and as I jumped through the narrowing opening I held out my hand to him. He looked wildly about, gave one last glance at the witch and — stepped into the sea-chamber. I protected him with my pistols as he entered. As the door came to I heard the sound of rushing feet behind it and then a scream of pain. A finger had been caught between the shutting sheet of copper and the side of the chamber and there it dangled, bleeding, before our eyes. It was the solitary digit of the dwarf's right hand! A strange memento it was for him to contribute to our flight, and had I been of hardier nature I should have kept it as a valued souvenir, but I allowed the ghastly object to remain hanging to the door.

CHAPTER XL

ATLANTIS MEETS ITS DOOM

We were saved, at least from fiends in human guise. There yet remained the perilous journey through the sea, but what were the terrors of the elements compared with those we had left behind? We rested a little and in various ways according to our natures showed our thankfulness and joy. As for myself I felt I had been resurrected from the dead. For months I had been restrained, repressed and suffocated under the yoke of social slavery, and the threat of dreadful death had hung above me like the sword of Damocles. But now I was myself again. My bonds were severed and a weight was lifted from me. Although the sea-chamber was low-ceilinged and watertight I could breathe again as I had not breathed for months.

The great copper sheet stood as a shield against the battering foe beyond. As a precaution I pressed the button used in closing the door so that if the enemy pressed the opening button on the other side it would be without effect. Then I gave a few directions to the doctor as to the opening of the hatch-lid of the boat and turned to the beautiful creature who had followed me with such a blind and trusting faith.

This was the first opportunity I had had since our flight began to say those things my heart urged the utterance of, and I made good use of it. For some minutes we spoke apart, rapt in our own happiness and unmindful of our friends. Then from the fullness of a soul overcharged with emotion she gave utterance to the wish that we might be married then and there. " For death may lie before us," she said with the simple innocence of a child, " and even if for only a brief moment I want you for my own."

The surgeon overheard and answered hesitatingly:

" Begging the pardon of you both, but your wish may be granted, if you desire, for I have the right to perform the ceremony under the laws of Atlantis."

" Good! " I exclaimed joyfully, " we accept your services, and when we reach the land above we shall have still another ceremony under the laws of the United States."

There in the sea-chamber fathoms down, with the water pressing on one side and the wretches crying for our death on the other, the surgeon pronounced those words that made us man and wife. The doctor, much affected, stood as the living witness of the nuptials, and though no register save that which is kept on high records the vows that made us one, yet two beings were never more firmly united than were Astræa and I that day.

The ceremony over, I led my bride to the submarine, while the surgeon stood guard over the door. We mounted to the conning-tower on planks which our two friends had removed from the interior of the boat, where it will be remembered the doctor and I had placed them to cover the gold and precious stones. When we descended the ladder through the hatch-way I hastily examined everything, to judge if the boat was ready for the sea. It appeared that no one had entered it since last the doctor and I had left it. Perhaps the minions of the State had been too lethargic, or perhaps they were unable to open the hatch-lid. To make sure the air-chambers were full and the batteries charged, the doctor and I started the gasoline motor, but, fairly satisfied that all was right, we stopped it quickly, lest the air in the chamber should become too foul.

We had been in the chamber some ten or fifteen minutes, and it became necessary that we hasten with what remained to be done. I now called on the surgeon to open the valves that let in the water from the sea, and it was soon spurting in torrents through

two large pipes. Suddenly I remembered that the sea-
door would not open unless the pressure on both its
sides was equal and how the button was to be pressed
to open it when the chamber was filled with water and
the four of us were in the boat with the hatch-lid down
was a problem that caused my heart to sink. I rushed
from the vessel and cried out in my perplexity, but the
doctor followed and quickly relieved me by pointing to
a rigging of timbers and boards that stretched to the
ceiling against one part of the wall.

" The crowbar there is wedged against the button,"
he explained, " and as soon as the chamber fills the door
will open."

He and the surgeon had been grappling with the
difficulty while Astræa and I had been engrossed with
each other.

Now the chamber was filling rapidly, and we stood
to our hips in the water watching the boat. Would
it float? At last we climbed aboard and stood by the
conning-tower. The water rose higher and higher
and now it began to lap the sides far up. The boat
trembled, rocked a little and then floated. Highly
elated we retreated down the hatchway. The boat
rose gradually until the open hatch-lid touched the
ceiling and then I closed it with a bang. The doctor
took charge of the steering wheel and signal buttons in

the tower and the surgeon and I placed ourselves
under his orders. Astræa also stood by to render all
the assistance she could.

The doctor gave orders quick and fast. First it was
to fill the trimming tanks to bring the vessel to an even
keel. Then the ballast tanks were filled, for, not knowing the buoyancy of the boat, it was well to guard
against a too sudden rise that might involve us in
overhanging crags or caves surrounding the wall of
Atlantis.

"We shall, if possible," said the doctor, "proceed
some distance near the sea's bottom until we are well
clear of the reefs."

The electric motor, now connected with the pro-
peller-shaft, began to hum. There was a grating
sound as the top of the hatch-lid grazed the ceiling
of the chamber. The steering-gear clanked, and the
propeller continued to revolve. The grating sound
ceased. We must have left the chamber! There
was a peculiar vibration to the vessel, and the
sound of the machinery prevented ordinary talk.
Were we going fast? It was impossible to tell. I
jumped to look at the depth indicator, but it told
nothing — it had not moved and perhaps was out
of order. The heavy glass in the tower through which
one could look into the sea was dark and impenetrable.

"We must go it blind," said the doctor in my ear. "We are like a lot of children with this thing. For my part, I must confess I have no idea of direction. I can not tell how fast we are going or where we are going, or whether we are ascending or remaining at the bottom. I hope and believe we are going out from Atlantis, but if you think best we will empty the tanks and make sure we are rising."

"Empty the tanks, by all means! As it is, we may be in imminent danger of running into a rock," I exclaimed.

The surgeon and myself applied ourselves to the task, but it was some time before we succeeded in blowing out the first tank. As we were proceeding to blow out the second one we heard the doctor, who had remained at his post, give a strange cry. Immediately I ran to his side. A dim light was coming through the glass and he was gazing into the sea.

"We are in front of the amphitheater!" he called out.

I looked through the glass and saw before me as wild and weird a picture as ever mortal eye beheld. There directly in our front was the gigantic pit brilliantly illuminated and still filled with a moving mass of humanity.

"We are going right into it!" I cried.

"We were, but we are not now," returned the doctor. "I am steering to port. However, we will cruise close by."

I called Astræa and then the surgeon, that they might see the wonderful sight. The surgeon, however, gave it only a brief look and returned below with the remark that he had seen it many times before and that his duty was with the motors and machinery aft.

"Finish the tanks," said the doctor to him, and then he continued to comment:

"This light gives me a good chance to practise."

He tugged at the wheel and under his manipulation the boat shot directly at the amphitheater and then darted away again. As we ran close in I saw that the multitude was greatly excited. The whole concourse seemed to be standing on the seats and waving their arms frantically. As for the arena, it was a mass of debris and human creatures. Perhaps the people were removing the dead who had been killed when the monument exploded.

"The boat is rising," exclaimed the doctor. The strange scene was sinking slowly before our eyes.

I turned away for an instant and looked at the sea in the opposite direction. As I did so my blood was almost congealed with terror. We had run upon the monster!

Immediately there came a frightful blow upon the deck and the vessel shivered in every beam. Then we began to sink and list. The motor still buzzed, but all progress seemed to stop. It was too evident we were in the grasp of the kraken.

So unexpectedly had it all come about that both the doctor and myself were completely unnerved.

"We are lost!" cried my friend.

I thought so myself, but only for a second. My experience in grappling at close quarters with death had not been for naught, and now my faculties quickly revived. I looked through the glass and saw the eyes and mouth of the monster at the very bow of the craft. It seemed to be trying to swallow us whole.

"Back the boat!" I commanded.

The doctor frantically endeavored to obey, but though the propeller was reversed and the motor was going at top speed the vessel remained stationary. But not altogether stationary either, for as I gazed the amphitheater seemed to be veering directly forward with the beast between. The boat now listed badly. A blow came upon the port side and then one on the starboard — surely we would be battered to pieces. In moments of danger the mind sometimes works automatically, and ideas shape themselves without our knowing how. It was thus that I suddenly recalled the torpedo that had been left in the tube. I gave a swift look ahead and saw the cavernous mouth of the beast apparently encircling the bow, while through two of its huge arms I caught a glimpse of a swaying multitude only a short distance away.

"The torpedo, the torpedo!" I yelled.

I jumped for the forward compartment, followed by the doctor. At my cry the surgeon also came running up.

"We must discharge it and trust that it hits the beast!" I continued.

"But first," the doctor put in quickly, "are all the tanks empty?"

"Emptied the last one before we struck," replied the surgeon.

"Is the motor running full speed?"

"It is."

We then determined that Astræa, who was standing by eager to help, should assist the surgeon in managing the torpedo. Giving them the needful instructions as to opening the bow port and turning on the compressed air, we closed the breech and the doctor and I returned to the tower. The doctor took hold of the steering wheel and brought into play the horizontal rudder. I looked into the sea and saw the monster directly ahead. The amphitheater, too, seemed closer than ever, and I warned the doctor that the transparent wall must be close at hand.

"Out with it!" I exclaimed.

I glued my eyes to the dead lights. But I had not long to wait. There was a thud and a sound of inrushing water — the torpedo had left on its mission. At the same instant the beast must have given a plunge, for the boat tilted badly forward and a resounding blow smashed against the keel. Had the torpedo missed its mark? For the fraction of a second I thought I saw it suspended in mid-sea. Then came a dull booming report, a great concussion and a white cloud of foam, blotted out the scene.

The vessel seemed to be thrown violently through the sea, but it recovered itself rapidly. The doctor and I had been thrown down and now we jumped again to our posts. Was the boat injured? It rolled heavily, and then righted itself on an even keel. Now it began to move — we were certain of it. Thank Heaven the monster, whether killed or not, had released its hold. The milky cloud against the glass was disappearing and I was gazing at the sea when suddenly I caught a glimpse of a most appalling sight. There directly before my eyes was the brilliantly-lighted amphitheater with a torrent of water pouring into the arena and thousands of creatures like ants struggling with the flood! What had happened was readily apparent. The torpedo had struck the Crystalline Wall and made a gap into which the sea was rushing. The doctor also saw and understood. With set features he grappled with the steering wheel.

Full of awe I continued to look into the sea. Should we escape the maelstrom or should we be hurled through the vent in the wall to become victims of the frightful cataclysm? Fortunately the impact of the concussion or else the frantic action of the beast had given the vessel an impetus upward which it had not entirely lost, and soon the effect of the horizontal rudder and the sturdy propeller began to tell in our favor. Slowly but steadily we made headway against the current that was setting in toward the gap. Gradually, too, the water cleared, and we obtained a plain view of the amphitheater as it sank slowly beneath us. We saw that the pit had become a turbulent lake, on the surface of which we could make out a scum of scarlet hue — the color of the common garb of Atlantis! The water still spurted over the scene like a geyser. The dreadful sight became dimmer and dimmer as it receded into the depths, and at last was blotted from our view.

Nothing but the blackness of the deep appeared against the glass.

By and by I again caught the faint suggestion of light through the glass. I had been looking for it ardently, and now I was rewarded.

"We are nearing the surface!" I called out, overjoyed, to my excited companions.

The boat began to roll slightly and the light grew gray. At last I raised the hatch-lid and, putting my head and shoulders through it, I looked on the full moon shining far up in the heavens while all about was the dark and heaving sea.

"And is that the sun?" asked the surgeon with awe.

"No, it is the moon, it is night," I replied.

"How beautiful is the world!" said Astræa.

"How sublime!" said the surgeon.

The doctor said nothing, but gazed as one whose emotions were beyond utterance.

CHAPTER XLI

CONCLUSION

Every story like a play needs an epilogue. When I began to write these memoirs I had intended to deal at length with the experiences of Astræa, the doctor and the surgeon under those institutions of individual freedom which are so familiar to us but which to them were as a new revelation of truth. But I find I have already spun my story to an unconscionable length, and, besides, the labor of writing is a wearying task to one who is long past his prime and seeks only comfort and leisure for the days that yet remain. Allow me then to lay down my pen with but half my object gained. It is with personal regret that I feel impelled to this conclusion, but I find consolation in the thought that the half that has been done is the more important half, since I who was there alone could tell of that strange land where socialism brought to a sad and evil pass a civilization once preëminent in the world. Others can report the things of the living present, but Atlantis is now dead and buried, overwhelmed by the wrath of God. My tale, I feel,

396

is crudely told, but it has the merit of veracity, and right glad am I that I have done my duty according to my light in preserving for mankind an account of the nation that through its worship of Social Equality went down to destruction.

A few words more, and I shall conclude. When we landed in our boat it was on the lonely coast of a small island in the West Indies. We buried our wealth and obtained food and shelter in the miserable hut of a native. After some days of anxieties and difficulties we were supplied with the habiliments of civilization, and one day a ship, which I had chartered, stood off the island and took on board an assortment of trunks and chests and a party of four, three of whom were much bewildered. In due time we arrived in New York, where one of the first of my pleasant duties was to lease a considerable space in a safety deposit vault. Returning after many days to the island, we searched for, but could not find, the submarine, which we had left in a little nook well-hidden by tropical foliage. It had gone to join the mysteries of the sea.

For some years we traveled, with one principal object in view, that of living where the temperature was neither hot nor cold. The summer found us far in the north, and the winter in the south. In the course of time my wife and our two companions became inured to the climatic changes, and to some degree also was their curiosity satisfied as to the many lands and nations that cover the globe. But they liked no country so well as the United States, and here we went into railroads and mining, employing many men and contributing our energy to the building up of the prosperity of the people. The doctor became greatly interested in scientific research, and was ever grateful to me for rescuing him from his miserable life in Atlantis. The surgeon developed a predilection for medicine, and became a man of note in his profession. He never regretted the day when, filled with grief, he took himself to the Hall of Curiosities to be as far removed as possible from the scene of my execution; and though one of the reasons that took him to the Hall, even on that occasion, was to bewail the failure of the project to remove the gold beyond the reach of man, yet I never heard him utter one criticism of the use to which I put our wealth. He became an individualist of the most ultra type, and both he and the doctor lived to a good age in the enjoyment of our liberties.

As for the beautiful woman who was my wife, many of my friends still hold her in endearing memory. While she lived she was inseparable from me, going with me on my many journeys, consoling me in my sorrows and partaking of my joys. In our mansion in town, overlooking Central Park, she was a charming hostess, admired and cultivated by the highest circle of society, not that circle which in vanity and display finds miserable pastime, but that circle which includes the noblest and most intellectual people of the day. When she died she left me a lonely and broken man. A mausoleum now stands where she is buried, and the flowers I put there never wither before fresh ones take their place.

While they were with me, my wife, my friends and I faithfully observed a compact made between ourselves to disclose nothing concerning the submerged realm. We did not think it well to inflame the minds of venturesome spirits by telling of the hoarded wealth that still lies buried in the Hall of Curiosities. I also had a fancy to keep secret the nature of our possessions, and then I had a dread of incurring ridicule and insinuations as to our sanity should we endeavor to take the world into our confidence. Now, however, I feel that the lessons taught by the social institutions of Atlantis should not be lost to mankind. By giving my story to the public a few may be encouraged to risk their lives in a search for the buried treasure, but they must understand I assume no responsibility for their conduct, or for the success or failure of their enterprises. Others there may be who will be incredulous, but what they say can affect me little. My life is now nearing its end and I am no longer sensitive to the criticism of men. Let the whole world believe my story or not believe — I still have done my duty and found some pleasure in the doing of it.

THE END

Utopian Literature

AN ARNO PRESS/NEW YORK TIMES COLLECTION

Adams, Frederick Upham.
President John Smith; The Story of a Peaceful Revolution.
1897.

Bird, Arthur.
Looking Forward: A Dream of the United States of the
Americas in 1999. 1899.

[Blanchard, Calvin.]
The Art of Real Pleasure. 1864.

Brinsmade, Herman Hine.
Utopia Achieved: A Novel of the Future. 1912.

Caryl, Charles W.
New Era. 1897.

Chavannes, Albert.
The Future Commonwealth. 1892.

Child, William Stanley.
The Legal Revolution of 1902. 1898.

Collens, T. Wharton.
Eden of Labor; or, The Christian Utopia. 1876.

Cowan, James.
Daybreak. A Romance of an Old World. 1896. 2nd ed.

Craig, Alexander.
Ionia; Land of Wise Men and Fair Women. 1898.

Daniel, Charles S.
AI: A Social Vision. 1892.

Devinne, Paul.
The Day of Prosperity: A Vision of the Century to Come.
1902.

Edson, Milan C.
Solaris Farm. 1900.

Fuller, Alvarado M.
A. D. 2000. 1890.

Geissler, Ludwig A.
Looking Beyond. 1891.

Hale, Edward Everett.
How They Lived in Hampton. 1888.

Hale, Edward Everett.
Sybaris and Other Homes. 1869.

Harris, W. S.
Life in a Thousand Worlds. 1905.

Henry, W. O.
Equitania. 1914.

Hicks, Granville, with Richard M. Bennett.
The First to Awaken. 1940.

Lewis, Arthur O., editor
American Utopias: Selected Short Fiction. 1790–1954.

McGrady, Thomas.
Beyond the Black Ocean. 1901.

Mendes H. Pereira.
Looking Ahead. 1899.

Michaelis, Richard.
Looking Further Forward. An Answer to
Looking Backward by Edward Bellamy. 1890.

Moore, David A.
The Age of Progress. 1856.

Noto, Cosimo.
The Ideal City. 1903.

Olerich, Henry.
A Cityless and Countryless World. 1893.

Parry, David M.
The Scarlet Empire. 1906.

Peck, Bradford.
The World a Department Store. 1900.

Reitmeister, Louis Aaron.
If Tomorrow Comes. 1934.

Roberts, J. W.
Looking Within. 1893.

Rosewater, Frank.
'96; A Romance of Utopia. 1894.

Satterlee, W. W.
Looking Backward and What I Saw. 2nd ed. 1890.

Schindler, Solomon.
Young West; A Sequel to Edward Bellamy's Celebrated Novel "Looking Backward." 1894.

Smith, Titus K.
Altruria. 1895.

Steere, C. A.
When Things Were Doing. 1908.

Taylor, William Alexander.
Intermere. 1901.

Thiusen, Ismar.
The Diothas, or, A Far Look Ahead. 1883.

Vinton, Arthur Dudley.
Looking Further Backward. 1890.

Wooldridge, C. W.
Perfecting the Earth. 1902.

Wright, Austin Tappan.
Islandia. 1942.

DATE DUE